ANYTIME

ANYTIME

Kim Louise

ANYTIME

ISBN-13: 978-0-373-22995-6

Recycling programs for this product may not exist in your area.

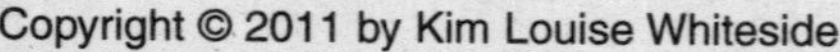

www.kimanipress.com

Printed in U.S.A.

Acknowledgments

I could not have written this book without the constant support, encouragement and camaraderie of my RWA chapter, Heartland Writers Group. So many of you have played a major role in keeping me growing as a writer and keeping my fingers typing even when I'd rather just veg and watch my latest Netflix rental. *lizzie, you are the best Goals Guru ever! And to everyone at Teri's Friday night critique, when the idea for this story really started to take shape—Jenn, Julie, Julie, Tina—your feedback and wisdom made such a big difference. A special shout-out goes to April, whose exceptional insights helped inspire many aspects of *Anytime.* Thank you for your candor and all the ways your brain dances in the story place. A great big thank-you goes to my writing sisterhood: Patti, Theresa, Dee Ann and Elaine. What would Monday evenings be without you?

To the regulars of my favorite coffee shop—and you know who you are—thank you for making me a part of the family. Can't wait for our next potluck!

To my literary sister-friend Niobia. To this day, we'll be on the phone and sometimes I'll think, "I can't believe I'm talking to one of my all-time favorite authors!" Thank you for being confident that I could write a book like this. Now I'm confident, too.

To all the readers who contacted me over the last two years and asked when my next book was coming out…I thank you. You all kept me going, kept me writing and kept me in the industry. I'm so grateful.

Those of you who said, "Make it hotter," here ya go!

For Kofi, who taught me about love, good love and angels.

I miss you.

Dear Reader,

The original idea for *Anytime* came to me as a mystery (one I may write one day) about a man searching for a mysterious woman. After several incarnations, it developed into a story about a man and woman searching for their own selves and needing each other's help to find the best parts of who they are.

I saw a documentary on the History Channel that chronicled the explosion of communes during the sexual revolution of the sixties. It made me wonder what people in the twenty-first century do to scratch that kind of itch. So, I asked around. Soon after, the idea for this book started taking shape. I have to say that the research I did for this book was…fascinating.

The story is set in Sedona, because I think it's one of the most beautiful places in the U.S. and it's home to a bounty of hot springs, red rock and vortexes that heal mind, body and spirit—just perfect for the couple I had in mind for the story.

For those of you who've read my books before… thank you. This story is a bit spicier than my usual. I hope you will find it just as enjoyable to read. If this is your first time reading one of my books, thank you, too! My wish is that this story fulfilled your expectations and was reading time well spent.

Feel free to contact me at:

mskimlouise@aol.com (email)
msklouise (Twitter)
kimlouise (Facebook)
http://klmusejuice.blogspot.com (blog)

Until next time, pour into your cup sweetly.

Kim Louise

Chapter One

They say hindsight is twenty/twenty—but that's only if you're brave enough to look back and learn.

Marlowe Chambers's long, thick fingers tapped rhythmically against the keys of his laptop. The motions sounded like slow rain in his hospital room. Oxygen from the tube in his nose made a faint, thin, whispering sound, the way fog might if you could hear it settling to the ground.

Marlowe would swear that hospital rooms were getting smaller and smaller, along with everything in them. The bedside table on his left was barely large enough for a water pitcher and tissues. The visitor's chair was barely larger than a card table seat, and the TV above the chair couldn't have been more than seventeen inches. Marlowe had to squint to see Wolf Blitzer's hairy face. A thick, white pull curtain separated his bed from the next bed, which was less than five feet to his left. If he'd had a "roommate," they would have been able to hear each other blink.

By the time we are wise enough and brave enough to look back at the lessons learned from the levees, it may be too late for us to see clearly. Until then, we must—

"You look like death in a white sheet," a voice from the doorway pronounced.

Marlow recognized that voice. Tuck Milsap, his current client. Marlowe's teeth clenched. A muscle throbbed in his jaw. He kept typing.

Stop doing what Leila DuPont called "humming with our ears covered."

"I'm surprised you aren't hooked to more tubes," Tuck said.

Marlowe watched his own words form sentences on the screen. "I was when they brought me in."

And start doing what the Village Vanguard *suggests: "Acknowledge the absurd."*

He was close now, he could feel it. Like the end of a good meal or the sweet release after making good love, Marlowe was about to wrap up another prize-winning story. It was writing itself now, making the case for due diligence and activism. Most days, Marlowe wished he could type faster, get the stories out of his head quicker, get paid sooner. But, at the end, at the sweet spot, where all his sweat, research, long days and pavement pounding came together, he'd slow down, take his time, drag it out until the last syllable—

"Chambers!"

"Yeah," he said, looking up for the first time.

Marlowe hadn't seen Tuck in months. As usual, the man was a long swatch of precision, from his shadow-fade haircut to his clear-polish manicure and mirror-shine shoes. Not one defiant hair, loose button, or wrinkle. Marlowe suspected the man had OCD and used a portable steamer to press himself throughout the day. "Yeah?" Marlowe repeated. His face tightened like a fist, and he realized his client hadn't come to check on him. He'd come to check on the story.

"I'm writing the end now."

Tuck hiked up designer pants so stiff they looked as if they could stand by themselves and took a seat in the chair across from him, careful not to scrape his knees on the foot of the bed. Tuck scratched a spot at the top of his head and glanced pensively out the window.

Omaha was waking up. From Methodist Hospital, he had an unobscured view of the eastern bulk of the city. The better part of seven hundred thousand residents locked into their morning commute. Dodge Street, the main artery of the city running parallel to the hospital, was choked with traffic. On the horizon, the sun's orange-red glow peeled away the dawn.

Tuck glanced back at Marlowe. His face much less tight and sour. More as if it had taken a pity bath and was still damp. “We need to talk.”

Marlowe’s fingers left the keyboard. He sat back against the thin, flimsy pillows behind him and breathed carefully from the oxygen tube.

“I need your advance,” Tuck said. The words rolled out of him like sharp-edged boulders.

Marlowe was sure he hadn’t heard correctly. “Say what?”

“They’re pulling your story.”

Marlowe lowered the breathing tube from his face. If he suddenly had to jump up and strangle the bull out of Tuck, he had to make sure he wouldn’t be yanked back by an air hose.

“They…or *you?*” Marlowe asked, already knowing the truth. At Hughes Enterprises, Tuck greenlighted all stories. He had a board he reported to, sure, but he had had that board wrapped around his pinkie for years.

“Let’s just start with the basics. Your stories never come in on time, man.”

“Whose do? Name one investigative journalist in my league who actually gets a story in on time.”

“Anthony Howard.”

“Man, kiss my ass. When has that close-up hog put his life on the line for anything?”

“That’s what you don’t get. He doesn’t have to. He’s a jour-nal-ist. Not a caped crusader. He *reports* the news. He doesn’t become part of it.”

Of course Tuck would bring up Anthony Howard. Another newsman who was just too tidy for his own good.

"I'll bet he's never even gotten a splinter from any story he's covered."

"Chambers—"

"Hell, if the wind blew and an eyelash got in his eye, he'd probably be on the next plane back to Atlanta."

"Chambers!"

"What?" Marlowe hollered back. He was so tired of people questioning his professionalism. It was bad enough when it came from random clients. But Tuck was a friend as well as a colleague. If he was going to get on his ass, too …

Tuck got up and paced under the TV. Blitzer's *Situation Room* marched on like a war story across the screen. "All I wanted was a follow-up. Six years later. And I sent you in because you're the best reporter I know. And I prayed—*I prayed*—you wouldn't let me down."

"Man, I got the story."

"And almost killed your lungs. The nurse said when they brought you in, you were coughing up tar."

"Whatever."

"No. Not whatever. *When*ever? As in when are you ever going to stick to the news? Focus on the story?"

"I helped clean out some office space. The whole

area was like Beirut, man. Or the apocalypse. Even after five years. I had to do something." He left off the part about Leila. That he had to do something for Leila—the beautiful woman from the Seventh Phoenyx whom he spent most of his time with—day and night. At least he thought he was just spending time until he found the *L word* jumping off the tip of his tongue. The thought of being in love so fast scared both of them. Soon they were backing away from each other, and it was all business and interviews until the day he left.

"You got…involved…again. I don't even want to know her name. The only thing I need to know now is whether you can write a check for the advance now, and if not, how soon I can expect it."

Marlowe stared at the masterpiece on the screen in front of him. Tuck was right. He was the best journalist he knew. He was one of the best in the industry, and he was one paragraph away from what his gut told him was his finest work.

"Tuck, one hundred words. No, ninety-nine. Just be still for a minute. Shut up, okay? I'll be finished in thirty seconds. Sixty tops."

"You're not hearing me. I came down here to do this face-to-face. You deserve better than a phone call or an email. It's done, Chambers."

"Tucker…man…"

"I mean it. I can't keep sticking my neck out only to have the very person I'm protecting chop it in half."

"Okay, I get it. But, you know me. I report from the inside out, but I always get the story. Always."

Tuck sat down again. Took another look out the window. "Yeah, but they take too long to come. And they're too expensive. Your week's stay in this hospital has already cost us fifty thousand dollars. That's what Dan the copy chief makes in a year."

For a moment, Marlowe wondered why Tuck would bring up Dan's salary. Then it made sense. Tuck's gripe might be with Marlowe to a certain extent, but it was mostly about the bottom line.

Marlowe's chest tightened. He couldn't tell if it was from his weakened lungs or the thought of his friend's newsmagazine going under. The economy had been hard on everyone, everywhere. Newspapers and magazines had taken hard blows. People didn't want to wait for news, and they weren't so willing to pay for information they could get instantly on the internet. Freelance reporters like Marlowe had compensated by trying to give the editors they contracted with more engaging stories. Some had even resorted to features that were more like reality TV on paper. It may have slowed the hemorrhage of the print industry, but it hadn't stopped it.

"How many?" Marlowe asked, seeing the layoffs riding his friend's tidy features. Tuck sighed heavily. He sounded as though he could use an oxygen machine, too. "Twenty-three…to start. The board wants to 'incrementally decrease the negative pecuniary strain on revenue.' That's corporate speak for we're looking at close to a hundred over the next seven months."

"Too bad you can't send me in on that. I could do a story on Hughes Enterprises. You can call it 'Black Business in the Red.'"

"As usual, that's a brilliant idea. But you'd end up spending more time with LaKayla in Accounting than you would on the story."

"Man, she's hella fine."

"Tell me about it," Tuck admitted.

Marlowe grinned. "I know you hit that."

"Hit it and quit it."

"My dog!"

The two men chuckled, and the tense air between them loosened up. "Seriously," Tuck said, "this habit you have of getting caught up with one-time-use women is going to get you in big trouble one day."

"One-time-use? No, man, I loved Leila."

"Leila? Is that who it was this time?"

Marlowe couldn't lie. "Yeah."

"And before that it was Shauntina, and before that Tomika, and before that…what's her name? The gal with the big hips—"

"Sally," Marlowe said with reverence. She was the best "no strings attached" fling he ever had. Mattresses were made for her movements. If he thought hard enough, he could still feel her on top of him.

Tuck grunted. "Yeah. Ride, Sally, ride. Her big hips cost me a thirteen-thousand-dollar video camera."

"And they got me the Ellie award. Don't act brand new. That California wildfire story put Hughes Enterprises on the map and turned *LifeWire* into a magazine people actually read."

"Maybe," Tuck mumbled.

"Maybe? Is that all you got for me?"

"Okay, all right, man. Damn. You did it. You've always done it. But the world has changed on us."

Tucker sounded far away, as if he were talking to that sun he kept staring at and not Marlowe.

"I can't send you off anymore and wait for you to finish your story whenever you get around to it—which is usually well after you come up for air after being buried between some woman's legs and right before you cost me something above and beyond what I'm paying you for the story.

"I'm sorry, man. And I know you've burned your bridges with other editors. I'm one of the last ones who would even take a chance on your ass."

Marlowe started typing again. He forced himself to focus away from what Tuck was saying. He shut out all the thoughts rushing into his mind about the balloon mortgage he could no longer afford and the advance money he'd already spent to buy the supplies he used to clean up Leila's office building after a terrible fire. His fingers tapped the keys, faster now. The words came as he knew they would, sliding into place like mortar-free blocks.

"Forty-five," he said. "Thirty-nine..."

"It doesn't matter. They don't want your story."

Tucker pulled a thin glossy magazine out of the inside pocket of his blazer. "They want this."

Tucker didn't have to unfold it. Marlowe could smell the cheap paper and matching stories from where he lay on the bed. Stories twisted so tightly they mangled the lives of the people they were about. Quotes taken so far out of context, they sounded as if they were spoken by someone else. And photos that were such an invasion of privacy, innocent bystanders should be able to sue for the offense. It was yellow journalism at its worst, and it made Marlowe want to throw those so-called "reporters" on their scandal-chasing asses.

"Get that out of my face."

Tucker opened the magazine and held it up. "No. You need to look at this, because like it or not, this is the way of the news world. At least, the part of the news world that still makes money. If you're not riding this gravy train, you don't eat. Period. Nobody wants to read about an organization still fighting the good fight in New Orleans when they can see a box office star like Carmela Moore getting her freak on at a sex party."

The mention of Carmela Moore got Marlowe to look close. The photo was definitely the award-winning Ms. Moore. Marlowe would recognize her body anywhere. Strategic areas on her naked frame had been blurred out. But it was her, riding what looked like a pommel horse with her arm waving and her head flung back in ecstasy. The caption read, "Gimme Moore! Carmela gets her ride on at the Chocolate Chateau."

Marlowe winced. "The Chocolate Chateau is a myth. That's grimy reporting."

"But it sells magazines."

Marlowe typed the last sentence in the last paragraph and smiled. If men could "exhale," this must be what it feels like, he thought.

"Okay. It's done." A few more clicks. "Not only is it done, but I just emailed it to you."

"You're not hearing me. This issue of *Hot Topics* alone sold more copies than the last six issues of *LifeWire* combined. We couldn't compete with that before, but we think we can now."

"By turning a respectable news source into a tabloid?"

"By doing what it takes to stay in business."

"I don't have your advance, Tuck. And I need the money from this article I just wrote for you from this hospital bed." Marlowe refused to admit to Tucker he'd been living off his 401(k) for three years. And now that it was almost gone, he was counting on money from his feature story to get him through the next couple of months.

"I can't do it. The board is tying my hands on this one. So, unless you've got photos of Tupac, Biggie and Michael Jackson alive and well on an island in the Pacific, or you have a Tiger Woods sex tape stashed somewhere, I have to pass."

Marlowe assumed Tuck's tied hands comment was code for "I could be next on the layoff list."

What was left of his 401(k) would cover the advance he got from Hughes. But then he'd be left with no way to pay his bills. He could keep his 401(k) and try to get other assignments. But with the tarnishes on his reputation in the industry and the state of the economy, the chances of him getting an assignment before Hughes took him to court over the advance were slim. And if that happened, what little reputation he had left would be ruined. He'd become like the tragic stories he wrote about. He could see the newscrawl now. *Award-winning journalist found homeless with only his laptop and his plaque.*

"Give me thirty days," Marlowe said, staring at the beautiful Carmela Moore and pulling an idea out of his ass.

"A month for what?"

"To get you a respectable story that will still sell issues."

"There's no such thing."

Marlowe glanced at the photo and read the headline again. "There might be. Just give me the time—one month."

"Man, I always give you a month. Then it's six more before I hear from you again, and you're usually in some kind of trouble."

"Not this time," he said, hoping he sounded convincing.

Tuck scratched the top of his head and let out a blast of air. "I must be smoking crack."

"Thanks, man," Marlowe said.

His friend stood and angled toward the door. "But I'm telling you right damn now, if you don't bring me thug life, baby-baybay, a smooth criminal or some hanky-panky in the Oval Office, I'm going straight to the legal department."

"I got this, man!"

"I mean it."

"Me, too, Tuck. Me, too."

Chapter Two

Carmela's phone rang again. The ringtone was a chopped up version of Michael Jackson's "P.Y.T." Gena frowned. Another client who refused to put their phone on vibrate during important meetings. Fantastic. If she wasn't the great and powerful Carmela Moore—the most important client at The Epicure—Gena would have told her exactly what to do with her phone.

"Hey," the actress said, her voice surprisingly soft.

Gena knew that tone. Only a man can soften a woman like that. Usually a man with some good lovin', Gena thought. And that had to be it, because offscreen the Magnificent Ms. Moore put the bitch in diva.

"What?...Well, you can take a number just like everydamnbody else. Now serving 3,085. Reporters have been on me all week behind that picture... I know you're a reporter, but you're also my Boo... are too...are too!"

Gena swung out of her office chair and walked to the wet bar. She poured tonic water into a glass and topped it off with a shot of orange juice. She stirred her drink with her finger and waited for Carmela to finish her call.

"If you're not my Boo, why are you calling?"

The actress's eyes grew narrow and she turned her attention to Gena. "You want to know where I was."

Gena's heart leaped to her throat. She knew Carmela's trust had been betrayed. It was Gena's fault, and she felt miserable for that. But she prayed that Carmela would honor her pledge to silence.

"Let's see," she said, pacing in the room but keeping an evil gaze on Gena, "where was I when that photo was taken? Hmm?"

Gena wondered what the public would think if they knew their beloved Carmela Moore, who'd won a prestigious industry award for her role as Judith Jamison, was a spoiled brat who resorted to blackmail whenever she couldn't get her way. Forget about the fact that she had a pommel-horse fetish and always left the one at The Epicure drenched and sticky with her juices after she finished. Or that, more often than not, the staff had to drag her off the thing in order to give the poor machine a rest. No, Gena thought extortion might get top billing as a headline, too.

"Three months," Gena said. "No charge."

Carmela smiled, but not wide enough. "Well, the rag said I was at the Chocolate Chateau…"

"Seven months," Gena offered. She calculated the figures in her head. Five thousand dollars seven times. Thirty-five thousand dollars swirled down the drain so quickly, the thought made a noise in her head that sounded like ka-ching! in reverse.

Carmela played with Gena's jade statute of Hotei. Rubbed its belly as if it were a cat purring on its side. "Well, Boo, as a matter of fact…the Chocolate Chateau—"

"A year," Gena said.

"Doesn't exist," Carmela finished, grinning widely. For a retaliatory second, Gena wished that the corners of Carmela's mouth would split. But Gena pushed the thought away and let go of the breath she'd been holding. Thanks to her monetary sacrifice, The Epicure, or as folks called it, "The Chocolate Chateau," was still a myth.

And Gena would do whatever it took to keep it that way.

What you won't do for love, Gena Bivens thought as the gorgeous starlet ended her conversation. The moment Gena had seen the photo of Carmela Moore in both the print and online versions of the gossip rag *Business In The Street,* she knew that she would have to pull out all stops to make her client happy and keep The Epicure safe. Gena loved her business more than anything in her life, and she'd do anything, include placate one of Hollywood's brightest, in order to protect it.

"Thank God I have the best publicist money can buy! She's spinning it as a still from an upcoming movie! But that's not the *point!* I want whoever took that picture fired; do you hear me! No, no, not fired! Thrown in jail for…for…invasion of privacy! Obstruction of justice! Stealing my soul!"

Gena held up her hand. "Carmela, please calm down. Let me pour you a drink. Roederer?"

That stopped the pacing. "I don't want any freaking champagne. I want my reputation back!"

Back to what, Gena wondered. The moment the child actress had turned twenty-one, she'd been in the paparazzi's lenses photographed as one of the wildest up-and-comers the entertainment industry had ever seen. The only time she'd been photographed without a drink in her hand was when she was on-screen. She'd been partying like that for five years since.

Gena's office was an indulgence of lipstick-red on the ceiling and in the filigree wallpaper on the four walls. The rich crown molding at the base of the ceiling, floor and around windows was a shiny onyx. Black satin sheers extended from ceiling to floor on each side of three windows. A silver chandelier hung low over Gena's desk. Flame-shaped lights sat in the center of swirling strips of chrome which dipped and bent around the lights in a sensual dance. Framed calligraphy decorated the wall behind Gena's desk, each featuring the words *sexual healing* in over fifteen languages. An enormous, custom-made standing mirror leaned against the right wall. Gena noticed Carmela staring into it and posing several times during her tirade.

She stood there looking like "blame it on the alcohol." She wore a turquoise cocktail dress that was half a centimeter away from being just a V of fabric draping over strategic places on her body. Shimmering dupioni silk plunged and swung in both the front and the back. There had to be a yard of fabric tape holding the dress in place. Carmela's bare legs were jammed into six-inch matching diamond-crusted sling backs with gold-tipped heels. Gena held her tongue and silently chanted "It's for The Epicure. It's for The Epicure."

Looking at her client, Gena almost felt *über*conservative and overdressed. With her tapered bob wig, Essence glasses, short black leather dress and black six-inch pumps, Gena's wardrobe appeared cheerless and flat.

Carmela not only brought in money which kept the center going, but clientele who kept the center growing. Whatever else she was, Carmela was a referral machine. And the people she referred were high dollar and surprisingly respectable. Gena had no worries about their discretion.

For someone so young, she had the most unique fetish allowed at The Epicure.

The entourage Carmela brought with her was ridiculous—although Gena had to admit they were all sweet on the eye. Seven overly handsome, muscle-bound men of various ethnicities.

Carmela put her cell phone in a silver lamé purse. She took a seat in one of three Asian-inspired lounge chairs in front of Gena's desk. "A whole year?"

It was the first time Carmela had spoken in a normal tone since she thundered into Gena's office. Gena leaned forward, grateful, but ready to bargain again if it meant protecting The Epicure. "Yes. One year. You can come and go as you please."

"Ooh, Gennnna!" Carmela squealed and clapped her hands together. "You are so good to me. I wouldn't be the same without you."

"Thank you for saying that."

"No, really. I couldn't do what I do, as good as I do, without this place. It chills me out in a way..."

Carmela's eyes misted, her lip quivered. "It's the only place where I feel normal."

Gena nodded. Even if Carmela was in actress mode and just feeding her a line, she would take it. She lived to hear that her center was making a difference for people—people who didn't fit so neatly into the sexual boundaries society set. And as a therapist and sex coach, she knew one thing: even lines come from some grain of truth.

"I just want you to know how sorry I am that this

happened. This is the first and, as far as I'm concerned, the last time anything like that has happened here. I know that's not much consolation, since the breach of privacy happened to you. I just—"

"I'm sorry, too. This…it just made me crazy. I went off like you took the picture. I know you protect us here. I know that. I just want—"

"What?" Gena asked, leery of what Carmela could demand but needing to know.

"I want to know who did this to me. I'm sure you want to know, too."

"I'm looking into it. When I know something, you'll know something."

Chapter Three

He'd checked his libido at the door...but that bad boy followed him inside anyway.

To turn it off completely, he stopped and noticed the golden-skinned woman snaking down the brass pole who had more junk in her trunk than three Southern gals. Her orange bra and thong were almost imaginary. Honey dust on her arms and six-pack abs glistened in the cheap lights of The Partyhouse and flashed like tiny strobes on brown skin.

She moved like water. Tonight at The Partyhouse, she was the headliner. Her body seemed boneless and flexible in a ghetto-yoga, "I can wrap my leg around my own neck," kinda way. As she twisted, wrapped and spun around the pole on the stage to a staccato of bass and nasty saxophones, Marlowe strummed his fingers on the bar.

He glanced around, noting the feral expressions on the men's faces. They watched her with wild, hungry eyes that soured his stomach. A nerve in his jaw pulsed. He looked away and stared at the glass of Courvoisier he had nearly finished.

The man sitting beside him seemed hungriest of all. An easy mark, he thought. No sooner had he thought "easy mark," the woman, who was all curves, silicone and thick thighs, slinked over, eight-inch clear heels snapping against the stage like whips cracking.

In an instant, her body popped down. A whoosh of perfume and sweat assaulted his nose as her ass made an arch and ellipses in front of the man's face. The guy held out a twenty. "How about a lap dance?" he said, patting the peak in his pants.

"I'd love to, baby." she purred. "For two fifty."

She strutted off the stage, chest leading the way, and straddled the man, who could have used a good drool bib. He reached into his pocket and pulled out his wallet while her hips did some slow corkscrew action against his erection.

Marlowe looked away. Drained the rest of his drink and tried to keep his lunch down. "I'll give you a hundred right now if you put your clothes on and meet me outside."

Her hips stopped in the middle of her circles. The man's eyes popped open.

"Let me see it," she demanded.

Technofunk marched out of the speakers, vibrated against the walls and Marlowe's bar stool. He reached into his wallet, fanned five twenties.

The lady in orange jumped off of ol' boy's lap with a quickness. "Sorry, Daddy. I'll give you a free ride when I get back."

She snatched the money from Marlowe's hand and ran backstage. "Five minutes!" she called before disappearing behind the black curtain.

"What the hell?" the man asked.

By the time she came out, fifteen minutes had passed. She emerged from the side door of The Partyhouse, waist-length ponytail swishing across her back and wearing a pair of orange sweats and white Nikes. She leaned into the passenger window, transformed from pole dancer back into Shereeta Chambers.

"What's up, cuz!" Shereeta said, smiling with big white teeth and deep, round dimples.

"Hey, baby girl," he responded out of habit, although his cousin Shereeta hadn't been a girl for twenty-seven years. As a matter of fact, for the past five years, Shereeta Chambers was a high-dollar call girl who specialized in servicing rich men with large companies and deep pockets. To top that off, she had a penchant for exhibitionism, which she indulged with periodic headlining stints at The Partyhouse, a strip club on the fringe of the city.

Shereeta eyed him suspiciously and hung back. “If my father sent you here—”

“Nah. He didn’t.”

She checked him out as though he were a customer instead of a cousin. “You lost weight.”

“Couple of pounds,” he admitted. Marlowe had always preferred his frame with some bulk on it. The challenge was, he had one of those metabolisms that allowed him to eat just about anything and not gain a pound. So, he had a regular gym routine and spent a lot of time on the weights. Three sets, eight reps, dumbbells, both close and wide grip. His routine worked and at six foot one inch, he made two hundred pounds of muscle look good.

Too bad his stint in the Methodist Hospital care unit trimmed almost fifteen pounds from his steady weight.

“I heard you were in the hospital,” she said, taking the seat next to him.

“Yeah?” he said, waiting for her excuse. She didn’t need one, though. Some cousins were close, others weren’t. Marlowe and Shereeta had never been that close, but maybe working on this story could change that.

“I’ve been in and out of town for the past few weeks. Traveling with my clients. Gotta keep ’em happy, you know?”

Did he ever. “I know.”

She smiled. “So, how’d you know my rent was late?”

"Your rent's always late."

Shereeta sucked her teeth. "I hear it runs in the family. Besides, it just kills me to fork over two thousand dollars for four walls."

"Four walls at Midtown Crossing," Marlowe said, ignoring her dig.

"True that."

Shereeta rented a one-room studio apartment with all the amenities of a four-star hotel at an enviable location.

"How long have you got?" Marlowe asked.

"About thirty minutes. After that, I'm back for an encore. "

Marlowe gritted his teeth. Shereeta's "profession" is what kept his aunt on her knees.

"So, what do you need?" Shereeta asked.

"I need some info for an assignment."

"I heard you got fired," she said, shaking sparkles out of her hair and onto the black leather of his interior.

"I work freelance. I can't get fired," he responded. But his cousin was close to being right. Getting kicked off the last story he was on left a sour taste in his mouth. When he'd started researching the Seventh Phoenyx House, he had no idea how involved he'd get. How much the social-class inequities would anger him. And how much satisfaction he'd get from putting in work himself. But once again, he'd crossed the line—the objective reporter line—that line that was supposed to keep him distant and impartial to the story he was telling.

But that was his way. It had been his M.O. since his earliest days as a reporter. He remembered covering a story of a wildfire burning out of control near Reno, Nevada, once. The damned thing had been burning for nearly a week and had crashed through a major firebreak. When it changed direction and started to threaten the suburbs, his station sent him to cover the evacuation of the residents. While interviewing a resident live, part of the fire broke through a fire line and quickly roared onto the property. Marlowe immediately put down his microphone and helped the man beat back the fire, at least temporarily.

For days, "Reporter Battles Fire on Air" was the popular news-video footage on every major network.

"You working on that earthquake overseas?"

"Nothin' like that."

"So, what then?"

"I thought I'd debunk an urban sex myth."

"Can't help you with that one. Black men really are bigger."

Marlowe laughed and checked out the sexy sister headed inside the club. The stiffening of his groin told him he felt a lap dance coming on. Then he remembered his promise to himself and to Tuck.

"That's Dominique. Her real name is Stephanie. Wanna meet her?"

"Yes," he said. "But I'm trying to cut down."

"What?"

"Yeah. A new leaf and all that. Anyway, I thought I'd do a piece on the Chocolate Chateau."

"You can't get in there. You gotta be invited or know someone."

"See, that's what I want to explore. People talk about this thing like it really exists."

"What if it does?"

"Yeah, right. A mansion where black folks go to get their freak on?"

"It's not a mansion. It's a resort."

Marlowe couldn't believe his ears. It must be groupthink. "I can get you four more bills if you know the location of this thing."

"I can't tell you."

"Well, that's a first. So far, people claim it's in Chicago, D.C., Atlanta, Denver, Minneapolis, Tijuana, and Mississippi. One guy told me it was here in Omaha, in Ponca Hills."

His cousin shot him a sour glance. "That's what you get for asking just any ol' body. How come you didn't come ask me first?"

"Hey, lady," a man walking past the car said. He looked like a ravenous wolf as he leered at Shereeta.

"Hey," Shereeta said.

"Honestly, you're blood and all, but you've got trouble on your shoulder twenty-four/seven. I just need to stay as far away from trouble as I can."

The sour glance turned rancid. "Really? So, why are you here now then?"

Marlowe thought about the two weeks he'd already wasted talking to anyone who might have a clue about debunking this myth. Following leads that took him nowhere. His desperation brought him to his cousin.

Shereeta waved her hand. "I get it. I'm some kinda last resort. Don't go to the nasty ho' for help. Some of her dirt might jump off on you."

"That's not true," Marlowe said, slightly insulted.

Shereeta leveled a hard gaze in his direction.

"Okay. You're right. I'm sorry. But you do keep stuff going. You know that's why most of the family keeps their distance."

"Well, I've changed," she said, checking her reflection in the passenger mirror.

"Since when?"

The cousins stared at each other and then laughed.

"So, then something big must have brought you my way—not just this story."

Marlowe pushed away the cloud of desperation threatening to form in his mind and focused.

"Yeah," he admitted. "It was something big."

Shereeta searched his face, trying to discern his meaning, he suspected, and a terrible thought occurred to him. Instead of stressing about the story, he could borrow the money he needed from cousin dearest, and instead of aiming for big stories, he could pitch more-mainstream articles to smaller magazines. Or, he could simply call Tuck and tell him not to wait the three remaining weeks and go now. Both options made him want to smash his fist into a wall.

"I'm sorry it took a miracle to bring you around my way," Shereeta said. Her voice sounded gruff now, agitated. "No one wants to come see about the troublemaker."

"Shereeta, look, I'm sorry if I made it seem that way."

Marlowe was starting to realize that it was a bad idea to visit his cousin. And he damn sure shouldn't have admitted that the family considered her the bad apple of the bunch. Truth was, of all the members in his family, he'd always found Shereeta's determination to march to the beat of her own drum fascinating. He could imagine very clearly what would happen if she decided to channel that determination into a more positive direction.

"One thing I know about you…when you put your mind to something, you do it. Now, most folks might make different choices than you, but most folks will live their lives without knowing what it's like to give everything they have over to something they want—something they believe in.

"I'd choose a different lifestyle for you, sure, but you and I are a lot alike. We both throw ourselves into what we believe—for better or for worse."

Marlowe watched as his cousin's eyes softened then welled up. If it was one thing that tied his stomach in knots, it was women's tears. They were like some kind of Achilles' heel that made him want to rescue a damsel whom he perceived in distress. Right now, he couldn't even rescue himself, let alone someone else.

"All right, cuz," he said, turning on his engine. "I was hoping that if anyone had any specific info about this place, it would be you. I better get gone. I've got some phone calls to make."

The streetlights blazed like tall torches in the parking lot. It was beyond well lit, Marlowe imagined, for the safety of the dancers as they left. It wouldn't do for some overdrunk patron to fool himself into believing the woman who'd just given him a lap dance really loved him.

Shereeta had a strange look on her face, as though she was struggling with something.

Marlowe gave her a friendly wink. "I won't be a stranger. I promise."

She nodded and nodded.

"Marlowe," she said. Under the hard light of the streetlights, Shereeta looked much less like a stripper/call girl and more like a regular woman with dreams, aspirations and a family who loved her.

"Yes?" he responded.

"I need to tell you something about that chateau."

That look came back—the look of struggle and wrestling. She looked both worried and eager at the same time. "It's about your story…it's about the Chocolate Chateau."

"What about it?"

"It's not a myth. It's in Sedona, Arizona. And, I've been there."

Chapter Four

"What do you mean, you've been there?"

"Two years ago, I hooked up with this guy. He runs some kind of computer company—only it's not the computers, it's what keeps them going. He said if it weren't for his company, cell phones couldn't do half of what they do. Anyway, I was his companion for a year. And when I say companion, I mean companion."

Shereeta's face turned serious. Her eyes glanced left and right as if she were checking for intruders or trying to make sure no one could overhear.

"No sex, we just hung out. Talked. Went to dinner, movies. It was like he was prepping me or feeling me out for something. Turns out, ol' boy is an exhibitionist. He *loves* to have sex; he just likes to have it in front of other people."

"Figures," Marlowe said, remembering some of the conversations he'd had with his boys. If their wives only knew what they really talked about sometimes—

"But when you're some muckety-muck, big-time computer guy and you got your face in *Wired* magazine and *PC World,* you can't just show up to a swinger's ball and get freaky."

Marlowe's investigative brain had already switched on and was cataloging everything his cousin was telling him. Even if there were no such thing as the Chocolate Chateau, he suddenly believed that there could be a market for such a place.

Lights from the street cast a silvery glow against the black leather interior, contoured bucket seats and cockpit dash. Marlowe tapped his fingers against the gear shift as article ideas duked it out in his mind.

"Then one day he flew me in his private jet to this place in Sedona, Arizona. We ended up at this *über*resort. And well…I had the time of my life. All of that exhibitionism came out. I've never come so hard or so many times in my life."

"Okay, TMI, but damn, you actually…liked it?"

"He was good. But it wasn't just that. It was like he belonged there. Something about that place brought out the best in him. He might be the best of the best at cell phone chips, but he was off the chain ridin' me in front of a bunch of folks enjoying the view. He…*we* were the center of attraction.

"I haven't been back since, but I damn sure wouldn't mind."

Marlowe opened the notebook app on his cell phone and tapped in a few notes. "Why didn't he take you back?"

"I don't know. I asked him about it a couple times. He said once was enough."

"How do you know this was the place? It could be just some swinger's palace."

"I can't explain it. I just knew. All of the rumors you've ever heard about the place are true. Wall-to-wall brown people. And not just anybody. It's a special type of party going on. And everyone had this understanding that the fact that this place existed was on the hush.

"I remember the doctor reminding us more than once about being discreet."

"What happens in Vegas, huh?"

Shereeta pulled a pack of Benson & Hedges out of her purse and lit up. "It's more than that. It's like a club with rules you just don't violate."

Disappointment churned in Marlowe's stomach like a bad meal. So much for Operation Rescue Marlowe's Career. His goal was to write about the power of urban myths, namely the Chocolate Chateau, and how rampant this particular myth was in the community. But if it actually existed, that means…

"How do I get in?"

Marlowe wished that in the warm blur of the streetlight, his cousin resembled an ordinary twenty-seven-year-old woman with a normal job and regular aspirations. The truth was far from his wishes. Outside the strip club, she looked more like a money girl than ever. Thin, blond braids, lifeless eyes, as if she'd been doing a thousand years' hard time on earth and hadn't smiled in centuries. He imagined that when she wasn't on the pole, she cleaned up better for her top-drawer clients.

"Are you on drugs?" he asked, noting how hollow she looked, sunken and eaten away from the inside out.

"No! If I look tired it's because I haven't been taking my iron lately. My doctor says I'm anemic, like really bad. If I don't take this big ol' green pill every day, I can barely get my ass out of bed."

"But that's what you want, right?" he asked with a chuckle. "To stay in bed?"

"Ah, negro, what kinda jokes you got?" she said, smirking, then chuckled. "But hey, if I can't laugh at me, nobody can, right?"

Marlowe wasn't sure what she meant by that, and he didn't want to know. What he did want was more information on the chateau.

"Seriously, Shereeta. How can I get invited to this thing?"

"You have to know somebody. Or the doctor invites you."

"The doctor. You said that before. What kind of doctor?"

"Dr. G., although I don't know if she's a real doctor. I think folks just call her that. But my client said that she invites people sometimes."

Marlowe stared into traffic and watched the few-and-far-between vehicles speeding down the highway. Smoke from Shereeta's cigarette tightened his lungs and threatened to make him wheeze. "You gotta put that out," he said. "And, you gotta hook me up."

She flicked the menthol cigarette out the window. "I wish I had it like that, cuz. If I did, I'd hook myself up and probably never leave that place."

"What about your boy? Can your client get me in? Or should I say, can't you *persuade* him to get me in?"

"What kind of story are you working on?"

"Urban legends."

"What will you do when you find out the legend lives up to the hype?"

Marlowe mulled over the question and didn't have an answer. He hadn't considered the idea that the Chocolate Chateau might actually be real. He gave it some thought…a story about a secret party palace would put him back in Tuck's good graces. Marlowe could all but hear a big electronic funds transfer now.

"Make this happen for me, cuz."

"And what?"

He paused for only for half a second. "And whatever."

Her eyebrow rose and her mouth curled into something close to a smile. It wasn't the flat line her lips had been since he arrived. "Well then, I guess I better get busy."

Marlowe turned on the engine and drove her up to the door. There were even fewer cars than when he first pulled up. He put his car in Park under the flashing Partyhouse sign and held his breath as Shereeta lit up cigarette number two.

She opened the door and blew out a small thundercloud of smoke. "How soon can you be ready to go?"

If Tuck okayed the story, he had to have okayed the costs. He'd charge everything he needed to his expense account with *LifeWare.* "Tonight."

"Dang, slow down. How about tomorrow? I'll call you tonight with the details. Get two tickets."

"Two?"

"Yeah." Shereeta stretched her thick legs out the side of his Nissan and stood. "I'm coming with."

"Hell no. No!"

"You just said whatever I wanted. I want to go with you."

"No deal."

"Then, no deal."

Marlowe rubbed the back of his neck in frustration. "God is going to punish you for this."

"God has already punished me. Now do you want your story or not?"

Shereeta had always equaled trouble in his family. And anyone who got mixed up with her always ended up in a mess of it. If Marlowe could get his finances back in order, maybe he wouldn't mind a little trouble.

She closed the door and stood back. Marlowe put his car in Drive and pressed on the gas. He stopped before he got ten feet away. Shereeta hadn't moved. He rolled his window down and cussed himself out at the same time. Tucker would have his ass along with his bank account if this didn't work out.

"Two tickets!" he called.

That did get a smile out of her as she pranced inside the Partyhouse like that iron she swore she needed was suddenly surging through her veins.

Marlowe drove off, not wondering if his cousin would get him into trouble, but wondering just how much.

Chapter Five

"How much did they pay you, Ward?" she asked, not even bothering to turn and look at him. Even a small glance right now meant she'd take one of her whips and there would be no safe word he could utter that would stop her arm. She needed another minute for her fury to subside.

"Who? Pay me w-what?" he stuttered.

"Business In The Street. BIS." Gena paused. Let those initials fall out of her mouth like hot boulders. She felt the pressure to slap the gleam off his teeth building inside her and bit it back.

"Word on the street is they pay pretty good. A few thousand for photos. A couple hundred just for a good tip. You must have made out like a smooth criminal since the photos appeared in their online and print publications."

They'd dated once. Well, that wasn't completely true. Their "dating" amounted to one late-afternoon slap and tickle. So, that didn't make them an item, but still, the man had seen her naked. She hated the thought of having bared her body to a shameless low-life.

"Is that the only reason you came here…to get info on my clients?"

"No."

"Then what? Did you approach *BIS* or did they approach you?"

Ward stood at the wet bar—as far away from her as he could get—and let out an exasperated breath. "I approached them. Last month. I guess seeing Carmela put thoughts into my head."

Gena lightly fingered her grass plant and forced herself into a calm state. "You mean dollar signs."

Thankfully the photos he'd taken were from a cell phone and blurry as hell. The image resembled Carmela, but it was too fuzzy to be sure it was her. Unfortunately, *BIS* ran with the story anyway, claiming Carmela was a sex addict and in need of serious rehab. No matter how close to the truth it was, it didn't give them the right to smear her on their home page like a flash plug-in.

"Whose idea was the all-night orgy?"

"The editor, I swear! Gena—"

"Keep it to yourself."

She kept her back turned and stared out the window of her office. The sun beat down hard. That April was turning into a dichotomy of hot-hot days and cold nights. After everything—security checks, background checks, screenings for both employees and clients—she'd come close to losing everything. Too close.

As a therapist, she'd made one vital promise to her clients: anonymity. Privacy. Complete, total, utter. If she couldn't guarantee that, she had nothing. Two things mattered to her in her life: her reputation and her soul. Right now, this poor excuse for a man had mucked her reputation.

Finally, she turned to face him. "I hope you kept that money, Ward."

He huffed loudly and blinked his round, moist eyes rapidly. A sure sign he'd been caught with his hand in the paparazzi cookie jar. She could barely believe how those puppy-dog eyes of his had persuaded her out of her clothes. "Hire yourself a good lawyer."

"What?"

"You know that employment agreement you signed when you started working for me? That confidentially clause means I'm going to sue your ass off. Every cent you own, every possession you have. I'm going to slap a badass lawsuit on you so far-reaching, your grandchildren will owe me damages."

"It was just a picture. It didn't turn out anyway."

He looked so out of place against the vibrant red

and sunlit backdrop of her office. Like gray soot smudged against a rainbow. "A *good* lawyer, Ward."

"Baby—"

"Baby?" she said, disgust churning in her stomach. Instinctively, she reached for the riding crop she always kept on her desk. The smooth, hard leather gave her something to focus on.

Her hand was itching now. It felt as if one hundred fire ants were scurrying over it. She really, really wanted to slap him. She just needed to.

"You really want to get the hell out now." She smacked the riding crop against her palm.

"Gen-na—"

"The longer you stay, the more your face looks like a punching bag. So, I'm telling you, it's about to be mama said knock you out up in here."

Gena hadn't kickboxed in six years, but she suspected her roundhouse and left jab were still on point.

Ward backed up slowly and then made an arthritic-like march to the office door. Gena turned back to the window where a black swan glided gently over the outlying pond almost trancelike. What's it like to be that tranquil? Gena wondered. To be that serene?

"Well, that went well," Narcisa said, closing the door behind Ward.

Gena placed the riding crop back on her desk and couldn't stop wondering how she could have been so careless…again. She'd thought she'd finally ended her stupid habit of choosing the wrong man. "I guess."

"He's a straight up scumbag, but taking money from his grandkids?"

First Gena smiled, and then she laughed. Not so much because it was funny, but because she needed the release. Social media was going to be the death of her. Between Facebook, YouTube and Twitter, Gena expected to look up on the internet one day and have news of her private sex parties wallpapering cyberspace. So far, so good. But she was going to have to step up her game to protect her clients. Otherwise, there would be no clients.

"I have to protect my clients, Narcisa. I let my guard down. It was stupid. But fool me once. You know? Never again."

She heard herself say the words just as a couple emerged from a limousine in the circle drive of the resort. They seemed courteous enough, but Gena could tell a front when she saw one. They were together but definitely not a couple. More like polite cordials. They didn't have a couple rhythm. Folks who had been together for a while knew each other, how to walk in space together—side by side and moving comfortably forward. They took on each other's cadence and created a new one between the two. Striding and arms swinging like a song in two-part harmony—even when there were problems. This couple strode together like sometime friends. Gena would have her work cut out with them.

"Who are they?" she asked.

Narcisa stood beside her at the window. "They're the newbies."

Gena hadn't approved a new couple for admission to the resort for a few months. Now, it was going to take a while to get beyond her suspicions.

"They've been screened. Don't worry," Narcisa said.

Gena checked out the man, looking oh so good. His hair was almost russet. The perfect hue of honor and fire, she thought. She stared at his eyes, feeling as though she could live in their depths for days and feed off of the raw sensuality she found there. He had an athlete's body and a jazz musician's swagger—sleek muscle over a smoky room backbeat. He walked as if he could handle himself on a soccer field, a dance floor and a bedroom.

Then she chided herself for her reaction. Ashamed of her reaction to somebody's else's guy. "I'm not worried. I'm not worried at all."

"Good," Narcisa said. "I'll go check them in."

"Then bring them here," Gena said. "I just want to double-check them. I don't want any more surprises."

"Yes, mistress," Narcisa said and strolled out of the office.

Chapter Six

If Marlowe didn't know he was on assignment, he'd swear he'd booked a weekend at the hippest urban resort in the northern hemisphere. The grounds sprawled east and west for half a block in both directions. The resort—styled from an avant-garde merger of English Tudor and Frank Lloyd Wright—looked fresh out of a young, ambitious and slightly twisted architect's mind.

The woman at the front desk had to be one of the finest he'd ever seen. Her hair was done in a curly brown beehive. Her makeup was dramatic and so over-the-top sexy that her face looked like a brown, red and orange work of erotic art. Around her neck, she sported a black leather collar with a D-ring hanging loosely from the front. The red leather miniskirt she wore was so tight, it could have been inside her skin rather than on the outside.

Marlowe fought the sensual awareness building inside him. After all, he'd promised to be good.

"How may I serve you?" she asked, big eyes bright and hopeful.

Marlowe struggled to answer that question without being disrespectful.

"We're checking in," Shereeta said, taking his arm in a phony possessive manner. "We're Mr. and Mrs. Chambers."

"One moment, please," the woman said, scanning an old-school guest book showing names written in calligraphy. Her slender, manicured finger slid down the list quickly and found their names, not in alphabetical order but at the end.

"Your first names?" she asked.

"Marlowe and Shereeta."

"Thank you," the woman replied. Her voice and mannerisms belied her appearance. She was subdued—took her time speaking and moved in a gentle, soothing way.

"My name is Narcisa. If you need anything while you're here," she gave Marlowe a scorching once-over and alluring smile, "please call on me."

"Thank you," Marlowe said, regaining his voice and giving a half nod in her direction.

"Emerald, please take their luggage to Room 428."

Marlowe bent toward their suitcases in protest. "Oh, no. I can manage."

"Yes, Mr. Chambers. I'm sure you can." There was that smile again. "However, Dr. G. wants to meet with you to complete your check-in and give you a proper welcome."

Concern tensed Marlowe's muscles. "Dr. G.?"

"Yes. She's in charge of The Epicure and will complete your…orientation."

The concern grew. He turned to his cousin. "Orientation, huh?"

"Don't worry about it," Shereeta said, smiling a little too sweetly. "Everyone has to be checked out before they can play. It's like a job interview."

"Anything else I need to know now that we're here?" he asked.

"Plenty," Shereeta said. "But first things first, okay?"

"Right," he responded. "Just don't make me resent trusting you. At least, not this soon."

Emerald loaded their bags on a luggage cart and headed off toward the elevators.

Shereeta patted the inside of his forearm. It made him feel like a child about to be schooled. "Be cool, okay? Relax," she said.

They followed Narcisa in the opposite direction.

Marlowe's Ferragamo shoes melted into the ultrasoft carpet. He was gliding more than walking. He made a note for his story that the place came built for pleasure and comfort all the way down to the flooring.

Until then, the place wasn't any different than any luxury resort he'd ever been to. With the exception of Narcisa and Emerald, who looked as if they could tie a brother down no problem and punish him for bad behavior, the lobby was not far from what he'd expected. One guy passed them in plain clothes with a stun gun, pepper spray and a baton attached to an oversized belt. Security, Marlowe realized.

"I guess I should tell you," Shereeta whispered.

Marlowe's gut knotted. "Tell me what?"

"This week at the Chocolate Chateau is sexual dysfunction week."

"So?" Marlowe said, letting go of some of his concern.

He took in the stucco walls. Rag-rolled with paint the color of buttermilk, they gave the hallway an upscale and relaxed vibe at the same time. Abstract paintings, sculptures and lamps lined the hallway of offices leading toward a large and open stairway. Marlowe wondered where such broad steps could lead.

"One moment, please," Narcisa said, stopping in front of a large red door. Marlowe and Shereeta held in place behind her as she knocked.

"Come in," came a voice from the other side. The timbre was as smooth as French silk. Marlowe couldn't wait to see the body that came with such a voice.

"Mistress, I've brought Mr. and Mrs. Chambers," Narcisa said, addressing the woman standing behind a long teakwood desk. She was leaning over a credenza and watering a plant that looked more like ornamental violet grass.

Through a skylight, the sunrays fell into the room in large, golden sheets. Antique gold fixtures accented the warm red-and-yellow walls. Marlowe's eye landed on the walnut hutch that doubled as a wet bar. He could go for a cognac.

Narcisa ushered them in and motioned them to sit opposite the desk.

Marlowe made a mental note. *Collared staff. Art-deco interior design. Mistress.* The article was starting off well.

The woman behind the desk finally turned to face them. She placed the watering can inside the credenza cabinet and smiled at their escort. "That will be all."

Marlowe had been straight-up wrong. Narcisa was just the visual appetizer. The woman behind the desk was the rest of a seven-course meal.

With her sleek, black hair straight and brushing the top of her shoulders and a shiny and tight black dress set off by a plunging neckline, she looked less like a doctor and more like a kinky glass of wine. Damn if he wasn't up for a tasting—almost literally. Too bad he'd sworn off...drinking. Just his luck to be in the presence of that much woman and not be able to fully enjoy it.

She casually inventoried the blindfolds, paddles, slappers and eye masks laid on her desk. A woman that sexy could have men lined up all the way to Connecticut. Just the dark depths of her eyes alone made him want to staple on a drool bucket. And the round hips inside a skintight black dress made him wish for a carton of ribbed Trojans and a deadline-free week. Just being in the same room with her was like unleashing a tiger. The caged animal in him wanted out immediately.

"Welcome," the woman said, extending a warm hand. "Please have a seat."

Marlowe suppressed a growl and quickly shut down his brain. But it was too late. His mind had already undressed her. According to his imagination, she was wearing a black-lace push-up with thin straps, see-through cups and no underwear.

"Not everyone here uses their real names. Your arrangements said real names were okay. Is that still true?"

"Yes," Shereeta said.

He heard the woman speaking and tried to concentrate on something other than undoing hooks and pulling down straps. It was hard. Just as he was going to be if he didn't focus. She looked like one of those calm, determined women who loved to stare into mirrors while rhythmically brushing their hair. He imagined she had people—to do her nails, her housework, her accounting…her body. And not lovers.

More like men she kept close and on call just in case she was in the mood for an orgasm.

Her voice was both confident and inviting. The lines of her body flowed long and easy—a question mark pulled nearly straight. She moved like a graceful and hot Sahara wind. As she sat down at her desk, she measured him with black, serious eyes and lips as perky as her breasts. Just right for…

It was lust at first sight.

The sooner he got his story, the better.

"So, Shereeta, good to see you again," the doctor said.

Shereeta grinned and blinked sweetly. "And you."

"Mr. Chambers, I'm Gena. Some people call me Dr. G. I answer to both. Thank you for coming to The Epicure, and congratulations on your marriage. When was the big day?"

Marlowe's mouth flew open, but no sounds came out. *Married?*

"A month ago," Shereeta chimed in. "And that's why we're here. I want our marriage to be the best it can be."

Every nerve in Marlowe's body coiled like a spring. "Married? We're not married!"

"You're not?" The look on Gena's face merged surprise with suspicion.

Shereeta fidgeted in her chair and smiled wildly. "Marlowe…poopkins…"

"This is not a singles' event," Gena stated. "If you're not in a committed relationship—"

"Oh, we *are,*" Shereeta assured her.

Anger built so quickly inside Marlowe, he could only gaze furiously at his foolish cousin and shake his head. His sharp disapproval must have had an effect. For a moment, Shereeta looked as if she was about to own up to her lie. Then Marlowe realized her admission could cost him the trip to the chateau and the story he needed.

"The truth is…" Shereeta began.

"We *were* married," Marlowe finished. He scrambled to come up with an untruth he could live with. "But we got our marriage annulled. So, now—"

"We're here because we want to try again," Shereeta chimed in. Her eyes beamed like two headlights on high. "We know we didn't give our marriage a chance. We *really* want to make it work this time."

She patted his thigh and Marlowe fought to keep his breakfast down.

Gena nodded her understanding. "Well, here at the center, we help individuals as well as couples enrich their lives through sexual discovery. I'm confident we can add to your…reconnection. Shereeta, you've been here before, so you're familiar with the guidelines. Marlowe, just to get you on the same page, our primary philosophy at The Epicure is discretion—meaning privacy, meaning confidentiality, meaning peace of mind. Without that, nothing else makes any difference or is even possible."

Marlowe was still stunned about the married thing. "Absolutely," he said.

"You've probably heard the phrase 'What happens in Vegas stays in Vegas.'"

He nodded. "Heard it. Lived it."

"Well, your discretion and confidentiality go beyond that. Our guests adhere to a code of honor."

"Where do I sign?" he asked, wondering if there was any written proof that the place existed.

Gena leveled an even gaze at him. "We accept nothing less than the most important contract. Your word."

Marlowe swallowed. This undercover reporter gig had set his resolve on edge already. Generally, he was a man of his word, even if he had to stretch out that word over a few weeks. He always kept his promises.

First his cousin tried to turn him into a married man. Now he's taking a vow he had every intention of breaking. This Chocolate Chateau story better be worth the compromises he was making. "You have my word."

A chord of guilt curled in his stomach like a salted slug. It darkened his mood. Damn his conscience. It never ceased to get in his way.

"We don't allow cell phones at The Epicure. If you have them, you'll have to turn them in."

She motioned to the floor safe next to her desk. "Don't worry about safety. I'll keep them locked away."

Shereeta pulled her cell phone out of her purse and

slid it across the desk. Marlowe, on the other hand, was not feeling so generous.

"It's a condition of your stay," Gena said.

Reluctantly, he pulled his smartphone from his back pocket and placed it on the desk.

"Thank you," Dr. G. said. "These days every cell phone is a movie camera. This is really for your protection. Also, if you have a digital camera or a laptop, I'll need those also. Again, for confidentially purposes."

Could she know who he was or what he was there to do? It wasn't possible. Even so, Marlowe wasn't about to give up his laptop.

"No can do, doc. No will do."

Shereeta sucked her teeth. "Marlowe, stop being so obstinate. Give her your laptop."

He stared into her eyes, bright with way too much makeup. Frustration slicing through him like a thin knife. "Haven't you said enough already?"

Shereeta shifted in her seat and angled her body away from him. "Apparently not. Dr. G., he's got a digital camera and a laptop in his carry-on."

"You'll need to bring them both to this office, Mr. Chambers. Immediately after this interview."

Game over, Marlowe thought. How could he write his story without his computer? The thought of using paper and pen was enough to make him ill. Maybe agreeing to the crazy notion now would buy him enough time to come up with another plan.

"No problem," he said. His voice sounded unconvincing, even to him.

The doctor's eyebrow rose. It was both serious and seductive. No doubt about it. Dr. G. was the personification of sexuality, and she knew it. Marlowe knew. Any man who saw her knew it. She looked, sounded, moved as though her libido never really turned off or shut down. It just went on high simmer.

"Now that that's out of the way, let's move on. I like to interview my first-time guests. To get to know them—what they want, what they need, any challenges or special requests they have. It also gives you a chance to get to know me and get comfortable with the center. That way we both can decide the best next step, which can mean staying at the center or leaving it."

"Got it," Marlowe said.

"Good," the doctor said then leaned back in her chair. "Now, what things have you tried to correct your impotence problem, Mr. Chambers?"

The I word. *Did someone just use the* I word*?* he wondered. He turned to his cousin. "My what?"

Shereeta cleared her throat. "That's what I've been trying to tell you, uh, Pookie."

Marlowe leveled a glance at her with enough fury to melt steel. "Impotence. You told them I was impotent!"

Shereeta offered the doctor a flimsy smile. "He's kinda in denial, but let's be clear. We have tried nudie mags, triple-X movies, Viagra. We tried sitz baths, hypnosis, acupuncture, herbal teas and magnet therapy."

Dr. G.'s eyes widened in surprise. "In such a short period of time?"

Marlowe grit his teeth. Shereeta worked her neck. "My orgasms are very important to me."

Gena smiled. "I understand. What happened after that?"

"Nothing." Shereeta threw a frustrated glance at his crotch. "And I mean nothing."

Marlowe had just about all he could take. "What? Shereeta, come on!"

"Well, there was that one time we had a threesome. Only it was really me and Rocky, our next-door neighbor. Marlowe watched us through a peephole. He seemed to enjoy that. Not enough to… you know—" Shereeta lowered her head and her voice as if she were speaking in church. "—get it up or anything. But Mini Marlowe woke up a little bit."

"Mini? Ain't nothin' mini about me. Get outta here with that."

The doctor leaned forward a bit. "Is there another side to this story, Mr. Chambers?"

Marlowe was jammed up bad. The only thing he could do was go along with his cousin's story so he could get his. Shereeta stared at him. A sharp look of "Say something; I dare you" plastered on her face.

"No," he said.

"Dr. G., it's just like I said. My ex-hubby has a problem. But I noticed that even the thought of me with someone else puts a jump in his Johnson. So, we figured if we came, and I actually spent the five days with someone else—maybe a few someone elses—that would be the best thing for our relationship."

Marlowe expected a reaction from the good Dr. G., but he didn't get one. He guessed she'd seen, heard and maybe even done it all. "Mr. Chambers, how do you feel about this?"

"Good," he lied. "Great, wonderful." He folded his arms to keep from choking his cousin.

"Excellent. Then I have just a few more things to cover," Dr. G. said. "Do you have nocturnal erections, Mr. Chambers?"

Marlowe said *yes* at the same time Shereeta said *no*.

Shereeta rolled her eyes. "Dr. G., I can't remember the last time I saw him with a stiff one."

Marlowe realized that if he did have an ED problem, coming to this place could cause more harm than good. Who would want to perform after this?

"How about nocturnal emissions?" the doctor asked.

Marlowe and Shereeta stared at each other to see who would speak first.

The doctor persisted. "Do you come in your sleep, Mr. Chambers?"

Shereeta leaned forward and looked as though she was actually distraught. "I don't think so, doctor. Now, I don't want to believe it, but I might have to. His dick might be dead."

Marlowe could take only so much. He turned to his cousin, anger rushing to the surface. "I should never have brought you with me. I knew better. I *knew* better!"

"Is there something else going on between you besides ED?"

"No," they both said flatly, holding a bitter stare.

Suddenly Marlowe wanted to get out of that office. As cozy as it was, as sexy as Dr. Gena was. He needed to regroup, replan and set his cousin straight.

"You've had the standard battery of tests?"

"If you mean have I been to the doctor, the answer would be no. But I can tell you my, uh…*alter ego* rises with the sun."

"And when you try to have sex with Shereeta in the morning…"

"I can't. Not that I don't want to. It's just, well, when I turn over, and I see her lying beside me…" Marlowe made a face as if he'd just bitten into a lemon rind.

"Bastard," Shereeta said.

"Hey, we're here. We might as well tell the truth," he said, thinking two could play this.

"Mr. Chambers, I want you to know there's nothing to be ashamed of."

He smiled. "Oh, I'm not ashamed."

She continued. "Over thirty million men in this country suffer from ED at any given time."

He winced at the second mention of that abbreviation. He had to be careful—stuff like that had a way of getting into your head and affecting you. He had yet to come away from an assignment unscathed. He was going to make damn sure he came away from this one unimpacted.

"Are you all right?" the doctor asked.

"Yes, I just…sometimes it's just hard to hear it said out loud. It's like you're trying to conjure it or give it some kind of power."

Dr. G. shook her head. "I have no desire to do that."

They eyed each other for a moment, with Marlowe wondering just exactly what she had the desire to do. She crossed one leg over the other and turned in her swivel office chair. "We could start with oysters. What they say about them being an aphrodisiac isn't far from the truth. The zinc stimulates blood flow."

"Nah. I'm not really a seafood lover. I can throw down on some catfish, but other than that, even hot sauce won't get me through. What else ya got?"

Her eyebrow rose. "Are you diabetic?"

"No."

"Do you use drugs…of any kind?"

"Just a little caffeine to get me jump-started in the morning. "

"Nothing else?"

"Nothing else…ever."

"Toxin-free body. Nice," she said. "Okay. When was your last complete physical? Erectile dy—your condition can be a symptom of the onset of heart disease."

He scratched the back of his neck. "About two weeks ago. Clean bill of health."

Dr. G. seemed satisfied with the answers to her questions. "So, is this…all in your head?"

"Or in my heart." He placed a hand over his chest. "My ex and I don't get along so well these days. It's done a number on our bedroom situation. She thinks that coming here will put some iron in the pole.

"Any more questions?" he asked the doctor.

"Just one. What are your expectations for the week?"

"I want to be able to arouse my man," Shereeta wasted no time in answering.

Dr. G. nodded. "Mr. Chambers, how about you?"

Keep playing along, his good sense insisted. "I just want to, um, get my groove back."

"Excellent. Sounds like you're both on the same page there."

Dr. G. steepled her fingers on her desk. "What questions do you have for me?"

"Where are the condoms?" Shereeta asked.

"There are condoms in every room, Mrs. Chambers."

"All right, now!" Shereeta said and beamed with a big, face splitting grin.

Marlowe shook his head. He felt as if he'd just been bulldozed.

"You look like you're in pain, Mr. Chambers. What's the source of that?"

He decided to be honest. "I keep thinking about your electronics moratorium. Your policy is taking a geek away from his gadgets."

Dr. G. sized him up. "You…a geek? You don't look like you have a geek bone in your body."

"Checking me out, huh?" Marlowe cringed. He hadn't meant to say that. The words just slipped out as they normally would. When he found a woman attractive, he flirted.

"I thoroughly check out any guest who stays with me."

"Is that right?" he asked.

Shereeta blew out a long breath. "Can we finish the check-in, please. I want to reacquaint myself with the place."

Marlowe knew that was code for "I'm going on a manhunt."

"Actually, we're finished here." Dr. Gena Bivens rose and extended her hand. "Mr. and Mrs. Chambers, enjoy your stay and see me if anything doesn't go one hundred percent to your liking."

"We will," Shereeta said.

"Count on it," he echoed and gave Dr. G. one last look.

In her heels, she was not far from six feet tall. She moved to the edge of the desk and leaned against the corner. The slit in the dress she wore revealed a luscious right thigh and the end of a tattoo. He couldn't make the whole thing out, but he sure would like to.

Marlowe exited the doctor's office herding his thoughts. He could get out now. He could say never mind and call it a day. No electronics was like cutting off his hands. Being with Shereeta was like salting those wounds. Corralling his sex drive with women like Narcisa and Dr. G. around was like being sliced in half by a buzz saw.

This was not his idea of a quick-and-easy story.

When he got to the hotel room, he didn't know if he would unpack his bags or grab them and leave.

Chapter Seven

"Have fun?" Marlowe asked. Shereeta came charging into the room as if she'd just gulped back a carafe of espresso. He didn't know where she'd spent the night, but she hadn't spent it in their room. He was grateful for small miracles.

"Not quite. I'm still looking for Mr. Right Up My Alley."

"Well, I'm glad you popped in between…dates. We need to talk about the game plan."

Marlowe typically worked alone, unless he hired a photographer or cameraperson. But having the tools of his trade stripped away, he felt like The Dark Knight without his utility belt. He could use all the help he could get.

"Plan? Sweetie, I have a plan."

Before he could say *Please, God no! My eyes!* Shereeta had stripped out of everything, dropping her dress and underwear to the floor and stepping clean out of them before heading to the shower.

He turned his head and choked back the two cups of coffee he'd had. "What the hell is wrong with you?"

"I need a shower, bad!" she called from the bathroom.

"You don't have an ounce of shame in your body, do you?" he asked, walking as far away from the crumpled heap as possible.

"Shame has no place in what I do, sweetheart. There's no room for shame in my life."

"People like you concern me. They usually have to be watched closely, otherwise they'll—"

"I can't hear you! I'll be done in a minute."

Marlowe shoved away all reservations about bringing his cousin. He would deal with them after he turned in the story. For now, he had to make the best of his limp-dick-lover cover story and no internet connectivity. If he was going to win this war, he needed another soldier in his army.

"Shereeta!" he called. "I need you to be a second set of eyes and ears up in here."

His request was met by silence and the tunneling hard spray of the shower.

"Shereeta!" The sound of the water turned off and

Marlowe turned toward the television before she had the chance to ta-da! out of the bathroom wet, naked and inappropriate.

"So what do you think?" he asked.

"I think I've kept Maynard waiting for way too long. If I didn't already know that you'd be holed up in this room this morning, I'd have brought him back here last night."

His hands stiffened. They ached as if he had arthritis. Not a good thing if he was going to be writing for five days. "Rule number one. You want sex, get it outside this room."

Shereeta bent into the outside mirror, fluffed her weave. "Oh, don't worry. I've got three big papas lined up already this morning, and two more behind them. If you see me in this room after today, it's probably because I got drunk and got lost *for real*."

"Hold on. We're supposed to be a couple."

"Shiiiii—. Shereeta gotta have it—money that is. And the quickest way to a man's bank account is through my—"

"Stop!" Marlowe said, putting up a hand. "Please don't make me regret bringing you," he said, although he already did.

Marlowe kept his eyes on the news while his cousin got dressed near the balcony. She did it so quickly, his mind didn't have time to come up with a coherent protest.

"Don't get it backward, cuz. I brought *you*. You

owe *me,* remember?" She high-heeled it toward the door and threw a self-satisfied look over her shoulder.

Marlowe glanced at his notes, or lack thereof. "Look, after I get my story, you can get your freak on with that statue in the courtyard if you want to, but until then...*cuz*...I need you to pretend that ring on your finger is from me."

"Ugh." She dropped her shoulders and stamped her right foot.

Marlowe grinned. "Thank you."

He gathered up the few notes he'd made on a tablet about his first impressions of the place. So far, the ambiance, and just knowing what people came there to do, made him want to grab Narcisa—or the sexy-as-sin Dr. G.—and do her, right there where everyone could see and cheer them on. Then he remembered his mortgage and, more important, two promises he'd made—one to Tuck and the other to himself. Being there gave new meaning to being on the grind for a story, but it was true. Maybe when it was over, he'd come back and see what life at The Epicure was like as a single man.

"You look like I feel," Shereeta said, interrupting Marlowe, who'd just imagined Gena Bivens naked except for black patent heels and a smile. "How much are they paying you for this, anyway?"

Marlowe thought for a moment. Back in the day, he could have gotten fifteen to twenty grand easy.

At three bucks a word, he might be able to squeeze a good ten out of Tuck. "Ten," he said, hopefully.

Shereeta's eyes got so big, he thought they would pop right out of their sockets. "Really?"

"Yeah. So come on. Let's go to breakfast, honey," he said, grabbing a pen. He had to get his mind off sex. Maybe food and an informant would do the trick.

If the entire group of Epicure guests wasn't in the dining room, there could have only been one or two missing. In the midsized space, it wasn't standing room only, but Marlowe almost wanted to ask those with empty seats next to them to raise their hands.

He and Shereeta moved through the buffet-style breakfast area along with one other couple and threaded through tables and chairs looking for a place to sit.

The dining area was set in rounds of four. The sun poured in through floor-to-ceiling windows and two glass walls, bathing everything in a warm golden light. Dusky blue-gray woodwork framed the baseboards of the room, and glazed earthenware accented the orange-and-harvest-green furnishings.

"Over here!" a man said, waving as though he were an old friend.

Marlowe decided to take the man up on his offer, and Shereeta followed him to the table near the west end of the room. Amazingly, there were two seats across from each other. Marlowe and Shereeta joined the man and a woman, who looked as if they'd been joined at the hip for decades.

"Colonel Bootney Barnes, U.S. soldier, Second Battalion, Ninth Marines," the man said before Marlowe and Shereeta could even sit down good.

The Colonel smiled broadly and offered a set of Clorox-white perfect dentures and a hand as big as any Marlowe had ever seen. "This here's my wife, Abigail."

"Pleasure," Marlowe said, taking the seat across from the man.

"Good mor-ting," Shereeta said, sounding like Madea. She took the seat across from Mrs. Barnes and grinned with an innocence she'd probably never had in her life.

Marlowe unloaded his tray and shook the man's hand. His own hand disappeared as Colonel Barnes's fingers, as big as Polish sausages, swallowed his.

"I'm Marlowe and this is Shereeta."

The older couple nodded knowingly. "We know," the man said. "New-booty news travels fast around here."

Shereeta laughed and took a timid bite of her link sausage that she'd picked up with her fingers.

Marlowe swallowed hard. "I'm sorry…new booty?"

"That's what the old guard calls the young ones when they come in."

Marlowe was intrigued. Not even twenty-four

hours at the place and already word had gotten around about the new people. He had to find out about this grapevine and get plugged in.

"How many old guard members are there?"

"Oh, we number about thirty-some. There's only eight of us here this week, though. And I must say, we're all mighty impressed with how you just laid your little problem right out, right away. Takes most men a few days before they actually admit they've got a poor saluter. Right, Ford?"

Colonel Barnes asked his question so loudly, all the guests looked up from their breakfasts. A muscle-bound man sitting across the room wearing a pastel-green shirt and white pants shot back a foul epithet. He looked and sounded like a thirty-year-old Erkel.

"Oh, isn't that sweet?" Shereeta said. "Since everyone knows of your…challenge—he doesn't like me to call it a problem—" she whispered "—you can get lots of advice."

"The first group starts in about an hour. You'll probably want to be there."

Considering the choice between finding a source for his story and sitting in a circle with a bunch of limp-biscuit men, Marlowe preferred searching for a source. "No thanks. I've never been here before, so I just want to get a lay of the land."

The Colonel stabbed at the scrambled eggs on his plate. "You won't get no kinda lay around here, unless you figure out what's causing your rising reluctance. Get it? Heh-heh!"

"Uh, yeah," Marlowe said, eyeing his own food. He'd gotten way too much. It would take him at least fifteen minutes to wolf down three scrambled eggs, four link sausages, hash browns and fry bread. And that was ten minutes too long to be around Mr. I'm ED, and I'm Proud.

He needed to find out about The Epicure, not all the messed up reasons why the men here couldn't get it up—or whatever their sexual challenges were.

"I know what you're thinking. You're wondering how a colonel, decorated war vet, career military commander such as myself could end up with this particular problem."

"If I say no, will you let me eat my breakfast without details of your particular problem?" Marlowe made sure his voice sounded jovial, but he was serious as hell. He shoveled a forkful of eggs into his mouth to avoid saying more.

The man seemed friendly enough. Maybe Marlowe could persuade the colonel and his wife to forgo "session" and spend time helping him get his bearings.

"Why, that's borderline disrespectful. Don't make me put you in a headlock!"

"Oh, Barnes," his wife said, jabbing him in the ribs with her elbow. "Don't pay him no kinda mind. He threatens to put everybody in a headlock."

"Yeah, well. I'll do it, too, if anybody gets out of hand around here. I'm still the Colonel, remember that."

"Sorry, Colonel. I'm just a little wary when it comes to that topic. So, how long does this session last?" Marlowe asked out of curiosity.

"Usually an hour, but if people get to talkin', it might run a bit longer," Colonel Barnes said.

"If I find you after the session, do you think you can show a newbie the ropes?"

"Are you kidding? I'm hoping that after the session I can get my missus in a compromising position."

Mrs. Barnes blushed, drew her shoulders up and giggled like an eight-year-old. Shereeta, uncharacteristically quiet, giggled as well.

Not wanting to whip out pen and paper at the table, Marlowe made a mental note. "Is that what usually happens around here? Guests leave the session and go get busy?"

"You should come to a session and find out."

The deep sultry voice came from behind him, but the image it created flashed hot before his eyes. Gena...with her fine, fine self. Everlasting curves and all. Only instead of black latex, she was naked and walking toward him in his room.

He felt a stirring between his legs and took a quick gulp of orange juice for distraction. "Good morning, Dr. G."

The others at the table exchanged pleasantries with the doctor.

Her dark eyes looked so mysterious in the morning. "Did everyone sleep well?"

"Yes," Marlowe answered quickly.

"That's not good." Her words came out at half strength.

"Why?" he asked, and turned as she came around into view.

Well, if she wasn't looking like a heat wave in black. All black. Low cut, button-down corset. Tight black latex, pants tucked into black platform boots. And that top halter button, small, shiny and smack dab in the middle of her breasts, looked as if it could pop off at any second from the strain. He couldn't take his eyes off it. Imagined her breasts springing free, perfectly round and nipples hard.

"The last thing you should be doing at The Epicure is sleeping—at least, sleeping at night."

That brought the first smile of the day to Marlowe's lips. He watched her closely as she came around to his left side. "I heard you mention a tour. I can get you and Shereeta a tour guide."

"I don't need a tour," Shereeta said then bit a sausage in half.

"I do," Marlowe said.

"I'll set one up for you."

Marlowe checked out the good doctor one more

time. Thinking tie me up, time me down. “Who leads the group sessions?”

Dr. G. smiled. “I do.”

Marlowe’s blood beat in his ears. “What room did you say they’re held in?”

Chapter Eight

Marlowe had the boneheaded idea of coming to the session with Shereeta in order to solidify his cover story, but "ex-wifey" was nowhere to be found.

He took a seat and extended a hand to the woman sitting next to him. "Hi, I'm Marlowe."

"Nice to meet you," she said and shook his hand firmly.

He waited for her name. She didn't offer it. Her only response was a polite smile and the movement of slender arms she crossed over a perfectly flat chest.

Similar things happened when he introduced himself to two other guests sitting on each side of him.

"I'm just curious," he said, speaking to everyone,

including the Colonel, "is there a 'no names' rule here?"

"No," the woman with bumps for boobs said. "Names are optional, and some of us prefer not to share ours."

Marlowe rubbed the back of his neck where a brick of tension had been building since Shereeta disrobed in front of him. "Damn. Even at an AA meeting you get first names."

That got a smile from most and a chuckle from a man two seats from him. A second later the man was up and offering his hand. "I'm Mike."

"Marlowe," he said with a nod and a strong handshake.

After that, others in the circle introduced themselves.

"Good morning," Marlowe said, checking everyone out quickly with a journalist's interest, looking for external hints that the people in the room with him were kinky and couldn't wait to get their freaky-deaky on.

There weren't any. They looked like anyone you would see in a mall, at a play, in a coffee shop. Regular Joes and Joellas. He wrote that down.

The real surprise came from the room itself, rather than the people in it. Marlowe had seen group-therapy rooms on television. He was not impressed. Most of them looked like stale interpretations and poor excuses for a treatment room. Walls washed with colorless paint, dime-store furniture and forgettable paintings made by artists with too much time and not enough talent.

Inside the avant-garde therapy room of The Epicure, he felt cocooned in luxury. Not a serenity poem or self-help quote in sight. Instead, ten high-backed chairs with thick padding took center stage. Verdant plants of every size and shape thrived in the corners, on end tables and from the stucco ceiling. Above him, wooden slats sloped to an overhang for the picture window that provided a massive view of Cathedral Rock. He sat closest to the wall with long sheers cinched in the middle. Footsteps of the couples entering hit the gleaming hard wood with loud, determined pangs. The room itself was like fine art. Marlowe glanced at his paper and pen, realizing he didn't want to write the details. He just wanted to soak them in.

"So," Marlowe said, settling back into his chair. "What are you in for?"

Before Mike could answer, Gena sauntered in with a big smile and bright sparkling eyes trained on him. She had a notebook in one hand and a riding crop in the other. He'd swear on a stack of Gideon bibles that her shiny, black outfit had gotten tighter.

"Hold on, newness. Asking that is my job," she said.

"Sorry," he said, but he wasn't. He'd do anything to keep that delectable mouth of hers moving. It was giving him ideas he'd promised to keep away. *A man can dream, can't he?*

"Did you say something, Mr. Chambers?"

"Yes, I said I had a dream last night."

Curiosity enlivened her face. "From all that sleeping, no doubt."

"No doubt."

"Well, hopefully, I can change that."

All of the guests sitting in the circle turned to Gena and then to Marlowe and Gena again.

They obviously sensed everything he was feeling. He and Dr. G. had a vibe between them. Dread cut off his momentary infatuation. *Note to self,* he thought, *stay away from Dr. G. This is the first and last session.*

"So, welcome everyone, and a special welcome to our newest guests. Mike and Jolisa, Marlowe and—is Shereeta coming to group today?"

"No," Marlowe said, still angry from her absence.

"Well, I'm glad you're here," she said to Marlowe. "I'm glad all of you are here. Thank you for choosing The Epicure. You all know we're about acceptance of the whole self here—even if that self is something others don't appreciate or understand."

Amens, yeses and murmurs of agreement followed her statement.

Marlowe took a deep breath. No camera, no tape recorder, no laptop. It was going to be tricky keeping all this stuff in his head. He thought back to his forensic-speaking days in undergrad. All those speeches he'd memorized.

"We start each session with a check-in, just to see

how we're doing, what's happened since our last session"—she sent a hot gaze blazing across the circle at him—"what thoughts are going through your mind right now."

"If only you knew," he mumbled.

"Mr. Chambers, would you like to start?"

"Me? No. I was just clearing my throat. You all go ahead."

"I don't believe in rules," Dr. G. continued, "but we do have some guidelines here. Would someone please share them?"

"Share what you want, when you want."

"No judgments."

"Support others in the circle."

"Tell the truth or keep quiet."

Gena smiled and sat forward. "I will qualify that by saying that not every truth deserves an audience. The filter we use here is whether your truth is affirming, kind or necessary. If it doesn't fit that criteria, it's probably a good idea not to share."

"In other words," Mike said, "this is an intimacy session, not *Celebrity Rehab.*"

Dr. G. nodded. "This is a safe space. What's said here stays here."

Marlowe almost choked on his own breath. A flash of anger throbbed at his temples. He cursed the economy and his own foolhardiness for the mess he was in. As badly as he needed a payday, he decided to write the story without disclosing too many names. That would probably cut his check by half, but he couldn't blow the whistle the way he'd first intended. Not completely, anyway.

"Will we all abide?" Gena asked.

"Yes," he answered with the rest of the group.

But he knew that wasn't true.

Group seemed to be going well. For some, it sounded as if it were same issue/different day. Most shared the progress they made and ideas for next steps. Gena had to interrupt the Colonel in the middle of his inch-by-inch account of the implant surgery he was considering.

And then there was the new guy.

New guests usually did more listening than talking during their first session, but Marlowe Chambers had taken over quite a bit of the conversation. Sharing very little about himself and his dysfunction, but asking a lot of questions. And the questions he asked were more about The Epicure itself and the backgrounds of the guests rather than the topic at hand. He'd explained his interrogation by saying he got off on knowing about people and things. Gena thought there was more to it. Hindsight was starting to kick in, and the week hadn't even started well.

"You say you're in medical equipment manufacturing. Is that ResMed?" Marlowe asked.

"Yes," Mike answered.

"So how does someone in the ResMed field hear about a place like this?"

"How did *you* hear about it?" Jolisa asked. Jolisa

was Mike's wife, although she acted like his mother. The frown on her face showed she was more than a little irritated by his drilling.

"My lady…she's been here before," Marlowe said.

"Without you?" she asked.

"Yes."

"No wonder your dick don't work."

"No judgments," Gena admonished.

"I'm not judging. I'm just saying…" Jolisa added.

There was a chuckle all around, and then Gena decided they'd had enough digression for one morning.

"This is your session," she said. "We can continue conversation in this direction or—"

"Nah," Jolisa said. "I just want to know how I can be crazy-attracted to my husband, want to ride him so bad my entire pubic area is in pain, and not get wet unless the lights are off. I mean not one drop. I got a whole Sahara Desert between my legs."

"What about KY?" someone asked.

"With all the KY we've bought, we should own half the company."

"How did it go with your doctor?" Gena questioned.

"She said everything checks out."

"Do you *ever* get wet?" Marlowe asked.

"Yeah, when I'm asleep. Then I'm the Amazon Rainforest, it's coming down so hard."

Gena made a note in her notebook. "Why do you think that is?"

"Well, I'm dreaming."

"About?" Gena continued.

"About…"

"Safe room," Marlowe chimed in, wanting to hear her answer.

"About…David Letterman."

"Da—"

"Who? What?" others chimed in.

"He makes me laugh. When I laugh, I get excited."

Mike drew his hand down the front of his face and shook his head. "Why didn't you ever tell me?"

"I dunno. I just thought you'd think it was weird. So, I never said nothing."

The Colonel gave a quick wink. "Uh, Mike, I suggest you write a stand-up routine and perform for your wife."

"Ah, he'd never—" Jolisa began.

"Of course I would! Why do you think I wanted to come here?"

"Really?" she said, eyes doeish and blinking.

"Knock, knock," he said, grinning.

"Who's there?" she asked, shyly.

Mike leaned over and whispered in his wife's ear. She giggled like a middle school girl. And then she licked her lips sensuously.

Gena loved the expressions on their faces. Content and appreciative. She lived for those moments when her guests found their way to the special places in their lives. Something made her glance at Marlowe to get his reaction.

His face seemed more appreciative than those of the now happy couple.

Too bad Marlowe's ex didn't join them. Gena had a feeling their relationship could use a shot of this kind of positivity.

For every event at The Epicure, there was usually one couple who required special attention. This time, it might be Shereeta and Marlowe. Suggesting that he come to group was a bad idea. Gena was way too attracted to the man.

Considering the power of his charm, it might be a good idea to turn over the group sessions to Narcisa.

"Let's talk about how to set goals for this week," she said, wondering if her goal would be to keep her professional distance from Marlowe Chambers or beg him and Shereeta for a threesome.

Chapter Nine

He was doing it again. Cornering her guests as if there was no tomorrow. Right there in the lobby between the zeezee plant and the Eros sculpture, he had Birdell and Ford Jordon in a verbal bear hug. He seemed to be latching on to them one by one. Either he was one of the friendliest people she'd ever met, or he was socially needy in the extreme.

Now was as good a time as any to give him the tour. As busy as she was, she could have arranged to have Narcisa or any other staff member do it. But Gena had thought of little else since she'd suggested the tour. And the reason why was simple.

She wanted more time with him.

There was no other explanation for her behavior.

She could tell herself, and Narcisa if she dared to ask, how she was extending hospitality and wanted to show the new guest around to help him get his bearings. But the truth was, she didn't want their time together to end.

She'd never done something this indulgent in all the years she'd been in charge of the center. It didn't take a personal escort to find one's way around. There were rooms for sleeping and rooms for play. That much was plain and obvious. What wasn't so obvious is why she wasn't ready to be free of Marlowe Chambers even though he'd just gotten there.

He finished his conversation and headed in her direction.

Gena wondered how in the world a man could look so impeccably cut and tailored and so raw and dangerously sensual at the same time. His chiseled, granitelike features and the way he wore everything, as if it was one of a kind and made only for him, never failed to arouse her. The cut of his shirt, tight where his arms were most muscular and always the top three buttons undone, revealing a crisp white sleeveless T-shirt underneath. Shoulders so wide they might as well have signs that said climb on, fasten your seat belt, it's going to be an orgasmic ride. Slacks pressed with a soft crease snug at the thigh and also the place where her eyes always rested. Brazen. Shameless, she knew, but she always went from his face to his crotch, hoping to see any hint, bulge or outline of brotherman's package.

He didn't walk or stand as *just anybody* would. He stood as if he were somebody important. His eyes were always so deep in thought. Neo-soul in the desert. Something serious and erotic always seemed to be going on behind those eyes. Marlowe Chambers didn't need to come to The Epicure to get his hot and heavy on. Men like him had it going on twenty-four/seven. He had the nerve to top off all that sexiness with a small, golden cross that hit the top of his undershirt and caught and held the halogens like tiny golden flickers of sunlight.

A man with swagger that strong couldn't possibly have any sex issues, could he? Nah. Obviously, he just hadn't found the right woman.

Gena gave Marlowe a slow, bold once-over. Their eyes locked.

"Cameras and mirrors," she said when he got close enough to hear.

"What about them?" he asked. He stood beside her in a possessive manner she liked. The wide-planted stance said *mine*—at least for the time being. It was an attitude he never displayed when he'd been with Shereeta.

Damn if his voice didn't sound as raw and sexy as he looked. "I'll bet you keep them all happy."

He grinned. "I could say the same about you. As a matter of fact, I will. You must make every mirror within six or seven hundred miles drool. And the men, well, men fight wars over women like you."

Gena tried to hold in the hilarity but couldn't. His

absurdity made her giggle. The sound was strange to her ears. It tickled her belly and reminded her that she could be other things besides serious. A few of the nearby clients stopped and took in her silliness.

"Why are they giving you the eye? Is there a rule that says mistresses can't laugh?"

Gena caught both her breath and her composure. "Maybe this mistress."

Marlowe's eyes sparkled mischievously. "I never had much use for rules,"

"Nor have I," she said honestly.

Their gazes caught and held. His smile broadened. "To…rule breaking."

"Hear, hear," she said and gave him a wink. "So, are you ready for your tour?"

He glanced around and seemed genuinely pleased with what he saw. "I'm at The Epicure. I'm ready for anything."

His husky voice soaked into her like hot rain. "Then let's start here," she said eagerly.

"The lobby is the all-purpose area." Gena walked slightly in front of him. She wanted to make sure he could see her hips and could watch her walk. It was as though the flash of his eyes turned up her womanhood dial and everything she'd done since he arrived—from licking her lips to swinging her hips—was involuntary and all for him.

"Guests use this area to socialize, relax, get a drink, get breakfast. We also have check-in, which you did yesterday, and our concierge service."

"Concierge?"

"Yes. Narcisa is in charge of seeing to our guests' needs. If there is something the guests want that we don't already have here, Narcisa will get it for you."

They strolled together toward the lobby entrance. "What are the most common requests?"

"Well, that's precisely why we have Narcisa. None of the requests are common."

"How about the most unusual thing?"

Gena thought for a moment. Of course, the most unusual thing had to be the pommel horse. Since pictures of it had already been big news in at least one gossip rag, she didn't believe she'd be violating any trusts by mentioning it.

"A pommel horse," she said.

Marlowe smiled. Her heart sank a bit. Maybe he'd seen the photo.

As they made their way from one end of the lobby to the other, Gena pointed out the lounge, the bell colonel's station and the business office for guests that was currently on lockdown.

They took the elevator down to the lower level. "This is where guests spend most of their time," she pointed out. "Vendors will be available starting tomorrow afternoon. They'll set up tables along this hallway. They'll be here twenty-four hours a day, in case you're interested."

"Interested in what?" he asked.

"What can you imagine?" she asked back.

"Condoms, toys, lingerie," he said.

"And much more," she responded. "Lotions, books…playthings."

Gena paused, her body tingling with attraction for the man beside her. "If you want it, you can get it."

"Is that right?" he asked, eyes dark and devilish.

Gena smiled in response. "Do you and Shereeta have an open relationship?"

"To tell the truth, I don't know what kind of relationship we have."

Rule number one, she reminded herself. Never sleep with a client. She bit her lip. Oh, how badly she wanted to.

"Do you have the kind of relationship you want?"

"No," he said, quickly.

Her mind told her to change the subject, before she strayed more into dangerous territory.

"As you can see, this is a full-service resort. We have an exercise room, swimming pool, sauna, cocktail lounge—"

"You mean a bar?"

"If you wish. Our business office has been shut down."

"So, your clients used to have contact with the outside world?"

"Yes."

"What changed?" he asked.

The image of the photo on the *BIS* site, the online gossip rag, bloomed in her mind like a wayward flower. And the vision of an upset actress played along with it like a bad movie.

"There was some impropriety. A photo of one of the clients enjoying herself here at the center got out…viral and print."

Gena hadn't meant to reveal how devastated she was by that picture, but her voice sounded so weak and so defeated. There was no mistaking the pain.

"That sounds like a bad thing, but is it really? So many people already believe this place exists. I hear jokes and insinuations about the Chocolate Chateau all the time."

Gena stopped. Marlowe's words turned her legs into concrete and set her teeth to a hard edge. "The people who come here have prominent backgrounds—CEOs, entertainers, political activists. They put their reputations on the line when they stay here. But more than that, the health of the clients depends on their full disclosure and involvement in the activities here. They won't be open or participate if they think their faces might end up on the cover of *Entertainment Weekly* or on the splash page of TMZ."

She squared her shoulders.

"The clients' protection and privacy is the top priority here. Without that, there is no Epicure."

Marlowe's golden-brown features turned ashen. "Are you all right?" she asked.

"Yeah, I, uh…just thinking about the protection of the clients. But the more the merrier, right? The more people know about this place, the better off it is. More money in the bank, right?"

"I...they don't do it for the money, Mar-lowe."

"Oh, I'm *Mar-lowe,* now, huh?"

"When you need to be set straight, you are."

She felt her back straighten. Gena walked a little prouder. Not strutting as before. More self-righteous. She couldn't help it. She wanted the man to know what kind of woman he was dealing with.

When people first met her, they tried to put her in a box—a stereotypical therapist—getting her jollies by pointing out what's wrong with people. Usually, she didn't care what others thought of her as long as they respected her facility and her house guidelines. But Marlowe Chambers was a completely different story. She wanted him to look at her with respect. He was just that type of man and had that kind of effect on her.

He stopped and stared at her. Their eyes locked. He might as well have had his hands on her, holding her in place. "It really means a lot to you, doesn't it?"

It's the only thing I have, she thought. "Yes," she said, more calmly than she felt.

"I've been officially set straight," he said, the playfulness in his voice getting inside her. It made her less tense and unwound some of her tight control.

"These three rooms are where the workshops are held." Gena walked inside the dark room and the motion sensor turned the lights on.

His gaze bore hotly into her. It said "Dare me, now." She could tell with the slightest push that they'd be in a raging lip crush.

If she didn't shift their focus, they'd be adulterers in sixty seconds.

He was walking so close to her. She could sense his warmth, smell his cologne. His mouth looked so delicious, it would be so easy to turn to him and kiss him in the room where they were alone.

She was dying to ask why Shereeta seemed to have a much more open relationship than he did. He was making her ache, so badly that she either had to get away from him or get on top of him. The urge to have a man in that way came so strongly and was so foreign; she didn't know what to do with her feelings. But she knew exactly what to do with her reason. Her better sense told her not to step in the way of a man on a mission to repair his relationship with a woman he cares about.

She gazed into his eyes and what she saw there wasn't lust at all, at least not the kind of carnal heat she was feeling. Attraction? Sure, she could see that. She had no trouble knowing when a man found her attractive. But most of what she saw in those warm brown eyes of his was worry and the duality of someone fighting strong urges. There was also an apology coming and a regret. She didn't want to hear either. She'd already seen them all too well in his stare.

He stepped forward, closing the gap between them and nearly pressing her into the side wall of the room.

"If I was here under different circumstances…I'd take you right now. That is…if you wanted me to."

Gena flashed with heat and struggled to control the dizzying torrent of attraction racing through her. She licked her lips. Yes, she wanted him to. So badly, she wondered how she would get through the rest of the week with a need like this boiling in her veins. Disappointment washed over her, taking her mind away from the man she wanted to see naked and focusing it back on the tour.

"I would definitely want you to."

She took a step away, out of the dangerous influence of her lust. "Let me show you the rest," she said.

Marlowe nodded.

She really did want him to see the rest of The Epicure. She was on a mission now and his presence was compelling her. It was as if all this time, she'd been waiting for Marlowe Chambers to walk through the lobby doors. So she could show off her masterpiece to him.

She took her time walking him through the workshop rooms and the group-session room and explaining how at night dividers were removed and the three rooms became one.

"We call it Erotic City."

"What happens here?" he asked, a half smile making him look damn sexy.

"Everything," she said.

One of her security staff passed them in the hallway. The woman gave Gena a nod and kept moving, but not before she gave Marlowe a good going-over.

"So, are you the official tour guide?"

"No. There are staff members who do that."

"I see. Why am I the exception?"

She stopped and gave him an unabashed and brazen appraisal from top to bottom. If she couldn't touch, she darn sure could look. "I volunteered. You are one of the most handsome men I've ever seen in my life. And I must say quite a few men have come through The Epicure's doors. There's just something about you that I wanted to be near for just a few moments longer. You have…a beautiful magnetism. It's intoxicating."

She paused for a moment then felt herself smile. "Yes. That's it."

As they approached the end of the hallway, he strolled closer. "So…are you saying I'm giving you a buzz?"

"I'm saying that the regular guests are surprised to see me give any one guest special attention. It's not usual."

"Well, then, thank you, doctor. I'm glad something about me is special."

Oh, there's so much, Gena thought to herself. *So, so much.*

"We're all special, Mr. Chambers."

At that, he gave her a slow, hot once-over. "Speaking of special, I feel compelled to ask something. I just wondered, are you…dominant? Most of the staff I've seen appears to be."

She stared into his eyes, surprised at how long she held their gaze. She'd never officially said or told anyone what she was. Did she like to tie men up, rule them, punish them for the bad things they claimed they did?

Yes. At least she used to.

It was a lifestyle choice she'd made years ago. If she couldn't control her own pleasure, maybe she could control someone else's.

"I didn't mean to offend you," Marlowe said.

Gena led him toward a collection of other rooms, realizing her hard memories must be showing on her face.

"No," she said, recovering. "You…I'm sorry. Please…ask your question again."

His smile and curiosity made a sexy combination. Gena's body flushed and tingled in every sensitive area.

"If I wasn't unavailable, what would you—" he began.

"I would take you into a private room and—" she tucked a stray lock of wig hair behind her ear "—do things to you."

They stared at each other, as if in a contest to see who would take off their clothes first. Neither gave in, though. Instead, Marlowe released a long breath and drank her in with his eyes.

"I think we should keep it moving," he said.

Gena nodded. “Right. Okay.”

They walked a few feet farther. The silence of the afternoon calmed her. She knew how loud and raucous it could be. The relaxed quiet was a nice change.

“This is the gift shop.” They walked up to a small, glass-enclosed room.

“We don’t keep much here because we usually have vendors on-site.”

She unlocked the door and they went inside. Marlowe began to browse.

Gena hadn’t given the official Epicure tour in at least two years. She missed it. Spending time with the new guests. Finding out more about them and their interests. Mostly she missed talking with the vanillas like Marlowe. Those who were so brand-new to the idea, and concept, of sexual freedom that talking to them about The Epicure was like seeing the center with fresh eyes.

Unlike standard fare in gift shops, there were no trinkets or mementos. No snow globes of the city. No white-porcelain bells with the state name on them. Oh, guests could buy things like mugs and postcards of Sedona and condoms by the box. But the other things, masks, riding crops, nipple jewelry and submissive collars, were specialized items. Most vanillas who came into the gift shop were either shocked into silence or embarrassed to the point of nervous giggling. Marlowe didn’t fit into either category.

“What’s this for?” he asked.

Gena eyed the plastic device shaped like a flaccid penis. It was hollow and had a padlock in the front.

"It's for male chastity. Total control over arousal."

Marlowe picked up the small accessory. He turned it around in his hand. It was obviously designed to create pain if a man became fully aroused. Pretending to be impotent was bad enough; he couldn't imagine *intentionally* shutting down his pleasure. "Does it work?"

"To the extent that people want it to. Some men enjoy the pain. The challenge of being fully aroused and having to fight to control it."

Marlowe's eyes rolled skyward.

"Well," she said, placing the device back on the display. "That's nothing you have to worry about, right?"

He did a quick take of her round rear. "I don't know. How much is it?"

"What?"

"Nothing. Nothing. Tell me about this."

He picked up a small rubber item with long flexible nubs on the end of it. Gena felt as though she were standing in quicksand. As if a force other than gravity was holding her feet hostage.

"It's a tickler," she said. "You put it on your tongue and put your tongue on a woman's..." She paused, wondering why it was so hard for her to finish that sentence. She'd put her personal challenge behind her long ago. But Marlowe made her think of it again... and hate it.

"I get the picture," he said. "I always wondered

about stuff like this. If it really works, you know. What do you think? Have you tried it?"

"No," she said. The word felt like an icy wind blowing inside her. Suddenly, her secluded penthouse didn't seem like such a bad place to be. "We should finish your tour, Marlowe. You probably want to get back to Shereeta."

"Oh, yeah. That's right." He placed the tickler next to the chastity device. Each item seemed to cancel the other out.

The disappointment she heard in his voice flattered her. She was enjoying his company as well.

The lower level of The Epicure was simply a long hallway of conference rooms that stretched the length of the center.

"So, this is where it goes down, huh?" he asked.

Gena wiped her hands against each other and frowned. "Where it goes down?" she repeated. "You sound like you're talking about a hooker and a business transaction."

"That's not what I meant."

"If you want to know if the guests come here to party, and be themselves, then yes. It gets lively down here at night."

"These are the workshop rooms. Concurrent sessions run all day."

"What? You mean like Bondage 101?" he asked, sarcastically.

"Yes," she responded. The word slid quickly and softly out of her mouth, as if she couldn't wait another millisecond to say it.

"Pole dancing, kiss 'til you come, erotic massage, the joys of toys, flying solo, come together."

His jaw dropped and his libido soared.

"Will you be teaching this week?"

"I haven't decided yet."

"Well, let a brother know. I'd like to check you out. Um, the class. I'll have to check out the class."

She flashed that sultry smile his way. "Either one is fine."

Another well-muscled man passed them in the hall. He nodded at her. His face was stoic and full of concentration. Dressed in a pressed navy cotton shirt and navy Dockers, he was the poster boy for drab, lifeless clothing. On Marlowe's law enforcement scale, the man, as well as the others he'd seen, measured at the halfway mark between mall cop and FBI.

"Why all the security?" Marlowe asked.

"Personal protection," she corrected. "There are three things I take seriously around here: anonymity, enjoyment and safety. That's why there are condoms in every corner and security in every hallway."

"Got it," Marlowe said, swallowing the discomfort trying to form in his throat. The guests' anonymity is exactly what he was there to expose, along with anything freaky-kinky those guests got into.

Funny, he'd always thought through his stories in

the past. He imagined the end and mentally worked out implications of what publication meant. But this was different. He'd only thought as far as getting what he needed to get back in with Tucker and the staff at *LifeWire.* It never occurred to him that the Chocolate Chateau would be anything beyond a place where people went to have wild sex. Mardi Gras, *Couples Gone Wild* stuff. What he'd seen so far was a high-end resort that came with *fascinating* fringe benefits. It changed up his plans, but he wasn't sure exactly how much yet.

"I'll never remember all this," he said. He took out a pen and the few sheets of paper he'd found in the desk in his room.

She frowned suspiciously. "It's okay, Marlowe. "There's no test at the end of the tour."

He jotted down some of the classes and underlined erotic massage. "That's good. That's good." He felt like the Grinch who stole orgasms trying to think up a quick lie to explain why he needed to write everything down. What occurred to him was more clever than he could have ever imagined.

"I, uh," he began, feigning hesitation. "I have this thing about school."

He formed the idea using a young man he had in his language arts class once as inspiration. Edrick. He was so eager to learn and to be recognized for learning that he never waited for Marlowe to ask a full question. As soon as Marlowe started a sentence with the words who, what, when, where, how or why, Edrick's hand was up.

At first, Marlowe found the kid annoying, but after time he recognized Edrick's passion for learning and realized he'd probably turn into a lifelong learner—taking classes well into the later stages of his life. Just so he could know stuff.

The doctor's face flickered with recognition. "Are you a good student or a bad one?"

"Oh, I'm good. Real good."

"Well, just so you know…"

Marlowe pulled the paper closer to his face, got his pen ready.

"If you're disruptive in the slightest, we have ways of dealing with…unruly pupils."

"Yes, Dr. G.," he said.

A rush of heat flared inside him like a torch flickering wildly in a desert wind. In the pit of his stomach the heat radiated with full force as he imagined flicking his tongue across her left breast, no her right, no both at the same time.

He licked his lips. She wished he were licking hers. "I can't say no to personal service like that, now can I?"

"I certainly hope not."

She started walking again, the hallway leading from stairway to lobby narrower than she remembered. The walls pressed them closer together. The warmth of his body flowed onto hers. She felt radiant in his presence. Years of Arizona sun, yet this one man made her feel as if the sun was being born *inside* her.

Off-limits, her mind said, but her body wondered just how far.

"You ever consider swinging, Mr. Chambers?"

The left side of his face looked as if it was arguing with the right. He truly had some issues with monogamy or commitment. Hopefully, he would use the group sessions to work through them.

"I have now," he said finally. "Before coming here, the only thing I would ever swing is a golf club."

He looked pensive, as though he had more to say. "Shereeta and I have an arrangement."

"An arranged union. I think that's a first for The Epicure."

Gena was disappointed by his vagueness. She wasn't sure if she'd gotten the answer she wanted or not. Her shoulders slumped as some of the strength went out of them. Another guideline flashed in her mind. Never get too involved with a guest, especially a guest in group. But Gena wanted to relax—or out-and-out erase that tenet. She'd been tempted before, but nothing as overwhelming as this. If Shereeta weren't in the picture, Gena would be all over Marlowe Chambers before he could even think about his safe word, let alone say it.

"I guess it's like they say these days. It's complicated," Marlowe said.

Gena considered the desires battling for control of her mind and body. “What isn’t?”

They arrived at the elevator bay at the west end of the lobby. A couple holding hands and smiling sweetly stepped on to the car moving in perfect sync. The doors whooshed closed and the numbers above them increased.

“There are more things to see,” she said.

He took a step closer. “Thank you for your time.”

Gena didn’t move. Instead, she stared into eyes so seductive she didn’t know if she’d be able to look away. “Like I said, the guests are important.”

“It’s nice to be important to someone.”

They were so close now. Both of them pulled toward each other by an attraction so strong it felt as if a rope was wrapped around them and was tightening with each second they remained together.

Just when Gena was about to say to hell with her guidelines, Marlowe stepped back and smiled. “I’m going to hit the weight room and then rent a movie or something. Thank you for the tour.”

Disappointment dampened her excitement, but she remained cordial. “You’re welcome, Mr. Chambers.”

He looked off into the distance as though it were a mile of desert rather than a hundred feet of hallway. “It feels like such a long way.”

Gena nodded and kept her eyes on his firm, round behind as he walked away. A crazy thought jumped into her head. Before she could stop it, the thought came out of her mouth.

"If you need anything, don't call the concierge. Call me."

"Don't worry," he said. "If I need anything, you'll most definitely be the first to know."

"Hey!" she said. "Are you going to First Night? It's a costume party."

"I didn't bring a costume," he said. "Shereeta didn't tell me that I needed one."

"That's okay. Not everyone wears a costume. But almost everyone wears a mask. Some people will wear masks all week. You can have one brought to your room. Housekeeping should have placed a catalogue on your bed."

"I'll think about it," he said.

Gena started off toward her office. It was the only way she could think of to dislodge the energy between them that was driving her crazy.

"What are you coming as?" he called behind her.

"A wallflower," she joked.

"What's it like?" he shouted, almost out of earshot.

"Wild," she said, then turned the corner.

Chapter Ten

Gena paced in her luxury suite in the penthouse of The Epicure. She checked the wall clock again. 8:53 p.m. Two minutes after the last time she checked it.

Although clients usually started gathering downstairs between 6:30 p.m. and 7:00 p.m. on First Night, she knew the festivities didn't officially jump off until 9:00 p.m. That's when her guests showed up wearing anything from Cleopatra's royal robes to Zorro's boots and cape.

Gena learned early on that her presence at the First Night ceremony distracted her guests. Many of them had commented on how her being there inhibited them, made them more restrained. For her guests, it seemed easier for them to recount their sexual escapades than to act them out in front of their sex coach.

So, she'd stopped attending and had relied on her staff to keep her apprised on the party status. Instead of seeing to her guests' needs personally, she'd left it up to the concierge, Narcisa. She used the time to rest and finalize plans for the upcoming week.

Knowing Marlowe might be downstairs was driving her nuts. She'd planned on updating the schedule of events but ended up staring at it—imagining Marlowe, wondering what things he would get into and whether Shereeta would join him. She turned on the television. *Set It Off* was on one of the movie channels. She'd managed to catch it right during the scene where Jada and Blair were doing the necessary in his apartment.

That looked like so much fun, Gena thought with a thin sadness. She'd given up experiencing that aspect of her sexuality. At least, she thought she had. Then along came Marlowe. With a face like Michael Ealy's, a voice like Allen Payne's and a body like LL Cool J's. That was how she imagined his body beneath his stylish and tailored clothes. All those feelings, needs, urges rushed over her in massive and breath-stealing waves.

The reserved and controlled Mistress of the Center who she'd always been disappeared the moment she saw him step out of the cab. Since then, for every moment she spent thinking, planning and working on her guest's activities for the upcoming week, she'd spent two fantasizing about the unavailable man with, of all the horrid things, erectile dysfunction.

The thing was, he just didn't seem committed.

And they didn't seem like a couple. There was no vibe between them. Couples have a habit of leaning toward each other when they sit together. They glance at each other. Walk into each other's sentences, recall memories together. There was none of that between Marlowe and Shereeta. And it was that absence that read like a crack or fracture with enough space for Gena to fantasize in.

"Shame on me," she said. "And shame on this," she added, standing in front of the full-length mirror now in full dominatrix regalia—a long, black-vinyl fitted dress with a wide side split and a lace reveal. She didn't throw on the sexiness for just anyone. Her full-on was usually reserved for special circumstances. Tonight was no special circumstance. She just wanted to be the center of attention and get Marlowe hard, by any means necessary. She knew that getting him hard would mean he'd be available for Shereeta again. But she tossed that thought out of her mind. All she could think about was creating the same desire in him that he'd created in her.

Gena walked to the door, reached for the knob and stopped. Guilt overthrew her selfishness. She couldn't do this, could she? Risk negatively affecting her guests just so she could parade herself in front of a man. Besides, her track record for choosing a good man was less than stellar, and *going after him* could seriously undermine her authority at The Epicure. But something about him made her want to strut around, jut her breasts out and swing her hips as if she was riding him. Oh, it was shameless. And not respectable at all.

Slowly, she backed away from the door, resolved not to make a fool out of herself or jeopardize her guests' stay.

But what if he's down there, her mind asked. There had to be a way for her to quench the insatiable need she had to see him, watch him during First Night at The Epicure, and stoke her fantasies. She'd love to be a fly on the wall or just invisible. Another glance at the domme in her mirror, and she realized that the best way for her to be invisible was to step into the party in plain sight.

But first, just as her guests did, she'd need a mask.

Marlowe felt the music in the elevator as he rode down to the lower level. A driving staccato and the unmistakable syncopation of a hard pounding, trip-hop, bass. It sounded as if the pulse of every guest at the center was beating in unison. It quickened both his own pulse and his breathing. He'd fantasized about orgies, sex parties, swingers clubs. He suspected that what he was about to witness was an erotic combination of all three. Now, he'd see some guests gone wild.

A couple in the elevator with him had already

started their festivities. Dressed in what Marlowe guessed were Jay-Z and Beyoncé costumes, the man and woman looked straight off a video set and had spent the entire ride down kissing as if the world was on fire. It was hot, and Marlowe decided he would stay as close as he could to the cold drinks. There was no telling when he'd have to pour one over his head.

The place was standing room only. Marlowe would not have believed it. There were twice as many people present as Marlowe remembered seeing even that morning at breakfast.

There had to be at least a hundred couples present. About half the crowd was busy getting drinks, getting massaged or getting busy. The other half was either deep into conversation or hanging back against the walls taking it all in.

Marlowe had to admit that there was quite a lot to see. He hadn't realized how much, or he would have brought pencil and paper. He just couldn't figure out where he would put those things, considering the "costume" he was wearing.

The atmosphere was part brothel, part dance club, part social gathering and all pleasure-seeking. He liked the red-gold lighting, steady throb of the music and adult-playground atmosphere. In the midst of such available sexuality, Marlowe would have to fight hard to keep his mind on his mission.

The guests had taken the costume party seriously. A few men and women—obviously security—mingled throughout the crowd to ensure the party didn't get overly serious. His eyes darted from a referee uniform to a Uhura uniform, Black Panther, a judge's robe, Santa Claus, Catwoman and Harry Potter. At first Marlowe wondered if he'd be out of place, but after seeing the array of dress or, in some voluptuous cases, lack thereof, he decided he fit right in.

He made a long mental note of the costumes he saw, hoping to keep them all straight.

The wait staff carried large silver trays of champagne, lubricant, chocolate covered strawberries and condoms of every size, color and flavor.

The area he'd toured just a few short hours ago had been transformed from empty rooms to staged places where people collected and were in various phases of exhibition or voyeurism. With the lighting, the music, the people who walked around like living décor, he felt teleported into a brand-new world. He hoped he wasn't staring or didn't come across as confused and lonely. He seemed to be the only one there without a partner or two.

He wondered for a second where the heck Shereeta was, if for nothing more than an escort into this adult playground. But that would have been too much to ask. Being solo, a twinge of awkwardness twisted in his gut. He ignored the twinge, adjusted his eye mask and moved on.

The guests had divided the whole downstairs into three distinct areas. In the first area, guests sat in groups, lounge-style at table sets, laughing, chatting, holding drinks. The middle area was more ambitious. It was the center of the music. Guests danced alone, coupled up or in groups to the technofunk pounding the walls and vibrating the floor beneath him.

Oh, but behind door number three. That's where the serious partiers came to play. Aside from a few stragglers hugging the sidelines, the intimate space was designed for skin-on-skin. Bodies in every hue of brown entwined like brazen dancers. Most in couples but a bold few in flamboyant groups groping, rolling, panting, sweating, moaning, grinding, pumping, banging and ass slapping.

He ran into a couple he thought he recognized from group. They were dressed as Oprah and Stedman. Their masks went beyond the typical and even avant-garde eye coverings most everyone wore and ventured more into a complete latex covering. He stopped to talk.

"Great costumes," he said. The music swallowed his words and carried them away like feathers in a vortex.

"Thanks," they said.

Even behind those elaborate masks, Oprah and Stedman gave him a once-over. "Who or what are you?" the woman asked, approval lifting her voice to his ears.

Marlowe smiled and shrugged. "Hugh Hefner," he responded, giving himself a half glance at the pajamas he wore. It was the only thing he could come up with at the last moment.

A waitress came over with a full tray. Each of them took a flute of champagne.

"It's workin' for you," the woman remarked.

"Oprah" sidled up next to him and, even behind the mask, Marlowe saw the wide grin. "We're looking for a swap, if you're interested…"

Her voice trailed off, but each word was coated with a thick helping of lust. He made another mental note for his article. The clients of The Epicure don't waste time with formalities.

He returned her smile. "Thank you for the invitation, but I'm having a little trouble in that area." It was the first time he could say it or even suggest it without cringing.

The woman edged closer. Marlowe imagined himself the only man in the past twenty years to be propositioned by Oprah. "I might be able to help you with that."

The man kept quiet, downed his champagne and kept his eyes glued to his companion. He seemed to genuinely enjoy her making a pass at another man. Article note number three, and he hadn't been in the lower level half an hour yet.

"I appreciate the offer, but tonight, I'm just going to watch."

The woman joined the man at his side and they angled off toward another couple. "If you change your mind—" the man threw over his shoulder.

"I'd look for you immediately," Marlowe responded.

A group of nine—six men and three women—sporting afros, bell-bottom jumpsuits and platform shoes had obviously come as The Jacksons. Marlowe wondered if they were planning on performing later.

Marlowe didn't mean to shake his head, but he couldn't help it. He was like a goose in a new world, and the new world was bold, sexual, open and unafraid to put its entire sexuality on blast. He had to get to the sidelines, where he could observe and file everything away in his mind without interruption.

On his way to a quiet corner of the room, he passed Princess Tiana and a dead ringer for Morgan Freeman. He would go ten rounds with Roy Jones Jr. for his camera phone right now. He'd learned his lesson. He'd never attend an Epicure event without pen and paper again. Even if he had to wear them around his neck. He had half a mind to go back to his room and get them when a woman on the other side of the room, alone and watching, caught his eye.

She had jet black microdreads that hung just past her shoulders. She wore a white tube top so snug he wondered how she ever got it on and, more important, what it took to get it off. The white skirt she wore hugged her hips and left plenty of belly open to the air. A gold-torch emblem on the lower front of the skirt matched the earrings she wore. The large, decorative mask she wore covered most of her facial features, but something beyond her attire gave her an international flair. Rasta or maybe Africa.

Even from across the room, she was mesmerizing. And oh so natural. No makeup. No gaudy jewelry or fake nails. Even her feet were bare and toes free from the glittery red polish that seemed so popular to nearly every woman in the place. He couldn't turn his eyes away.

He swapped his empty glass of champagne for a full one, thinking some people might assume the woman had come as an island girl or African princess. Marlowe's keen observation told him that the woman's natural grace and elemental elegance was front and center.

A woman like her will keep your back straight, he thought. He took a long drink of the Jean Milan sparkling in his glass, fighting the overpowering urge to strike a masculine pose. To strut, flex his muscles or just knock someone out cold just to display his prowess. The most urgent thing he wanted to do at that moment was undress her, take off her mask and slide in and out of her until she clawed his back and yelled his name.

He was in danger of proving that he'd been suddenly and miraculously cured of the problem that brought him there in the first place.

She was alone. For five minutes. Ten. Fifteen. Narcisa stopped briefly and spoke with her. Beyond that, not many had made contact with the mystery single woman. For a moment, Marlowe wondered if his “ex” was with the woman’s husband. If so, he owed it to the woman to provide her some company.

Her eye mask was black with gold-sequin trim, gold accents and a plume of gold and black feathers cascading off the right side and cradling her hair. Marlowe had never heard of anyone working a mask, but baby-girl was doing exactly that.

He started walking in her direction, asking himself who he thought he was kidding. The woman was crazy fine and he wanted to know if she was with someone. Even if he couldn’t do anything about it right now. If she was there alone, maybe they could pass the time together. But since this was couples week, she had to be with someone, right? Well, he would find out in a moment.

I love it, Gena thought. It had been so long since she’d spent First Night with her guests, she’d forgotten how exciting it was, the level of activity and how liberating wearing a mask and freely expressing oneself could ultimately be. It did her spirit good to see her hard work was not in vain. Everywhere she looked, she saw people talking, laughing and bridging the gap between who they present to the world and the people they really were.

She’d walked around, rather self-indulgently, just taking in all of the couples and the way they’d chosen to celebrate the upcoming week. Gena strolled through the long hallway and spent time in every room and every area, taking in the fruits of her labor.

On any other occasion, the sights and sounds would have contented her. But not tonight. Tonight she was looking for a special kind of contentment that would come only from seeing the man she hadn't been able to get out of her mind since yesterday. She hoped he made the decision to come to the costume party. If he had, she hoped that among all the Zorros, ninjas and French maids, she'd be able to pick him out.

Her eyes roamed the room, looking for signs of him. She stole away in a corner for a clear view and took a chocolate covered strawberry from Narcisa as she made her rounds in the room. As she took a bite, a man in black silk pajamas caught her eye and made her shudder with gratification. Marlowe. He was talking to a couple, or more like the couple was talking to him. If Gena knew her couples, Ronalda and Philad Blue were probably propositioning him to be a star in their show. Gena watched closely to see if he would take them up on their offer. When he declined, a cool wave of relief washed over her. She watched closely to see what he would do next.

Gena made her way to the other side of the room. Marlowe took a fresh glass of champagne and drank as if he was completely uncomfortable and needed the alcohol to balance his unease.

Behind the refuge of her mask, she indulged herself and admired Marlowe openly and languidly from top to bottom. He'd definitely chosen the right costume. The silk pajamas were sheer, nearly see-through, showing buttery and sinewy skin beneath.

He wore the shirt completely open revealing a panty-wetting set of washboard abs, with just the whisper of fine hair growing beneath his belly button and thickening as it went down. His pants fit snug and low against his hips, the drawstring pulled tight and satin hanging loose.

The conservative black eye mask he wore made a clear statement. He wanted to be compliant to opening-ceremony requirements, but he didn't care that everyone knew exactly who he was. Maybe he wanted people to know it was him. The thought of his boldness was so sexy.

On the end of her thorough appraisal, Marlowe looked up and saw her. He went still. Her heart beat a quick time in her chest. She held her ground, choosing to be as courageous as he.

As Dr. G., she was bold, and baaad, and brash and brave. The wig, makeup, fetish outfits, American accent and heels so high she could get nosebleeds helped her create a persona that didn't have a shameful past. But now, here, stripped down to her real self, she was caught between two worlds. She didn't know if she had what it took to be daring, and she didn't remember what it was like to be vulnerable.

If there was such a thing as mind sex, she and Marlowe were having it. In her head, she had torn that silk off, shoved him onto the floor and was riding wild and halfway to orgasm. From the heat flowing from his gaze, he must have been imagining something similar. Dr. G. would want to act it out. Gena Bivens would be too ashamed to.

Marlowe leaned against the wall, crossed one leg over the other and stretched an arm across the length of the wood molding. Looking like the master of all he surveyed. Slightly apart from the festivities. The handsome stranger who'd just come to town. He created a perfect vision for a photo shoot. He would make even the highest-paid fashion photographer fill an entire memory card. Whatever it was he was selling, the part of her that craved an orgasm was ready to buy.

He didn't stand still for long. Either he'd heard her thoughts or he was as powerless as she felt to control the attraction between them.

She swallowed quickly as he moved toward her.

Gena braced herself. So much of her wanted to be bold right now. But brotherman was spoken for. Keeping her mind on that truth would keep her mouth and her hips, ass and breasts, in check.

He walked straight toward her. As badly as they wanted to welcome him, Gena reminded her legs and arms to stay closed. But she would talk with him. For as long as he wanted.

"Are you enjoying yourself?" was on the tip of her tongue, when he turned and headed in the opposite direction. Toward the dance floor.

Her shoulders slumped from disappointment. The inside of her mouth tasted bitter and stale, as if the sadness was not just something she felt; she could taste it, too.

Gena hadn't spent the past two hours debating what to wear and whether or not to attend, and hoping like hell that he'd be here, to pass up an opportunity to talk to him. She slammed back her sparkling cider and followed him.

He weaved in and out of the guests. His body moved with the music somehow. She memorized the fall of the shirt against his backside, his firm, round, two-handful backside, and moved as if they were tethered together. He was pleasant, speaking to guests as he made his way through the dance area and back toward what she called Erotic City. He stopped to drop off his flute and picked a chocolate-covered strawberry from the tray. Allowing Gena to catch up.

"Hugh Hefner, right?" she asked when she got close.

He turned to her, the full onslaught of his handsome features stealing her breath and all her intelligence. He smiled appreciatively.

"Yes."

She took in the expanse of his chest, realizing that without her heels, she was perfectly mouth level to his nipples. "Very nice."

"Thank you. You're the first person to get me. Everybody else thinks I'm Peter Pan or somebody."

She gave him another bold appraisal. She couldn't

stop herself. "I'm not getting Peter Pan from you at all."

"Good, 'cause in a place like this, I don't want nobody to mistake a brother. You know what I'm saying."

She folded her lips to keep from giggling. She couldn't imagine anyone mistaking him for anything other than what he was: one hundred percent grade A male.

"So, what about you? I was checking you out back there. I know you saw me."

"I saw you," she said.

They moved aside as a threesome ran past them giggling and throwing packets of lube.

"I can't put my finger on it."

He walked around her, assessing. "I'm getting this tropical, island, African vibe from you. Are you Lauryn Hill?"

"No," she said, but she appreciated the compliment. "I came as me."

"Ah, no fair. Everyone else dressed up."

Just as he said that, a man and two women buck naked and jiggling walked past them on the way to Erotic City. "Well, most everybody," he corrected.

Gena took a deep breath. "My day life is so different. For me to come as myself is almost like wearing a costume."

"Um," he said. "I respect that."

Her heart galloped. "Thank you."

Marlowe bit into the strawberry he'd been holding.

He did it slowly, gently. Juice from the large, round fruit covered his bottom lip. Glistened like lip gloss. Gena's tongue was nearly on autopilot, ready to lick his lip clean.

She realized she would kick a chicken to be that strawberry. To have her juices on his face. He licked his bottom lip with the same slow deliberation that he used to bite the strawberry. If Gena had had a clitoris, it certainly would have been vibrating like crazy. As it was, she had only her customary tepid arousal and a slight moistness to mark her excitement.

"I'm Marlowe," he said, offering his hand.

"I know," she said, closing her hand around his. She noted the firm smoothness of it and how it seemed to radiate more heat than three kitchens.

"So, I don't get a name?" he asked.

"Maybe later," she said, allowing some of Dr. G.'s boldness to creep into her words.

He nodded and popped the rest of the strawberry in his mouth. "Sounds like a woman who has something to hide."

They started walking together, passing whirling, dancing, gyrating guests as they went.

"Don't you?"

"Don't I what?" he asked, clearing his throat.

"Have something to hide?"

He stopped and stretched his arms. "Now, as you can see, I got nothin' to hide."

And he was so right. That sheer satin left nothing to the imagination. Nothing.

Gena stared at the blessing between his legs. It had been hard to see when he was on the other side of the room, but now—her hand floated to the base of her throat in an *Oh, my* gesture. Well-endowed would have been a nice way to put it. But Gena wasn't feeling nice at that moment; she was feeling straight-up nasty, and *hung* was the word that caught in her throat.

"Thank you for being so…unrestricted," she finally looked up and said.

He put his arms down, but not before several woman took note and admired the view.

"Have mercy!"

"Damn!"

"Rain on *me*."

Were several of the numerous calls of appreciation.

Marlowe gave a half chuckle and a dazzling smile.

"You're free with yourself," she said. "But you have some modesty or else you wouldn't have worn the pajamas."

"Don't tell me," he said. "Psychology major."

Gena's stomach clenched. No matter what she did, she was always going to diagnose people, try to get inside their heads, figure out why they do what they do. She had to stop that, or he'd know who she was.

"I'm just interested in people."

"Do you ever focus your interests on one person?"

She straightened her mask and fidgeted with her dreads. "Like who?"

Marlowe looked around as though he was trying to talk himself out of speaking further. Gena could sympathize.

"A man, a boyfriend, husband."

"No," she said, honestly.

The group of guests who'd come dressed as the Jacksons struggled with spontaneous choreography. Collapsing into a heap after an epic fail.

"Girlfriend?" he asked.

"No. There's nobody." As soon as she said the words, she was aware of how hollow they sounded and how alone they made her feel.

He looked surprised. "So, how's that work during couple's week?"

"I get special treatment."

He looked her up and down. His lips curled into a grin. "For everything, I'll bet."

She thought of all the special treatment she wanted from Marlowe right now. His mouth on her breasts, his tongue in her navel, his hands gripping her ass. A shiver of desire surged through her.

Gena took one more look. Burning the image of Marlowe's long, thick penis into her memory probably forever. "You sure you're here for sexual dysfunction week?"

Marlowe blew out a breath. There was real pain in it, as if he was struggling with something onerous and unruly. "That's my story and I'm sticking to it."

* * *

Saturday, Sunday, Monday, Tuesday, Marlowe thought. Four more days and he could stop saying that phrase.

"You're new, but you don't act new," she said.

"Is that a good thing?" Marlowe asked. He looked the woman over. She was petite, with skin that was beautifully and flawlessly dark.

"That depends on you." He recognized her accent. East African. She sounded as if she was singing rather than speaking. Behind the mask, her eyes were large and round, like gold coins. Pretty. They could have been gorgeous, but they were too full of pain. Marlowe cringed inwardly. A woman who seemed so beautiful deserved to have a life as beautiful as she was.

"Are you from Kenya?"

"Close," she said, eyes brighter. "Tanzania."

Marlowe shrugged. "I took a shot."

She leaned against the wall and gave him an approving glance. "It's more than most people do. Have you been to the region?"

"Yes," he said, remembering all the weeks he'd spent at a beach club in Zanzibar. He'd gone there to cover a story on the evolution of HIV/AIDS prevention. After he got the story, he hung out at the bar, handing out condoms and advocating the merits of safe sex. "I was an AIDS educator," he said. That wasn't a big stretch of the truth.

"Thank you," she said.

He gave an exaggerated wave-off of accolades. "I'm just a concerned citizen. No need to thank me."

"Well, a lot of people say they're concerned..."

"Tell me about it," he said, noticing her round hips and liking them.

"So, what brings you here, tonight?" she asked.

Marlowe took a sip of champagne. "Ladies first."

The sadness rumbled in her eyes like storm clouds. She smiled anyway. "Voyeurism. I like to watch."

"That seems to be a common theme around here. Now, a brother can enjoy the hell out of a triple-X flick. But watching from a distance will never replace the TKO of the real thing."

She laughed. It sounded like gentle bells ringing. He liked this woman.

"I've never heard it called that before," she said.

He finished his drink and set the flute on a nearby receiving tray. "Hey, stick with me. You'll hear a lot of things for the first time."

She gave him a full, teeth-gleaming grin. It was beautiful enough to brighten the entire lower level.

"What? Is that a smile?"

"It is," she said, covering her mouth.

Marlowe pulled her hand away from her face. Her skin was soft and he allowed himself the luxury of its warmth. "No. Don't hide it. The whole world should see a smile that beautiful."

She took half a step back and gave him a whimsical appraisal. "Well, aren't you something."

"As a matter of fact, I am."

She squinted her eyes, as if she was considering something. And then she said, "Why don't I show you around."

"Oh, you got it like that?" he asked, hoping he finally found someone who could give him some information.

"Let's just say I've been around The Epicure block a few times," she said. "So yes, I got it like that."

She guided him to one end of the floor. The texture of the walls on the periphery caught his eye. The crimson, amber, burnt orange blended together like acrobatic lovers. The colors seemed poured and combed together in thick circles and waves. "Nice walls," he said.

"Thank you," she said then smiled. "We'll start here at the more…reserved end."

They strolled like easy lovers down the spacious first-floor hallway that stretched the entire length of the resort. They were flanked to their left and right by room after room—each one offering its own unique delight.

Opaque silk screens divided the rooms into common areas. "This is the piano lounge. If you just want to relax, this is a good place to relax."

The area looked like a small jazz club with ten round tables for two. Several couples gathered at the bar, and a dark-complexioned woman with waist-length microbraids and a Mardi Gras mask played the piano in the corner of the space.

"On the other side is the game room."

Sure enough, couples were animatedly playing bid, rummy, poker and what looked like a rousing game of strip dominoes.

"Boston!" an older woman cried. She slammed down a card and made it spin in the middle of the table. Her denture-wearing partner scooped up the book while the other two players threw up their hands in exasperation.

"If you're looking for something more lively, you can get your party on in the Arena."

Guided by a DJ wearing headphones and rocking three turntables, guests jammed *Soul Train*-style to hip-hop on full blast. Not even tight kimonos, Fillmore Slim pimp suits or insanely high platform shoes kept the couples from ravelike gyrations in the black light and flashing strobes.

Behind a screen above the DJ's stand a woman danced suggestively, casting a hauntingly sexy shadow.

Since he'd arrived at First Night, the thought of him being on assignment left his mind almost completely.

"It's so easy to lose yourself here," he said.

She tucked a loose lock of hair behind an ear. "It's not as easy as it looks."

What would it be like to exist in a world without certain boundaries—a world without deadlines, he wondered. Marlowe took a second to check out the two topless women in see-through thongs and shiny red heels performing synchronized pole dancing to his left. "Maybe the costumes are the clothes we wear every day and this is what's real."

She grinned. "Now you're speaking my language."

Marlowe noticed that he no longer heard the piano from a few rooms back and realized while at the piano lounge, he hadn't heard the strumming bass vibrating the floor now.

"Do you know how they compartmentalize the sound?" the reporter in him asked.

"I'm kind of a fixture here, so yeah, I do. It's the walls you liked. They're sound-absorbing panels. We can get as loud as we want in any section we want without disturbing each other."

"Your idea?"

"Yes," she said.

He gave her an admiring side-eye. "Smart move."

She nodded. "Thank you, again."

Was it his lusty imagination or were the woman's nipples getting harder the farther they walked. He had to admit, there was something about her. Aside from her beauty. She had such an easy way with herself and all the happenings on the first floor. Just her comfort with large groups of people being sexual in her presence was alluring as hell. The closer they got to the other end of the hallway, the more he felt as if he was not being escorted but being seduced. And walking around with a dick so hard it felt as if he was swinging a Craftsman hammer between his legs was evidence of her seduction.

Two-thirds of the way down the hall, things started to get interesting. Couples walked close-bodied or posted up against the paneled walls in lip orgies. They felt each other up wildly and moaned over the background of slow-grinding soul instrumentals. Marlowe's groin stirred to life.

"Now, if you need something more tactile, you'll like this space."

"No doubt," Marlowe agreed.

As though somebody had flipped a switch, there was a lot less talking and a lot more skin showing. The costume crowd tapered off into women in string bikinis and men in thin, bulge boxers, but most were wearing masks only. Marlowe had never seen so many melon-sized breasts in one place in his entire life.

He glanced at her. She gave him a slow, burning up and down. Her eyes stopped where evidence of his arousal grew by the second.

She swallowed hard then smiled alluringly. "Find something you like?"

He glanced around at all the mouthwatering flesh surrounding him.

To his left and right, both spaces were arranged like upscale living rooms. Low dropped chandeliers, overstuffed chairs, long sectionals, end tables with lamps, coffee tables with table runners, all on top of plush carpeting. Marlowe half expected to see a wall clock, fireplace and panel TV, but instead he filled his visual appetite with couples on every inch of every piece of furniture, writhing, humping and moaning their way to oblivion.

"This is where guests come to improve their lust lives."

Marlowe could barely contain himself from licking his lips and joining in the fun. He was sure the look on his face must have been raw, animalistic and ravenous. Ms. Masquerade, on the other hand, couldn't have looked more at peace. He could tell she was excited, but her face was also brightened with a genuine contentment.

"Admiring the view?" he asked.

"That and other things." She gave him another scorching once-over. This one hotter than the first.

"Thirsty?" she asked.

Marlowe glanced at the skirt he wanted to rip off her hips and imagined the meeting of her thighs beneath it. "Yeah. I could drink somethin'."

They walked into another bar area, where the bartender was handing the couple in front of them something fruity. "What can I make for you?"

The mystery woman winked. "Two Nasty Nookies, please."

"Coming up," the bartender said.

Marlowe couldn't help the grin on his face. "Nasty Nookie?"

"Mmm-hmm. It's an aphrodisiac."

"Really? What's in it?"

"Well..." she smiled playfully. "It's mostly Squirt, but it comes with a shot of pineapple, a shot of white grape juice, a dash of vanilla and a pinch of nutmeg that's blended and poured over crushed ice."

Their drinks came and they each took a sip.

Curiosity danced in her eyes as it had in some of the guests he'd seen. "Well?"

"Not bad," Marlowe said, knowing he didn't need an aphrodisiac. Just the atmosphere alone had him jonesin' for a woman. And his beautiful escort was the object of his First Night desire.

Marlowe drained his drink and set the glass on the bar.

"Would you like another?"

He glanced down at his penis, stiff and nearly painful at the front of his Hef-wear. "Do you think I need another one?"

His mystery woman folded her bottom lip into her mouth and rolled it between her teeth for a second. "No."

They set off strolling again, slowing to watch a set of couples having a position competition. Side by side, they humped hard through missionary, reverse spoon, lap dance, butterfly and doggy style. They declared the game over when one woman did the splits while straddling her lover.

"I'll have what he's having," Marlowe said, eyeing three women in another area who'd surrounded a man wearing only a Zorro mask. The man was quaking on the floor while one woman slipped her fingers into his mouth, one woman swallowed his engorged dick and the other tongued his balls.

"Some people get off on special treatment," she said.

No sooner had she uttered the words, a woman on the other side of the hallway cried out while one man sucked her right breast, another her left and a third man buried his head between her legs.

"Forget the piano bar," Marlowe said. "This is the place to be."

"We feed many appetites here," the woman said. "Is this more your style?"

Marlowe licked his lips and rubbed his hands together. He'd found it. Nirvana. A Bower of Bliss. *The Chocolate Chateau.* The realization quickened his excitement. "I may never leave," he confessed.

Desire built in him so hotly, his body felt as if he was swallowing fire. Marlowe knew he had to get off soon or his dick would blow up like a super M-80 in a microwave.

Most couples made out on the couch or the chairs. A few guests rode the erotic vibe using a steady rhythm, with the loudest ones taking on a more pile-driving-like pace.

Couples clustered into groups. The group members finger-fed each other truffles, figs and other libido-enhancing foods. Some engaged in mutual hand jobs, others went for straight up, hard-driving lovemaking. One ambitious group of five formed a daisy chain of oral satiation on the carpet.

One woman stood on her hands while her partner held her thighs and dipped his tongue into her core. Marlowe and Gena looked on together and tilted their heads to get a better view.

Everyone seemed lust-drunken even though each guest had been limited to two glasses of champagne maximum. They were so focused on pleasure, a nuclear blast wouldn't have disturbed them. One woman in particular caught several people's attention. In platform boots only, she danced and stared transfixed into a mirror obviously performing just for herself.

By the time they got to the end of the hallway, Marlowe was so stoked, he only wanted to know one thing.

"So, what do I have to do?" he asked. He didn't finish his sentence. He didn't have to. Her nipples were so hard they looked as if they could slice her blouse open like diamonds. And her eyes looked drugged, lusty.

"Marlowe—"

"I need to lay you down. Right now," he said.

The sexy woman before him just stared with her lovely mouth parted.

"Just let me kiss you," he continued. He hoped like hell that if he kissed her right, she'd let him sex her right.

He bent down to her lips. Just before he pressed into their softness, she turned away. "Not here," she whispered.

He was in pain now. Nearly doubled over with need. He didn't think he could make it to his room. Going someplace else to get busy would have been a waste of carnal lust and disrespectful to the whole idea of First Night. If she wanted to be discreet, maybe there was a way.

He grabbed her hand. "Let's go."

He maneuvered them through the guests as discreetly as possible and stopped at the place where the shadow dancer still performed. Four couples watched as the music moved through her and projected against the screen. "How about hiding in plain sight?"

"Wanna take a break?" Marlowe asked the dancer. In a skintight, opaque body suit and a tiny red mask, the woman smiled, nodded and left the space behind the screen.

Strangely, she seemed nervous, and he was wondering why she was concerned about getting her freak on in an active pleasure den aptly named Erotic City. If it weren't for her legs calling his name, he would have asked about it.

"Get naked for me," she said, with a hand caressing her shoulder and flowing down to her forearm.

"Nothing like a woman who knows what she wants." Marlowe tossed off his see-through silks in seconds. "Your turn," he said, stunned by all the eagerness in his voice.

She removed her top, skirt and a black-lace thong.

She had high round breasts, a soft sensuous waist, mouthwatering hips as round as planets and legs like a gymnast—smooth and tightly packed. Marlowe's dick throbbed like a long, thick heart. "You look good."

The spotlight behind them made her skin glow almost too brightly, washing out all the details. But that didn't matter. Marlowe wanted his mouth on all of it. He shook his head approvingly. "Damn, where do I start?"

"How about here?" the woman asked.

She backed up toward the middle of the screen where the spotlight was the brightest and lay face-down on a square cushion. It was flat, not quite the size of a mattress, but it looked as if it was made from memory foam. The cream color made an exotic contrast to the snatches of nut brown on her arms and neck still visible in the concentration of light.

She spread her legs in wide invitation.

Like a spray of confetti, packets of condoms and lube surrounded the cushion. He quickly rolled on protection, eased down on top of her and slid his fingers under her belly. "Um," she purred. "Play with my nipples."

Marlowe didn't have to be asked twice. He fingered her breasts where her flesh had turned as hard as small stones. Then putting his weight on his left side, and because he couldn't wait another second, he slid himself inch by inch into her core. He took it easy, not wanting to push in too fast, but at the same time teasing her with the sensation. Her wet pussy welcomed him and made him feel right at home.

She sighed loudly and Marlowe released a groan of his own. Fingering her breasts again, he caught a rhythm and stayed there until she moaned again, this time louder than before.

"Am I strokin' you right?" he asked.

"Yes," she said. The word trickled out of her mouth so soaked with lust, he barely heard her.

He took some of his weight off her, leaning again to his left. This time, he pulled her to his chest and lifted her leg to get in deeper. He stroked her calf, her thigh. He licked his fingers and went back to an exposed nipple that seemed to be calling him to flick and twist it. Marlowe matched his finger play with his thrusts.

The woman shuddered. "Ride me."

Her words set his blood on fire. He rolled onto his knees, taking her hips with him. He grabbed her thighs and placed her legs against his chest. Her eyes fluttered closed as he kneaded her breasts as if they were slow-rising dough. Her walls tightened against him. Inside her hotter, wetter core, he slid easier now. No matter where he moved or how he controlled the tempo, she matched him.

She slid her hands up and down his arms. Her ripe breasts bobbed on her chest. "Ride me."

Desire streaked inside him. He lowered her legs to his sides and shifted his weight until he was on top of her again. Face-to-face this time. A lustful smile crawled across her lips. Light from the spotlight illuminated the feathers at the side of her mask. He stared at her mouth.

"Kiss me," she said.

"Kiss *me,*" he said back.

Instantly, she leaned up and captured his mouth in hers. Marlowe's dick felt as if it had doubled in size. He moaned in her mouth.

The mystery woman put her arms around his neck, massaging, smoothing, caressing. "Why didn't we do this the second we saw each other?" she asked.

"We did…our minds," he replied.

"Time to get real," she said.

With a gentle but powerful shove, she pushed him backward. A few gasps and intakes of approval came from the other side of the screen. Marlowe had forgotten all about being watched. He only concentrated on the woman maneuvering on top of him. Though wearing a mask, she was sexy as hell.

Without breaking their connection, she laced her fingers between his, tucked her legs beneath her and began to bounce. Marlowe sucked air from her moves and her movement. His toes curled and uncurled as he matched her.

"Ride me," he said.

Using his arms for leverage, she placed her feet flat on the cushion, knees up, hips pumping and rocking against the head of his dick. "Uh-uh-uh," he said. Marlowe watched the intensity on her face. She looked like a woman who loved being in control.

"Keep ridin' me," he repeated.

The expression on her face went molten then. Hot enough to melt steel or make his dick explode. "Hold me," she said.

Marlowe set his hands on the soft, pliable skin at her waist, right where the narrowest part started that slow, sweet expansion to her hips. Balancing with the cushion, she damn near spun on his dick until she was facing away from him. In a swift movement that looked like a bow, she bent forward and grabbed his calves. She snapped her hips, as if she was pop-locking on his dick. If Marlowe hadn't been lying down, the pure pleasure of it would have knocked him over.

"Ah, damn. Damn!" he called, watching her sweet ass working him, draining him wickedly. "Come *now,*" he insisted. The pressure in his loins rushed forward like a runaway train. He shoved his hips up, driving into her as far as he could go. "Come with me now."

Marlowe came so hard, he hoped the force of his semen didn't destroy the condom.

She rode him strongly until he'd emptied himself all the way. He held on to the condom while she rolled off and lay beside him. He saw the contentment behind her mask. She smiled and settled into the nook of his arm. "I'm feeling all kinds of ways right now," she said.

He was still breathing fast and listening to his heart as the pounding eased in his chest. He glanced down at where she looked so relaxed beside him. "Good ways, right?"

She turned, raked her teeth across his nipple. "Really good."

Marlowe stroked her forearm and thought he heard applause on the other side of the screen. Her damp, smooth skin was lusciously hot beneath his fingertips. It was only his first event at The Epicure, and he was already anticipating the next time he could be inside her. He was in the middle of hoping for *later that night* when he got a knock on the door of his consciousness. It reminded him about past mistakes. About the dangers of time spent sexing instead of writing. He stared at his mystery woman, looking so ready for round two, and realized he could get into trouble at The Epicure.

Serious trouble.

Chapter Eleven

Marlowe unwound in his room, relieved. He'd kept Mr. Happy just excited enough to keep him quiet, but just barely. He didn't know how much longer he could keep up the facade. And, fool that he was, he had strong ideas about going back into the den of iniquity tomorrow night.

But he had to admit, it was fun. Exhilarating, actually. The freeness in the sexuality was palpable. It lived in every breath he took. And seeing all the guests being so free made him want to be free, too. Try something different, like swing from the proverbial chandelier, get his freak on in front of people, strut naked, break his vow. He'd seen enough tonight to start his article off with a bang—literally.

The only thing missing was names and titles. He needed the who's who to sell it big and to get the big dollars he needed. He'd work on that next. He made a note to interview as many people as possible and to record and remember names. Then he could pick and choose the ones who could blow the doors wide open.

A wave of regret threatened to capsize his plans. Dr. G.'s determination to keep identities on lockdown concerned him. He hoped that he was right about his instinct. Having proof positive that this place exists would throw her client list into the stratosphere. She'd make a killing. She'd have enough money to do whatever "goodwill" work she wanted to with whomever she wanted to do it with.

He gathered his notes, imagined the story coming and sat down to write. It was 3:00 a.m. before he took a break.

The key sliding into the lock broke his concentration. He didn't bother to look up. He had no interest in seeing what lewd costume Shereeta was wearing. He was certain that whatever it was, it disrespected her.

"What are you doing up?" she asked.

"Working," he said.

"Me, too. Okay!"

She pranced into the room, and he was absolutely right. She had on too much makeup, too much perfume and not nearly enough clothes. "I'm working on this big baller. His bankroll is so fat, my stuff clenches just thinking about it."

Marlowe wiped the sleep from his eyes and gathered the notes on the desk. "Spare me."

"I'm gonna kick all these other clowns to the background. Everybody else in this place can kiss my ass, but I'ma have me a sugar daddy by next Tuesday!"

"Shereeta…"

"I don't care if I never see another strip pole again in life. Although I hear there's one downstairs. To put some of these prissy biddies in their place, I might have to break off a little something on Last Night."

"Shereeta!"

"What!"

"Get another room," he said.

"Oh, no, you didn't! And oh, no, I ain't. Sorry, boo, but one thing I firmly believe in, and that's plan B. You, cuz, and this room are my plan B. Not that anything would really prevent me from hooking up by Tuesday. But just in case, I'll be checking on you from time to time.

"Now, if you need your privacy, put the sign on the door. Uh-oh, that's right. You're experiencing technical difficulties."

She had the nerve to throw her head back and cackle like a witch.

He put his head in his palms, fatigue finally setting in. "Remind me to change families. Change my last name. Disown you."

She kissed him on the cheek. Her lips were cold

and had no doubt left a big red lip print on the side of his face. “You know you love me,” she said and headed toward the door.

She paused as she stepped outside. The thud of the subwoofers downstairs wafted in through the open space. “All I really want is for someone else to love me, too.”

Her voice was so weak and cracked with pain he barely recognized it. He turned around, but she’d already stepped into the hallway and closed the door behind her.

Chapter Twelve

Marlowe paged through his notes in his room. He hadn't had to handwrite so much information since grade-school book reports.

"Life before computers..." he muttered. He thought about the History of Communications class he'd taken in undergrad. He thought he would get extra credit for using a manual typewriter to write one of his research papers. The whole thing was a disaster. First trying to assemble the parts, correcting mistakes, making a carbon copy in case something happened to the original. The tips of his fingers were black and red for days from touching the ink ribbon. The result of his bright idea was a bump from a B+ to an A and reverence for all those who created mass media before the CRT.

The pages he had looked like a collage project. Notepads, napkins, Post-it notes. It was a conglomeration. He'd used anything he could write on, including the palm of his hand once or twice, to start on the story. So far, he had only enough to paint The Epicure in a vague light of debauchery, since all the celebs kept their masks on.

What he *did* have told an interesting story.

The Epicure was a blessing on the hill. It was the much-needed respite, spa, therapy, light-at-the-end-of-the-tunnel place for anyone who had the least bit of a hang-up about sex, their own sexuality or the sexuality of others. The Epicure was a safe, nonjudgmental haven where people could work through their issues without ridicule, stigmatization or down-looks of any kind.

He understood why folks came back again and again.

The notes for the article he had would make for a phenomenal story: success, seclusion and sex. Marlowe had the beginnings of what he needed to paint that picture. It's the story he'd much rather write.

Marlowe needed to talk to Tuck. Grease the wheels. Convince him that the story he came to get was not the one he should leave with.

Marlowe finished sorting his notes and stacked them into piles, realizing it would be a tough sell, if not impossible. But he had to try.

Marlowe sat back and fished inside his pockets. He tossed out what he found there.

Knowing that he had to contact his editor at some point during his stay, Marlowe had kept an eye out for anything that could help him pick a lock.

He smiled at the memory of the woman who taught him the fine art of breaking into lockboxes, file cabinets and safes that had simple locks. He had been doing a piece on recycled people—individuals who changed their lives for the better without the help (or hindrance, some might believe) of the system. The star of the article was a big-boned woman with the longest legs he'd ever given a tongue bath. Picking locks wasn't all she'd taught him.

"Um, um, um," he said, picking up a paper clip and twisting it into the shape of an L.

Then he took two other paper clips and straightened them. They were jumbo size. No matter what was going on at The Epicure, they seemed to want to do it big. All the way down to the paper clips. He envisioned the floor safe, thinking he could get one in the gap easily, but two? Three if he needed it? He wasn't sure.

Marlowe picked up a hairpin. It was black, sturdy, and shaped like an A without the crosshair. Instinctively, Marlowe drew the hair accessory to his nose. It smelled like an erotic dance of smoke, incense and femininity. Just as he imagined, there were hints of her aroma on it.

Irresistible, he thought. If he could keep it between

his fingers, it might just be the leverage he needed to force the tumbles apart. Just a feather touch and a hook pick to open the lock.

He rolled his tools into a napkin, shoved it into his back pocket and headed for Dr. G.'s office.

The hallways were relatively empty. Dr. G. was having her group session, others were in workshops, working out, getting Reiki or sitting in the enchanted grotto soaking up the vortexes.

Marlowe smiled and nodded at the few attendees he passed and kept a keen eye out for his cousin. With her knack for ruining the best laid plans, he couldn't afford whatever running in to her might lead to.

Marlowe made his way down the hallway, a faint fragrance that reminded him of Nag Champa garnishing the air. From the gold, deep red and bronze of the resort decor to the vendors and their sexual wares and finally the women open with their eroticism, he felt like a kid in the greatest candy store on the planet.

Skin, skin and more skin. Marlowe loved the skin. He couldn't believe fate had thrown him into a place like this and not allowed him to…indulge himself. He checked out a woman so curvy his eyes almost crossed trying to follow all the ways her body meandered like a river.

She smiled at him with her whole body. He flashed his killer smile out of instinct.

"Where're ya headed?" she asked.

He whipped out the response he'd prepared just in case he was stopped. "I'm looking for Shereeta."

The two paused in the hallway where the light was good. It illuminated every luscious brown ounce of her legs. For Marlowe, it was like being given the best present ever but not being allowed to unwrap it.

"You're the impotent one, right?"

Marlowe chuckled. "I see word continues to get around."

She sized him up as if she was making an important assessment. "I'll bet I can help you." She took a step, closing the gap between them and pressing against him like a purring cat.

"I'm sure you could, but I'm really here to work on my relationship," he responded in an attempt to deflect her advance.

"You sure?" she asked and began stroking his thigh.

Why did he go along with the impotence story? Why couldn't he have said he had priapism?

"Look, uh—"

"Sophie, get off of that guy!"

Sophie was a platinum blonde with Gwen Stefani hair, stop sign-red lipstick, a short, silver halter dress and silver stilettos.

A man who must have weighed 280–300 pounds came charging toward them. He was wearing a blue T-shirt, two sizes too small, tucked into black Dockers. The brown-skinned Bluto came complete with stomach overhang, knit cap and big thick knuckles.

"Uh-oh," Sophie said, but didn't bother moving her hand.

Marlowe's body tensed, anticipating the oncoming altercation.

The big guy grabbed Sophie and hugged her tightly. "I missed you, baby!"

The Incredible Black Hulk kissed Sophie's forehead then turned to Marlowe. "Sorry, man. Sophie likes to rub against people. It makes her—"

"I get it," Marlowe said.

"Come on, Sophie," the man said. "I need a back rub."

The man gently pulled her away and Sophie obliged, feigning reluctance. Her bottom lip stuck out as though she was a kid and someone had taken away her teddy bear. She kept her eyes on Marlowe the whole time down the hallway.

"You got hard," she said, pointing.

Marlowe glanced down at the rock-solid evidence of the turmoil he'd been in since he'd arrived. *Paper plates, books, ash trays, bees, rocks, cardboard boxes,* he repeated in his mind. He continued to Dr. G.'s office, imagining as many nonsexual things as possible. Picking up the pace now, he figured it would be just his luck for the good doctor's session to finish early.

"Chambers?"

"Yeah. It's me."

"Damn, negro. I've been calling you nearly every hour, on the hour. What the hell is going on?"

"Well, this thing exists. The Chocolate Chateau. I'm here and I've got a story."

"You got pages to back that up?"

"Yeah."

"What about photos?"

"No photos."

"Get some. Then send me everything you got ASAP."

"That's not gonna be easy."

"Why do you sound like you've got cotton in your mouth?"

Marlowe hunkered down, kept his voice low. "I'm trying to be quiet. They have every gadget on lock-down. Cell phones, laptops, iPods. Everything. I had to break into the main office to call you."

Marlowe's cell phone beeped in his ear. His stomach twisted sharply. *Low signal.* Tuck really had been blowing up his phone.

"Look, Chambers. It's been almost three weeks. This is the first I've heard from you."

Frustration blew out in hot blasts. "Did you hear me? Did you *hear* me? I'm like MacGyver up in here. I feel like a safecracker. I just called to tell you I'm on it."

"You better be. I already promised the board this story. And they promised me Haiti."

A surge of hope charged through Marlowe in

large waves. "What?" he asked, much louder than he should have.

"Haiti. We need someone to cover the rebuild in Port-au-Prince. It's a long-term assignment. If you can redeem yourself with this story, the board is willing to send you. They know you're the best. Just get back on your feet, man."

"Tuck," he began. More beeps in his hear. The light on his phone was flashing now. He was running out of time. "This place, it's called The Epicure. It's not as wild as you might think. It's more like a resort with—"

The line went dead.

"Sexual self-help," he finished.

His heart pounded in his chest like a fist. *Haiti.*

When the earthquake occurred, he was on the other side of the world. The assignment he'd been sent to get was late as usual, but damn good nonetheless. He'd called everyone he could think of to get an assignment. A few of them had already sent people. Those who hadn't wouldn't touch him with a ten-foot live feed. They were so interested in the quick, cursory story, they didn't want to invest in stories with depth and meaning. But this long-term assignment in Haiti was everything he'd wanted to build his career around. Those kinds of stories were far and few between for any journalist, and for him… freelance and tarnished rep, sometimes they didn't come around at all.

Marlowe placed the cell phone back into the safe.

Hopeful about his career for the first time in over a year. He could replenish his 401(k) and keep his lifestyle with an assignment like that, and, more important, he could repair his standing in the industry.

Marlowe checked to make sure anything he might have disturbed was put back in place and headed back to his room—his mind already packing his bags for Port-au-Prince.

Chapter Thirteen

The new day slipped in like a thief, stealing the comfort of sleep and blaring at Gena with the realization that once again, she was waking up alone.

Gena tried on four outfits before she decided that the look she needed was a combination of outfits two and three. Short dress to show off the confident legs she stood on every day and lace accents to emphasize the femininity inside her that had taken her over since the moment she saw Marlowe step out of that cab.

She wanted to get as far away from the weak-willed woman she'd been on First Night as she could. That woman had very little control over her emotions and her actions and had handed those things over to

Marlowe on a silver condom-laden platter and hollered: "It's yours, Mista Big Stuff!"

Big was the operative word. She could barely take her mind or her eyes off his size. As a sex coach, she knew that men with especially thick penises had a greater chance of bringing women to orgasm. Experts said their girth created greater friction in the muscles surrounding the clitoris. But "How thick is your dick?" isn't a question men liked to be asked on the first or second date. And with Gena's sexual challenges anyway, she realized that it was probably sexually useless to date a man with a small or even average-size penis.

She'd grown discouraged with trying to find a man who would go the sexual distance with her. The few men she'd been with had either been turned off by her missing organ, unconcerned as long as they got theirs or thought they could solve her "problem" by pounding her harder. If she heard the phrase "Wow, well, that's okay" one more time, she would cut someone.

It wasn't okay.

Gena had dreamed of being with the kind of man who wasn't appalled, who cared about her condition and was willing to work through it with her. So far, the order had been too tall to fill. Being with Marlowe last night put ideas in her head she hadn't allowed herself to have in years. The vaginal orgasm she'd had was the glorious proof.

She adjusted her wig, put on fake lashes and

chanted "Back away from his fine ass" in her head. After her fiasco with Ward, she knew she needed to put her lust on lock. The problem was…could she?

When she arrived in group, most of the session guests were already there. Narcisa had done her job and placed bouquets of fresh flowers on side tables. The strategic splashes of color helped to wake up the room, which was already glowing with sunlight.

She greeted each person and trained her eyes on Marlowe's forehead, afraid that if she didn't, she'd only be able to stare tongue-tied at his crotch and she'd have to cancel the session.

"I'm sorry I'm late. I've gained some weight recently and none of my really cute outfits fit me."

"I can't tell," Ronalda said.

Philad shrugged his shoulders. "You look okay."

"Looks good on you," the Colonel said.

"It sure does," Marlowe agreed.

"Thank you, and enough about my pudginess. Did any of you go to First Night?"

Everyone indicated that they had, and Gena used the previous night's festivities as an icebreaker for the day.

Then she asked each couple to share their plans for the day and whether they had met any part of their goals last night. The conversation was lively, but no matter how mesmerizing the talk, Gena's thoughts drifted toward Marlowe sitting alone again, taking his notes and looking intense and confident doing it.

Instead of fighting her urge to gaze in his direction and garner his attention, she decided to give in to it.

"So, Marlowe, you don't strike me as someone who's typically this quiet, especially after yesterday's session. Am I wrong?"

He looked up from his notebook—no doubt compliments of Narcisa's concierge magic. It looked like the kind of tablet first-graders used, with the dashed line between two solid ones. Of all the leather, sex toys, and bondage aids, that notebook struck her as the most unusual thing she'd ever seen at the center.

"I'm just trying to take it all in."

"Are you getting what you need?" she asked.

He tapped his pen against the page, which was nearly full with his handwriting. "So far, yes."

Gena smiled, thinking of First Night, and was both happy and sad to hear his response. "And what about Shereeta?"

His expression went sour. "I'm sure she's getting whatever it is that she needs."

"And that doesn't bother you?" she pressed. Others in the group looked on, curiosity growing in their eyes.

He kept silent. His lips pursed as though he wasn't sure how to answer the question.

"That's why Jolisa and I have a *completely* open marriage," Mike Titsworth said. "That way, there's no hurt feelings, misunderstandings or…equipment malfunctions."

The guests fought to stifle their laughter.

Gena had to admit, that was a humorous remark. But it was completely uncalled for. "Mike, what are our group standards?"

Mike shifted in his seat. "No animals; no forced interaction; no unreasonable objects."

A woman next to Marlowe chuckled.

"And no disparaging remarks," Jolisa finished. "I'm sorry for laughing, Marlowe, but I'm just saying. When you have a clear understanding, things like what you're going through don't happen. And to tell the truth, last night, when I was doing the slide in the Arena, I would have sworn you were hard as a steel rod."

"He wasn't hard. He's just huge," Ronalda said. "When you got it like that, you just look stiff."

"And heavy," Birdell finished.

"Care to comment, Mr. Chambers?" Gena asked. A flurry of desire rose inside her like a rabble of butterflies. "Were you able to get an erection?"

All eyes were on Marlowe. He placed a hand on his mouth and wiped it down to his chin. He didn't look like a student anymore. He looked like a man who just got busted with another woman.

The expression on Marlowe's face changed from *Damn, I've been caught* to *I got something for ya.* A sly grin crawled across his face. "I never said I couldn't get it up. I said I couldn't get it up with Shereeta."

If Gena's feminine lips could clap, they would

have at how happy that thought made her. Now, instead of wondering if what happened between them was a fluke, she could exchange hopeful thinking for wild fantasies.

"What is it about her that turns you off?" Ronalda asked.

"She's no good in bed. She thinks she knows how to work it, but I've had better sex with partially inflated blowups."

"Damn, that's cold," Philad said.

One of the more silent members of the group, Eleanor, glanced at her husband Luke then shook her head slowly. "Oh, what a shame."

"In case you haven't noticed, she's not exactly committed to our relationship. The last thing I want is sloppy seconds, thirds and fourths. So, when it comes to the missus, the dick don't."

Gena waited a moment for everyone, including herself, to digest what he was saying. "Since Shereeta isn't here, there's no way to confirm what you're saying. There's also no way for you two to set a joint goal to address this situation."

"You see what I go through?" Marlowe asked.

He dropped his head as if he were ashamed or weighed down with disappointment.

Gena longed to help him. "Don't feel bad. Shereeta owns her behavior. Even though she's not here to defend herself, the fact that she's been a no-show twice speaks very loudly."

"Thank you for saying that," Marlowe said.

“What would you like to get out of your remaining days here, Mr. Chambers?”

His expression went pensive. He looked like someone thinking way too hard about something. “I would like to make sure that this block that I have with Shereeta doesn’t get any worse. If we were to, say, get divorced, I don’t want the next woman I’m involved with to suffer because of what she is putting me through.”

Gena felt sad and angry at the same time. She was saddened by Marlowe’s sexual difficulty and how terrible he seemed to feel about it. She was angry with Shereeta for treating what appeared to be a good man so badly.

Ronalda cleared her throat. “Since Shereeta is living an open lifestyle, maybe you should, too.”

His eyes grew large and he relaxed the grip on his pen. “That…might be something to consider.”

“Yes,” she said.

“Sure is,” another woman agreed.

Ronalda’s husband folded his arms over his chest. “I know you see me sitting here.”

“Sorry, Philad. We agreed to be one hundred with each other, and Mr. Chambers is fine as hell.”

“Hmm,” came an agreement from one of the women. Gena couldn’t tell which.

“We agreed to keep it one hundred. That doesn’t mean you have to throw your creepin’ tendencies in my face.”

“Who’s creepin’, Philad? Who? Was it me who

went next door and sucked the neighbor's toes on her back porch?"

He scoffed and held up one frustrated finger. "One time! Six years ago!"

Ronalda rocked her neck. "Yeah, well, whose toes did you suck yesterday? Huh?"

"They damn sure weren't yours!" Philad shouted.

"Whoa," Gena said. Leaving her seat. She stepped between the couple and stretched her arms out like a ref at a boxing match. Others in the circle shifted in their seats and mumbled their concern.

"Jolisa already repeated the rules, so we don't need that again. But we do need some civility," Gena insisted.

"Rabid dogs don't deserve civility. They should be put down." Ronalda rocked her neck so severely, Gena thought she could give herself a crook or a bad muscle cramp.

"You're kidding me, right? I've sat here next to you while you undressed this man with your eyes and humped him in your mind. Then you wanna talk about how *fine he is* and I'm just supposed to pretend like that don't hurt. Well, quiet as it's kept, my ED is just about you, 'cause I sure don't have no trouble with nobody else."

The security person hanging back from the circle sprang into action and grabbed Ronalda. He held both of her arms behind her back and pulled her to the other side of the room. The woman flailed and spat out a string of epithets so foul, they would make hard-core rappers blush.

A wave of frustration coursed through Gena. Philad and Ronalda had been her problem couple from day one. They thought that healing their sexual dysfunctions would heal their entire relationship. No matter how thoroughly Gena explained that their sex life was a *part* of their relationship, but not the sum of it, they came back each year for more of the same. This year she'd warned them that it was their last trip to The Epicure. Gena thought she was prepared for any repercussions, fallout or hard feelings that declaration might cause. Unfortunately, she hadn't anticipated this.

With all eyes on her now, she knew she had to do something above and beyond her normal discussion, analysis, action planning. She just hoped it was the right thing. The kind of exercise she had in mind either brought people together or proved to them it was best if they parted ways.

"I'll be right back," Gena said.

Ronalda finally settled down. She looked as if she'd been running in an emotional windstorm. "I could never hurt you as much as you hurt me," she said and stopped struggling altogether.

The doctor nodded for the security person to release her. Ronalda sank down into a chair next to the Colonel.

Dr. G. came back holding a silver tray of ceramic

cups. They were all colors and each one was soup bowl size. She placed the tray on a counter then handed each person in the group a cup.

"May I have some of your paper, Mr. Chambers?"

Panic struck him for a second. He couldn't let her see what he'd written. He'd be busted for sure. He flipped the pad to the back. "How many sheets?"

"One for each person," she said.

Marlowe tore out nine sheets of paper and handed them over.

Dr. G. distributed them along with the pencils she'd brought in.

"I'm going to ask you all some questions. The most important thing I'm going to ask is that you be completely honest with your responses."

This woman who was zipped into a *don't-even-think-about-breathing* leather outfit was a far cry from the soft, accented woman he spent time with last night. Sexy as she was, Dr. G. seemed like a straight-up control freak. Last night's masked woman was like a sweet package just yearning to be unwrapped.

"Every time you write down an answer, I want you to tear it away from your paper and drop it in the cup."

Everyone nodded.

"Regarding the time you spend with your spouse, are you present, somewhat present, or absent? If you get less than four hours of quality face time per day, you're absent."

The small room filled with groans and then the sound of ripping and tearing.

Since Marlowe didn't have a significant other at the moment, he decided to substitute his relationship with his closest friend and colleague, Tuck. He thought about the assignments he'd gotten from him over the years and realized that the only significant chill time they'd had in years was three weeks ago when he was in the hospital. Marlowe added his groan to the others. He wrote *absent* and dropped it into the cup.

"Would you say that most of your interactions with your spouse are negative or positive? There's no middle of the road here. Even if the percentage is 50.9. People tend to fall heavily to one side or the other."

Another groan. The last few conversations Marlowe had with Tuck had been negative. "You're late!" "It's coming, just hang on."

It occurred to Marlowe that he'd been incredibly selfish and self-indulgent to assume that just because he was good, all rules would bend for him.

"When your spouse comes home from work, are they welcomed, ignored, or pounced on? In other words, what's it like being married to you?"

Marlowe barely acknowledged Tuck when he walked into his hospital room. He treated him as if he was an annoying ghost. That was no way to treat a friend. "Damn," Marlowe said.

"You all right over there, Mr. Chambers?" Gena asked.

"Not really," he said honestly. He didn't like this exercise and hoped it would be over soon.

"This is some bull because she pushes my buttons," Philad said.

"Are you or are you not in control of your own actions?" Gena asked. "Because if you're not in control, let me know. People who aren't in control of themselves need psychiatric care or medication or electroshock. I can go get my prescription pad right now or check you into St. Agnes down the road. Is that what you need?"

"No."

"Then write down your response, please."

Dr. G. continued with her questions. Praise or putdowns? Loving tones or yelling? Reaching toward or turning away? Delightful or demanding?

"When you're stressed do you turn to your mate or on them?"

They kept tearing off responses and putting them in the cups. Finally, they ran out of paper.

"There is a saying. You can only get out of a relationship what you put into it. So, please, hold up your cups."

They all did as they were instructed.

"Now think about all the things you've put into your cup. Close your eyes, lift your cup to your lips and imagine what it's like to drink what's in your cup."

There were numerous groans, moans of protest. A couple of people even put their cups down on the floor.

Dr. G., who hadn't sat down since she returned with the cups, paced around the group circle and stopped near where Philad and Ronalda were seated. "Considering what's in your cup, would you marry you?"

"I can't drink that," Philad admitted.

Dr. G. knelt beside him. "Why not? You've been asking your wife to drink it on a daily basis. Have you been putting in the ingredients for a successful marriage?"

"Nah. What's in here is, uh, it's uh—"

"It's what?" his wife asked, eyes moist with tears.

"Foul. Just straight-up nasty," Philad said and put his cup on the floor.

"Let's not even talk about the aftertaste of this mess," Ronalda said, staring at her cup and then placing it on the floor.

Philad's eyes filled with sorrow. "Damn, babygirl. I'm sorry."

Dr. G. rose and took a moment to glance at everyone. "The rest of you are not off the hook. What does it taste like? And that's not a hypothetical question. Sit with it a moment and then somebody answer."

She went back to her seat. You could have heard a cotton ball roll in that room. With the exception of a few long sighs, everyone seemed in stun mode and seriously considering the answer to Dr. G.'s question.

"Say something, somebody," she insisted.

"It's bitter. What's in that cup tastes like garbage," Ronalda said.

"Mine tastes like all the things I've been resenting," Mike added, and the Colonel agreed.

Gena leaned forward in her chair. "Be more specific."

Abigail cleared her throat. "Maybe like bile. It's like I'm throwing up all these cruel things."

One by one they shared what they thought the contents of their cups tasted like. From ashes to roadkill, each flavor was stomach churning. Except for the youngest couple among them. Luke and Eleanor. They said what was in their cups tasted like warm milk and honey.

Dr. G. stared across to Marlowe. He knew it was coming. His whole body felt heavy with remorse. "What about you, Mr. Chambers? What flavor have you been serving up?"

"I don't know. Bad, I guess."

"What does bad taste like if you have to swallow it?" she asked.

Marlowe couldn't put a flavor to it. All this group session stuff was new to him. These people were probably pros at sharing and naming their feelings. He hated that thought of what he'd put Tuck and the other editors he'd worked for through, not to mention the women he'd had brief relationships with. "I'm just not sure. But it's nothing I'm proud of."

"Oh, what a cop-out," the Colonel said.

"Hold on," Dr. G. said. "This is his first time. Not everyone is comfortable putting everything out in the open. All I ask from you is that you share as much as you can, and step out of your comfort zone sometimes."

Marlowe felt as if he'd just become a cast member of a reality TV show.

Gena crossed her legs and looked fearless in her black leather and lace. "If you found this helpful, we can do other exercises like this. I'm going to keep saying this until you get it. Lovemaking starts outside of the bedroom. You all have to learn how to sex each other from the outside in."

"You've been saying that, but this time, I finally got it," Ronalda said.

Philad nodded. "Yeah, I've got some things to think about."

"Don't think," Dr. G. said. "Talk, to each other. Do something to change that foul and bitter taste."

All of the couples shared looks and glances. Marlowe kept his eyes on the miracle-working doctor and sex coach, Gena Bivens, who'd just changed a slasher film into a Disney movie. He had to admit, that was some exercise. And it was the right exercise at the right time.

He'd planned his whole day and would get to the interviews he needed. But first, he had to talk to the good doctor about her technique.

"Well, I know it's not been the full hour," Dr G. said, "but why don't you couple up and spend the rest of the time sharing your thoughts and feelings about the exercise? You don't have to say what was in your cup. Don't ask what your spouse put in his/her cup. Just stick with the feelings."

The couples thanked the doctor and filed out—some hand in hand. Marlowe remained in his seat.

"Is there something wrong?" she asked him.

"No. I just wanted to talk about the exercise, if you have time."

Dr. G. stood and gathered the cups. "I think it would be better if you talked about it with Shereeta."

"It's not about what's in my cup. I just wanted to ask you how you came up with that." Marlowe gave her his cup and helped her pick up the rest.

"That one came to me while I was listening to a couple berate each other the way Philad and Ronalda were starting to do. I just wondered if they realized all the drama they were causing the other person."

"I see."

"I just wanted them to get a taste of their own medicine, so to speak."

Marlowe could think of several times in his life when he could have probably used a taste of his own medicine. "What happens when the person doesn't change?"

"You've chosen the wrong person."

"That's cold," he said.

"The cold hard truth. If you're trying to make a relationship work, but no matter what you do you get dogged, why would you continue that relationship?"

Painfully, Marlowe thought about his relationships with his editors. They'd generously given him assignments, and time after time he assumed they would wait for his *genius.* For the great Marlowe Chambers to turn in his work. No wonder they were kicking him to the curb.

"So, what should a person do?"

"You start by making better choices. Everything else flows from there."

Marlowe nodded, hoping he understood her correctly.

Together they dumped the slips of paper from the cups into the trash then placed the cups back on the silver tray.

"May I ask a personal question?" she asked.

"Yes."

"Was Shereeta *outgoing* when you married her?"

"Shereeta's been Shereeta since day one."

"But you decided to be with her anyway. Why?"

He scratched his forehead, discomfort crawling under his skin like ants. "The audacity of hope, I guess. I thought she could be different. I thought I could *make* her different."

"Ooh, I wanna say something so badly."

Marlowe shook his head, knew what he had coming. "Go ahead."

They walked toward the door, the doctor's face full of mischief. "How's that workin' for ya?"

The two shared a laugh and Marlowe felt a connection. Funny, the connection was more like a recollection. As if he was remembering something special between them. Right then and there, he felt relaxed and content. And peaceful. *Don't get too comfortable*, he told himself. *You've got a story to finish.*

"Well, the workshops will be starting soon. I think I'll go to the one on positions. Then I'll hit the weights."

The doctor grinned. A bit of naughtiness rode the corners of her mouth. "That's one of our most popular workshops. You'll probably need the weights by the end of it."

"No doubt."

She gave him an electrifying smile. It struck a chord in all right places.

"Have a good time, Mr. Chambers," she said.

He headed out the door and before he could get through it, the question that had been nagging him since the moment he saw her stopped him.

"What about you, Doctor? Did you choose the right person?"

"I most certainly did," she responded. "I chose myself."

Chapter Fourteen

Marlowe made the rounds before the workshops started, chatting with guests and trying to get the 411 and anything else they were willing to share about why they were there. Couples talked freely about The Epicure and how much they appreciated the service it provided. Beyond that, he didn't get much. Very few personal details regarding how long they'd been coming or what their favorite activities were. When Marlowe pushed further, he ended up standing alone while the couple moved off to check out vendor tables or sample some of the refreshments set out along the perimeter of the rooms.

Slightly discouraged from his failed attempts at covert interviews, he considered walking around the grounds and writing about the landscaping to add ambience to the article. When Narcisa notified everyone that Sedona was on a scorpion alert and that the staff recommended that guests stay inside, he decided he'd just go to a workshop room and wait for it to begin.

Marlowe arrived before any guests. It was just him and the presenter. Damn if it wasn't his mystery woman from last night. No wonder this workshop was so popular. The woman was eroticism on two legs. He bet the men came in salivating. He knew he was.

In her own petite way, she was stacked like a million-dollar poker deck. Melon-sized breasts, small waist and hips that curved for days and days. She had the nerve to cover all that with a lace negligee. He hung back for a second, hoping she would turn sideways.

"It's you," he said.

"It's me," she replied, face glowing despite the mask. And that accent—he'd never get enough of it.

Marlowe smiled all over. "Hey, me."

He walked into the conference room tentatively. Instead of rows of chairs arranged auditorium-style, these chairs were arranged in groups with tables in the middle. Good, he thought. He'd get more interaction with the guests that way.

"Will you help me with this?" she asked.

"Sure."

Marlowe put his notebook down on a nearby table

and trotted over to the lectern, where she was busy unpacking thick packets of paper stapled together.

"Handouts," she said. "One for each person."

"Got it," Marlowe said, taking a stack. He and the mystery woman headed in opposite directions, putting a packet in front of each participant space at each table. He smiled at the image on the front. It was hand drawn and showed a man and woman pretzeled into a position only a contortionist could love.

"Is this even possible?" Marlowe asked.

"Yes," she said and blinked innocently. "I'll be demonstrating that as well as other positions today."

His mouth watered. *Of course she would.* He could tell last night she had the positions thing on lock. "I can't wait."

The innocence in her eyes turned hot. "Care to volunteer?"

Marlowe chuckled yet throbbed with curiosity. "Me? Nah. Thanks for the invite though. I'm just not that flexible or in that kinda shape," he lied. He was just too eager to watch.

"Really? You were in perfect shape last night."

Desire flashed inside him with her compliment. "Thanks."

With both of them putting out the handouts, the work went fast.

"So, you got a name for me yet?"

Her eyes twinkled like stars. She folded her bottom lip in, and just when it seemed as if she would tell him her name, she shook her head no.

"Uh, I don't know how much longer I can stand it," he said, wondering how a woman so hot could be so demure.

They finished with the front-table groups and started toward the middle. "So, think you'll stay the week?"

"Yes," he said. "Don't most people?"

"As a matter of fact, they do. But you don't seem like most people."

"Oh, yeah? How do I seem?"

"Like a man in perfect control of his sexuality."

The woman did wonders for his ego. "I wouldn't use the word *perfect.*"

They finished placing the packets. Ms. Masquerade went back to her boxes and pulled out multicolored markers. She smiled sweetly. "Just toss a handful on each table."

"Aye-aye, Captain," he said, taking an armful of felt tips. He made sure each table had a variety of colors to choose from. "I hear some pretty famous people show up here."

"That's right," she said absentmindedly.

"It must be nice to look around and see someone you recognize from, say, the movies or television."

"Yes, it is."

"Who's the most famous person you've ever seen here?"

She stopped digging in the box for markers. Her body went still and she looked caught somewhere between wanting to slap him or give him the finger.

"Did you meet with Dr. G. before you checked in?"

He straightened a little. Fought the wave of defensiveness rising inside him. "Yes."

"Then I'm sure she shared our don't tell, don't ask policy."

"She did indeed."

"Then why are you asking me to violate it?" Her beautiful mouth flattened into a thin line. Her eyes grew hard.

"I'm sorry. I assumed the policy applied to people outside of The Epicure. If you're here, I figure we're all seeing them, so there's no harm in discussing it, right?"

Marlowe's stomach went sour. Discomfort sloughed around in his belly as if he'd actually swallowed all the things in his cup from the exercise. His behavior was making him sick.

"Wrong. The people who come here are pretty much hand-selected."

"What does that mean?"

"It means there are certain things we just don't mention."

The expression on her face was thunderous. She was more than irritated or put off. She was insulted.

Marlowe could add impolite to his cup now.

"Hey, I apologize."

People were starting to filter into the conference room. A few stopped to fill glasses of water on a back table and then wandered in. The stream of people was steady. Marlowe could tell the workshop would fill quickly. He was glad he got there when he did.

"I'll accept your apology on one condition."

"What's that?" He placed the last few markers on the remaining table, believing that even a yoga master would have trouble with the position on the cover of the packet.

"You volunteer for one of the positions."

Her invitation set every nerve ending in his body on fire. "No can do," he said, knowing his buddies back home would kick his ass for passing up this kind of a chance.

"Trust me. It's easy. And for the position I'm thinking of, you don't even have to take off your clothes. You just have to have strong arms."

Marlowe nearly killed his brain trying to come up with a position like what she was describing. When he couldn't, he decided it was an experience he could add to his article. Plus, he kept his biceps on point.

"You've got a volunteer."

"Excellent," she said and smiled warmly.

He smiled back, remembered how her hips had worked him. "Just don't hurt me."

"Not a chance."

Because he didn't know how erotic the workshop would be, Marlowe took a seat in the back just in case his front and center decided to take center stage. He was flanked a few seats to his left and his right by a couple of guys who obviously had the opposite idea.

He'd recognize their ravenous grins from the one and only time he'd gone to a triple-X movie theater. He knew they were there to do a Pee-wee Herman during the presentation.

"No sitting in the back," she insisted. "Join a group, and behave!"

All three of them groaned and then each one joined a different table group.

As its name implied, Fifty Positions in Fifty Minutes was a high-speed ride into the world of smack it up, flip it and rub it down. Marlowe had never seen such agility. He was mesmerized. So much so, that he didn't have time to interview his tablemates. He barely had time to use the markers to highlight the positions he liked, those he wanted to try or the ones he didn't care for. And there weren't many of those. When his demo time came around, Marlowe felt as if he'd just been treated to Cirque du Sex. Surprisingly, it was more educational than strongly erotic. So, he was able to keep his sex drive in check.

The woman and her…assistants kept their clothes on; however, the demonstration used every prop in the room. Tables, chairs, a couch, a bed as well as the wall and good old floor. The speed of the demonstration squeezed his brain. He tried to keep up, but it was difficult. By the time he'd made notes about a particular position, mystery woman was on to the next. She was so bad, her sexual gymnastics often got an enthusiastic round of applause from the audience. She was a leg-flipping, backing-that-thing-up, dropping-it-like-it's-hot tour de force. She made each twist and movement look so easy and made nearly every position something Marlowe wanted to try. Although he'd need at least a year of Hatha training for a few of them.

"Please lay on the couch," she said.

He got into position quickly so any awkwardness he might have wouldn't throw her off schedule.

"Scoot down so your thighs are against the arm."

He slid down.

"Now hold me," she said.

Before he could ask how, she'd vaulted on top of him, holding on where his knees were. He caught her at the waist, and to his surprise her black-lace thong was directly above his face.

"All right now!" came a shout from a woman in the audience.

She turned toward the audience and smiled. "This is called Face Time. But brothers, brothers, don't bury your face. Just lift and lower as my able-bodied partner will demonstrate."

Marlowe didn't have to be instructed twice. He lifted and lowered her just as he would a barbell. Her thighs were infinitely better than weights. He especially enjoyed the view of the blazing torch tattoo just below her waist on her upper left thigh. He'd caught a glimpse of it last night, but he preferred the full image now. It seemed…familiar.

This was no time to contemplate skin art. He flicked his tongue out of his mouth for show and because he couldn't help himself. He didn't make contact, but a millimeter closer…

All the women in the room moaned.

"Thank you," she said to Marlowe.

"The pleasure is all mine," he said honestly.

He lowered her gently to the floor. As quickly as Marlowe had gotten up there, he was back in his seat, exhilarated and writing notes in his mind quicker than he could get them down on paper. He'd never seen anything like it. The *LifeWire* readers might not even believe it. The details rushed to his hand, and he used his pen like a paintbrush to create vibrant pictures.

If Dr. G. was responsible for this session, and she seemed to him the type of leader who would have special control over every single thing that happened in her center, then the woman was brilliant. She was a triple threat offering coaching, education and entertainment. Everything he'd seen so far was a broad combination of all three. The approach covered every possible base and would become the focus and format of his article.

He looked up at his mystery woman for a moment and wondered for the first time if one article would do The Epicure justice. A documentary might be better.

If the other workshops were as enjoyable as this one, Marlowe would do his best to attend every one. He flipped through the few empty pages of his notebook. He'd have to find more paper. He'd already filled up two-thirds of it. Until he could get more paper, he'd write small and get as much on each page as possible. He'd also use both front and back sheets.

"Whadaya think?" a man in a T-shirt and long, wide shorts asked.

"I think if someone had told me about this place when I was sixteen, I would have run away from home and come straight here."

"This is my second time. The first time I came when it was a party goin' on. You know what I mean?"

"No. Why don't you tell me?"

The man glanced at Marlowe's pen and paper. His grin faded.

"Naw, man. That's all right. I just wanted to check you out, seein' as you was part of the show and all. You go 'head. Do ya thing. I'll catch you later."

The man moved on. He walked as if the sole of his left shoe was made out of lead. Marlowe figured that was his cool stride. *Rapper,* he guessed.

Most of the others filed out also. Those who stayed had his mystery woman hemmed up near the lectern—their eyes bright and mouths wagging. Marlowe didn't want to be intrusive or obvious. But he did want to hear what they were saying. He moved toward the closest seating group and began to pick up the left-behind markers, papers and miscellaneous cups and napkins from the table. He pretended to sort the items into piles while the groupies talked, appearing to worship their Position Goddess.

"You were *so* amazing! It must take years to get that good," Eleanor exclaimed.

"I hope not, because I need you to be able to do all that tonight," her companion said.

"Oh, Luke!"

The smile broadening across their presenter's mouth could compete with the Arizona sun and win. "It didn't take long, actually. I had a good teacher."

"Really? Who?"

"Dr. G."

At the reference to Gena Bivens, Marlowe nearly choked on his own awe.

"Dr. G.?" Luke said.

"Wow!" the woman replied. "Well, you're fantastic."

"I'm not half as good as the doctor. She can do things with her body that would make you drop your head sideways."

"Oh, yeah?" Luke asked.

"Don't get any ideas!" his companion admonished.

He frowned. "I thought we came here for ideas."

The woman snickered into her hand. "You know what I mean."

Marlowe imagined holding Dr. G. the way he'd held his mystery woman. Then that lift-and-lower thing. He had just started getting into the fantasy when the markers he held slipped out of his hand. He must have started squeezing them and not noticed. They all looked over at him.

"Don't let me disturb the groove," he said, wanting to hear more.

"Well, I've got to clear out for the next workshop," she said.

"Okay," the two replied. "Thanks for everything!"

They left bumping into each other playfully like a brand-new couple. "You remember all that? I hope you remember all that," Luke asked.

"Not all of it."

"Well, we 'bout ta have a pop quiz up in the room."

Marlowe felt good for the couple. Whatever their issues were, they sounded ready to move past them.

"Did you like the workshop?"

Appreciation washed over him. Between their time together last night and finding out she was queen of positions, he felt closer to her. Almost as if they were in a relationship or something.

Or something, his mind repeated.

"I liked it very much."

"Do you think your wife will like it when you try the positions on her?"

"Who knows? Uh, sure," he said.

Some of the fire in her eyes went out. It made him want to be General Electric and bring the light again.

"Are you going to another workshop?" she asked.

"What do you suggest?"

"Joys of Toys is good. People love Make it Last, too. It might be the best thing for your relationship?"

"Do you have a favorite?"

"Yes. I like Touch Me, Tease Me."

He stared at her mouth and wanted to roll it wet against his. "Then that's the one I'll go to."

Some of the light came back. It warmed him like a caress. "I'll let you know what I think."

"Can't wait to hear. And thanks for your help," she said.

Marlowe placed the markers back into her box. "I helped set up. I can help tear down."

"Actually, I meant the demo."

"Oh, that. That was…nice."

"Think you'll try it?" she asked. She licked her top lip and sucked on her bottom one. Marlowe longed to feel what she was doing with her tongue on a spot just below his belly button.

Images of her naked crowded his brain. His body flushed from head to toe and every erogenous zone he had caught fire. "I damn sure would like to."

They finished packing the markers and papers. They tossed all the trash into the receptacles. Marlowe picked up his pen, tucked his pad under his arm and carried her supply box. They walked toward the door together.

"You say Dr. G. taught you that?"

Her eyebrow rose in surprise. "So, you were eavesdropping."

"Eavesdropping is such a strong word."

"How about heavy listening?"

He chuckled. "Heavy listening. I like that."

"Yes. Dr. G. taught me. She taught most of the staff just about everything they know."

"How's that?"

"Well, the staff came onboard like Dr. G. disciples or something. Groupies maybe. They orbited her like satellites and moons."

"I get that. She seems pretty cool."

"At first, she did everything. All the workshops. All the arrangements for the evening activities. The coaching. She wore herself so thin."

Marlowe could see that, too. Typical workaholic personality. "She's either totally dedicated or half-way nuts."

"She ain't nuts. She knows what she's doing. And, after four years she started trusting others to do the things she'd been doing. Then she could focus on intake and the coaching sessions."

"When you say intake, what do you mean?"

"I mean the guests. I'm sure you noticed it's easier to get a car loan than it is to get in here."

"Yeah. I noticed. Listen, I'd like to talk to you some more about this place. Since it's my first time. I don't really know the ropes. I was hoping you could show me."

Her eyes softened and she smiled as though she wanted to pat him on the head rather than help him. "Just ask Gena. She'll tell you everything you need to know."

Marlowe almost lost the wind being in the session had put into his sails. It was day two and he was getting nowhere. He needed details. Nitty-gritty stuff. What he had now was good, but it was superficial. A lot of it anyone renting the latest indie porno could get.

"Information is surely at a premium around here."

"Yeah. I can't help you with that. But if you decide you want to hang out in the evenings, I'll be around."

He followed her out into the corridor. "Where would you like this?" he asked, nodding toward the box.

"In the storage closet. It's this way."

Marlowe took some time to appreciate her walk. A brown hourglass in a black negligee. She walked as if every erotic thing came from her hips. It matched the environment. The whole place was a sexual smorgasbord. *Why oh why did I pick now to have an alibi about my sex drive?* he chided himself again.

The after-session cleanup did little to cool Gena's need. The sessions always kicked her desire into overdrive, but today with Marlowe, she'd been more excited than she could remember. Her sessions always left her wet and wanting. She'd put her wetness right where Marlowe could see it and was not ashamed at how damp her thong must have looked to him.

As they walked down the corridor and passed guests heading off in various directions to their sessions, she replayed their face time position again and again in her mind. Sweat dampened her skin. She was grateful that Marlowe was carrying her boxes so that her hands were free to fan her face.

"I feel like a Roman candle," Marlowe said, speaking her thoughts. His face bore the expression of a man on the verge of a slow-building orgasm.

"I'm hot, too," she responded, on the verge of something herself.

Marlowe licked those easy lips of his in a way that told her he'd be good at licking her feminine ones. "How hot?" he asked.

It was a dare. She knew it. An irresistible one. Why did she insist that he help her demonstrate a position? Why had she told him about the position session at all? One reason. To ride that big dick again.

With her heart and her lust racing, she took his elbow. "Come with me."

With her two Ms—Marlowe and her mask—she felt a swelling freedom and a recklessness that kept her as hot as a pot on a constant boil. She tossed away notions of all the mistakes she'd made with men. For as long as that big, sweet dick would salute her, she would be wet and ready for it...anytime.

She'd heard of people with missing limbs having phantom sensations. Pains and itches in places where an arm or a leg used to be. Since Marlowe's arrival, she'd had phantom jumps, trembles and pulsations from her missing organ. The imaginary tip of her sexual mountain tightened and pointed straight at a man so sexy, his presence made the needs of every other guest vanish like ghosts in a dream.

She led him downstairs and across the hall from Erotic City. A handful of couples had meandered below to make out or talk away from the crowds. Gena and Marlowe glanced casually at a few and marched past the rest.

The current passing between them was so strong it should have been visible as white-hot electric charges. Tiny lightning strikes ricocheting from body to body. Gena fished a key card from the box and passed it in front of a square panel. To most guests, it looked like a flat sangria-colored box on the side of a wall. A slight push revealed a large door that opened into a room she'd designed herself.

"Um," was all Marlowe said when he went in.

Gena didn't know if that was a sound of approval or surprise.

The room was reserved for special guests—those who were really into a more *toyful* lifestyle, as she'd once been herself.

It was called the Grand Chamber. Studded, black-leather walls, red ceiling and devil-red laminate floor. The space smelled like fresh cedar and new leather. Gena kept the ornate room stocked with toys for nearly every fetish imaginable. The soundproof and isolated VIP area came complete with a worship area and throne, pleasure table, racks of toys, shelves of whips, face masks and dildos. A red body harness hung from the ceiling, flanked by a tie-and-tease chair. Her pride and joy was the five-point suspension punishment stand at the rear of the room. She walked straight for it.

Marlowe smirked. “Guests make *servants* here?”

“Or break them,” she answered.

Marlowe took a condom out of the box of materials and placed the box and his things on a table near the stand. Not a moment too soon. Gena couldn’t stop her hands as she pushed him toward the wall. They did whatever they wanted—pulling and tugging on Marlowe’s slacks. Yanking his clothes off until he was gorgeously naked. She’d seen plenty of guests lose control. The need to join so profound, they couldn’t make it to a bed, a couch or the floor. They’d just slammed against the wall and humped until their eyes rolled back. She understood completely now.

Her fingers moved frantically over his hard muscles and she stared at them in amazement. Suddenly, the queen of control found herself in the middle of losing hers. “I…don’t…I don’t…understand—” she began, unable to believe how reckless and lustful she felt.

Marlowe ripped open the packet and rolled the condom onto his hardness. “Here’s how it works,” he said, voice low-toned and bottomless. “I’m going to put my—”

“Shh, please, just…”

The position demo was all the foreplay they needed. Gena and Marlowe groped each other in a frenzy of blind desire. Each tugging on shoulders and pulling on hips as if they wanted to merge from head to toe rather than groin to groin. As if they were trying to tear each other's skin off.

She shoved him against the wall. He hit the leather, grunted and stretched his arms out and slightly above his head in mock surrender. But the fire smoldering in his eyes told a different story. She shuddered with the intensity she saw there. Grabbing his wrists, she tugged his arms straight up and reached for the restraints. It had been a long time since she'd had a submissive. All at once her body craved the experience.

Just before she secured the bonds, Marlowe's eyes flashed. He grabbed her waist and swung her against the leather wall. He tore at her clothes as if they were demons and threw them to the floor. Quickly he pushed her arms up and pulled the bonds into place around her wrists. A half smile curled across his lips.

"What? Whoa," she uttered, realizing her predicament. Her thighs quivered in anticipation.

"So," he said, taking a riding crop from rack of crops and whips next to the bondage area. "You like to be in charge?"

He dragged the fringed leather at the end of the crop across her collarbone. Her knees turned to jelly. "Yes."

She strained against her restraints, so eager to get her hands on his hard-muscled flesh. "I want to touch you."

That half smile of his broadened as he shook his head. "No," he said.

A thin spark of fear flickered through her. This was the first time she'd been on the other side of the bondage role. She glanced down at the long and thick length of him that was getting longer and thicker by the second.

"A safe word," she whispered. "I, I don't have one."

As the one in control, she'd never needed a safe word, but now…

"Guess you'll just have to trust me," he said.

Starting with her neck, he passed the crop over every inch of her body. Shoulders, arms, nipples, belly. He placed it against her opening and twirled it like a baton. The fringe spun against her delicate flesh. Gena trembled with the rush of explosive currents stoking inside her.

Marlowe kept on with his teasing, brushing the crop against her thighs, behind her knees, over her calves and ankles. The sensation was so glorious, so potent, all she could do was shiver and pant while her shoulders heaved in response. Gena felt wetter than she'd ever been. Her juices trickled down her thighs like tears.

"Mar—lowe…" she pleaded, helpless and aching.

He saw her strong need and tossed the crop aside. His entire body seemed so much bigger with his clothes off. He stood back a moment, to let her see him and just how much he wanted her. Then, their bodies connected like magnets. He kissed her neck, her shoulder. "You taste good," he murmured. His voice pressed against her cleavage. Moans leaked from her throat like tiny songs.

She couldn't decide what she wanted more: his mouth on her or his dick in her.

She nipped his shoulders and sank her teeth lightly into the fleshy part underneath. He moaned. His skin tasted like salted caramel. Marlowe's allure overwhelmed her. He made her want to scream *yes* before the dick even got inside her good.

"Don't stop," she said, nervous that he might discover her secret.

"I won't," he responded and slammed into her core.

Gena whimpered from the intensity of the tight fit. Even with her juices flowing easy, he filled her completely. Her feminine walls clamped around his thick length instantly.

"Damn," he said. His breath came in a hot burst of air against her cheek. "You okay?"

Gena nodded. There were no words. He simply felt like a homecoming.

He pinned her against the leather. Their thrusting became a fierce dance of tenderness and abandon. They rode each other swiftly. Tasting and feeding. The heat and intensity drove them on. Gena closed her eyes while her head fell back and pitched forward. His dick was one long onslaught of pleasure, so heavy inside her. She dared to think that this time… maybe this time…

There was a hurricane taking place in the VIP. A tsunami. A sexual tantrum. He brought every Celsius degree of the desert heat with him and pressed it against her skin. He looked at her so intensely, touched her so deliberately, it didn't matter what he asked at that moment. Her answer would be yes, he could have anything. And what he didn't ask for she would beg for him to take.

His hands were hot against her skin, as if he'd just taken them out of an oven or they'd just come from between her legs. Gena was so desperate to come. So sex frantic. Already in that ain't no stopping us now place. The paparazzi could come, they could threaten to put her freakiness on YouTube, and she'd keep right on rocking. Her pussy walls clamped down, like two hands clapping her approval. She gripped him tight, pretending that if she held on to that sweet dick hard enough, the sensation would go on for days.

Gena inhaled Marlowe's soapy, sweet aroma as if it were new air. She couldn't get close enough. She wanted to swallow his dick whole with her body so that she wouldn't be a separate entity but completely one with him. He seemed to be caught up in the same need. He pulled her so close it hurt, hurt so damned good. She gasped and ground while his thrusts stopped and started time.

He draped his flesh over hers. Pressed in hot and

tight. She wanted so much to grab him. He yanked her hips. Instinctively Gena wrapped her legs around him. With one arm under her buttocks and the other cupping a breast, he sucked firmly on a taut nipple. Still slamming. Still grinding. His teeth raked against the tight pebble while his tongue flicked across the front. Gena flopped like a fish missing water and rode his length in an urgent fury.

"Yes," he said.

She burrowed into the crook of his neck and inhaled. He smelled like a wet dream. They groaned together, both too out of control to stop, slow down, breathe. His sweat bathed her like hot water.

Gena opened her eyes then. Watched the brutal pleasure passing over Marlowe's face. He grunted and ground into her. Finally releasing her breast and rolling his powerful hips into hers. She gasped and let the feeling charge into her body.

"So close," she said, clamping her thighs tighter around his waist. "I'm so, so…"

Perspiration glistened across his sturdy chest. Gena reveled in the sound of their sweaty flesh smacking together like lips. She met him thrust for thrust, consumed by the way he filled her inch by luscious inch. The leather wall behind her squeaked rhythmically from their wild movements. The chains holding her bonds clanked above them and seemed to drive them further. They sounded like wind chimes on sex packets.

His hands kneaded the flesh of her buttocks, fingers sliding up and down the crack of her behind.

The movement quickened her breath and sent her blood pounding in her throat. Gena watched for a moment, transfixed as his thick length thrust in and out. Marlowe saw her watching and pushed into her even more deeply. She gasped on the verge and craved completion.

Marlowe's sexy brown eyes bored into hers. Then he kissed her fast. His tongue hungrily explored her mouth. Desire streaked through her as Marlowe claimed her with his prowess, the sensation emotionally and literally stealing her breath. With each plunge into her core, he unleashed the passion that had been building inside her for much too long.

"How close?" he murmured.

Their sweat flowed together now, merged like their sex, their passion.

"Right now," she whispered.

A tide inside her surged forward. She let go as it struck her wave after wave after wave.

Marlowe's fulfillment came only seconds behind Gena's. His body slammed into hers and then stiffened while her core still quivered deep inside, clenching against his jerking dick.

A rush of satiation overcame her along with the knowledge that with this newest exchange, she would walk out of the Grand Chamber a new woman—one for whom the rest of the world was now blurred out. She would see Marlowe in her therapist notes, smell him on her body, feel him between her legs. As he unfastened the leather straps holding her wrists, she hoped that she hadn't once again given herself over to the wrong man.

Chapter Fifteen

After recovering from his delicious tête-à-tête, Marlowe spent the rest of the day in workshops. History of Sexuality, Touch Me, Tease Me and a Joys of Toys session presented by Honey Ambrose-Pace. Each session was thorough, unique and, considering the subject matter, very professional. He'd pit the Better Bondage workshop against any workshop he'd taken or ever would take at a professional journalism conference any day.

He'd called the concierge for more notebooks. They were delivered to his room two hours later. He felt as though at The Epicure, he'd been given carte blanche to do anything he wanted, whenever he wanted. Two days and he was living rap-star righteous. Whatever he wished for, if he snapped his fingers, he could have it.

"What are you writing, a novel?"

Marlowe sat in the dining area, furiously summarizing all the events so far that day. "No. I just like to keep a journal of everything I do and think. It's a compulsion. It keeps me calm."

Marlowe was getting tired of so many people asking him about his writing. He understood it. But it still got on his nerves. But he supposed people were tired of his questions, too.

Why are you here?

How long have you been coming?

What's your favorite part?

And the question no one would answer: *How did you hear about this place?*

To tell the truth, people still weren't forthcoming about the answers to most of his questions. They were as vague and evasive as the mystery woman had been. So far, Marlowe could describe The Epicure from top to bottom. He could give an account of the workshops and First Night and even depict the clientele, at least from the outside. But the meat of the story, and what he considered the magic of his approach to article writing—the memorable human interest—was missing. Aside from Carmela, the actress he'd dated a while back, he didn't think he had many real names of clients nor did he have any real insight into what drove them to a place like this, what they got out of it or what really made The Epicure tick.

The personal minutia was his signature. His brand. Without that piece of unique grit, the shell of his story would never produce the pearl of an article.

When he'd agreed to do a story on the Chocolate Chateau, he'd known that the subject matter wasn't up to his usual standards, but he always believed that his writing would be. He had to find somebody willing to open up to him. At least one person who could give him the goods, not just on the place but their experience there. Otherwise, Tuck would not only take him to court for his past advance, he'd skim his new story and sue him for breach of contract.

Determined to stay on track, Marlowe picked up the schedule of events to see what was on tap for tonight.

The event schedule for that evening said *Buffet*. Well, Marlowe supposed even sexually challenged couples deserved to be well fed. He'd go with a big appetite and lots of questions. His mind immediately conjured a vision of the woman with the striking mask and sexy dreads.

Damn.

The more he fought thinking about her, the more thoughts of her consumed him. He tried to picture what she looked like without the plume of feathers off the side of her face. He couldn't help but wonder if tonight he'd find out.

* * *

Gena was ready. She'd taken off her wig and pulled her locks into a ponytail. Removed all her makeup, contact lenses and expensive jewelry. She'd replaced her domme attire with a plain white tank top and a multicolored sarong that she'd tied with a side knot at the top of her left hip. She abandoned her eight-inch skyscraper stilettos and slipped into a pair of barely there sandals that showed off her arches and polish-free toes.

Fully clothed yet she felt completely naked. Without the armor of her domme persona, Gena's vulnerability was the only thing standing between her and the world. She'd never been this bold to risk letting someone see the other side of her. The sun-kissed and soft-walking half-Bantu woman who sometimes dreamed of quiet nights under purple skies. Who urgently yearned to be held and protected and even rescued like some silly damsel in distress.

The excitement in her belly was so strong, it made her want to rest her hand there to see if she could feel it fluttering against her palm. She was the happy secret shopper, observing the events she'd helped plan and put into place. If tonight went anywhere close to last night, she'd have another success to celebrate and be thankful for.

She secured the mask to her face, relying on it once again to keep her secret and allow her to talk to Marlowe. She looked forward to seeing him again. No, there was more to it than that. She needed to see him again. Gena wanted to do the right thing and assure him that all was not lost. He could repair his relationship even if it took every ounce of energy he and Shereeta had. If they both committed to it, they could make it work. Gena had seen reconciliations happen all the time. It was the driving force behind why she had the dysfunction/immersion weeks in the first place.

Marlowe Chambers deserved to be happy. His confidence, charm and good looks compelled her to help him be happy. If he attended the Buffet, she would try to talk Shereeta into participating in the activity.

Gena left her penthouse, allowing the fluttering wings of all the butterflies in her stomach to float her down to the lower level, where she searched for Marlowe.

When she stepped off the elevator, everything was just as she'd planned it. Bowling ball-size clay pots of condoms placed in the hallway on tables, on decorative pillars, on counters and in Navajo woven baskets hanging from the ceiling. Red lights and wickless candles provided the only illumination and created an atmosphere of sensuality and seduction. For this event, wall-size paintings had been mounted on the walls. Each one contained abstract images of bodies entwined, joined, interlocked. She'd chosen them because to her they represented that "can't stop" energy.

"Would you like a drink?" Narcisa asked. She

stood eager, with her beehive hairdo, leather collar and black-lace, baby-doll dress. She cheerfully brought guests tonic water, soda, and a fruit orchard of juices.

After First Night, there was no alcohol allowed. Gena discovered in the early days that not enough people could handle their liquor. And suddenly couples who'd sworn they were all right with their significant others playing with someone else turned into jealous, raging maniacs who sometimes had to be shot with a stun gun into calm, submissive states and removed from the premises in headlocks.

"Ginger ale, please."

"As you wish, mistress."

Gena grew concerned. She considered the fact that others might recognize her, and hoped that wouldn't become a problem. She just hoped that she was wrong. "This week, in the lower level, Narcisa, you don't know me."

The woman nodded. "As you wish, mi…ma'am."

Narcisa threaded her way through the milling crowd. There were plenty of seats, but most people stood talking and stayed as close to the buffet line as possible. It was almost time for the entrées to be brought out. It was obvious to Gena that certain clients, including Ronalda and Philad, wanted to be first in line.

As Gena thought about what it meant to want to be first in line at an Epicure event, the man she'd stand in line for strolled toward her. Here come those sexy eyes, she told herself. He was dressed much more conservatively in a short-sleeve shirt, open, revealing the snug white tank underneath and dark denim jeans, but it didn't matter what he had on. Her mind substituted the see-through PJs and bare feet.

The butterflies in her belly flapped so wildly, it felt as if she was lifting off the carpet.

"I thought costume night was last night," he said, stopping beside her. He smelled as if he'd just stepped out of the shower. Gena flushed. *Where's my ginger ale?* she wondered.

"As you can see, lots of people like wearing a mask here."

He had a drink in his hand. It looked like Dr. Pepper—something with several flavors coming together in one. In the other hand, he had the notebook he'd been tethered to. Gena wondered what he'd written in it. She'd have to talk to him about it before it got too close to the end of the week. There was no way she could allow him to take the notebook with him. He could write whatever he needed to while he worked out his problems, but afterward, he'd have to turn it over. She couldn't risk another breach, even one so innocent as a child-player's journal.

"Will you?" he asked.

"Will I what?" she'd been so caught up in his notebook, she hadn't heard his question.

"Will you wear your mask all week?"

"Yes."

Guests milled closer now, queuing up in impatient rows.

"Did you attend any more workshops?" she asked.

"Oh, yeah. And that one on touching and teasing that you suggested was pretty good. But yours was definitely memorable."

His words turned up the pride meter inside her. "In what way?"

He chuckled and took a sip from his soda. "First of all, I never knew a woman's body could do all those things. But now that I know, I wanna know."

Gena laughed at his honesty. "Anything else?"

Marlowe looked up and squinted his eyes. He looked as though he was struggling with the memory, making it straight and plain as he went over it in his mind before setting it free.

"I learned that just about any damn thing can be sexy. I mean anything, if you do it right."

His face brightened and he shifted his weight. She was about to ask him to continue, but she could tell he was excited to talk.

"Even a blink. If the person who blinks is full of confidence, maybe has a sexy thought or two on the brain, or is with someone they'd like to have sex with, they can make something as simple as a blink sexy as hell."

"Show me," she said.

"Hold up," he said. "Let me get in blinking stance."

She chuckled. "There's a blinking stance?"

"Oh, yeah. You didn't know? How long have you been coming here?"

"Nine years."

"What? Nine years and you don't know about the blinking stance? Woman, get ready 'cause here it comes."

Anticipation fired rapidly inside her. Marlowe placed his notebook and his soda on a nearby table and struck one of the sexiest poses she'd ever seen. He stood sideways, turned his head toward her then placed his hand on his chest—in a gesture that looked as though he were pledging allegiance to her. Instead of undressing her with his eyes, he let a blink do it. It was slow. About a second short of a wink and sexy as hell. He obviously knew he was fine and had figured out a way to work all that fineness when the occasion struck him.

Narcisa finally returned with her soda. Gena turned up the glass once and downed it in quick gulps.

He held the pose for only a moment. Then he was back to normal and picking up his soda and notebook, a wide, sexy grin splitting his face. "Huh? Huh? How ya like me now?"

"I like you just fine," she admitted.

"Told you. See, don't play with this! You'll get your feelings hurt. I'm telling you!"

Smitten. That's what you'll get. Or *strung up in the Grand Chamber babbling like a baby.* Her insides were all fluttery. And below her belly, she just felt starved. Like the desert lived there instead of outside the building. This was bad. Gena knew how easy it would be for her to fall for Marlowe. More than that, she wanted to. She wanted to give in to everything inside her that felt alone and needy when he wasn't around. She didn't understand why his ex-wife didn't see him the way she did.

"What's wrong with Shereeta?" she asked without thinking first.

The expression on his face turned from fun-loving to frustrated. Gena realized it didn't take a gun to kill. She just murdered the jovial bond they'd struck between them. But she had to know. Did they fight? Did he neglect her? Did he just make a really, really bad choice. What was it?

"If I had a dollar for every time someone has asked me that, I could pay for another day's stay here."

Gena regretted her intrusion into his personal life. He wasn't in a therapy session now. The "frustration" she saw on his face made her wish she could take back the question.

"How many times can I say: It's a free country; To each her own; We have an understanding; or It's complicated?

"I know what I'll do. I'll put all those answers on three-by-five cards and keep them in my pocket. Every time someone asks, I'll just pull one out and hand it to them."

Regret troubled her mood. "I'm sorry."

"Not more than I am. I care about her. When I think about her aunts, uncles, cousins—hell, even her own mother—most of them kicked her to the curb a long time ago. I wonder why I didn't."

"Probably because you're not that kind of man."

"Even if she never again in life respects me, all I want is for her to respect herself."

Gena touched his shoulder. It was hard muscle tightened by tension. "No matter how much *you* want for other people, nothing will change until *they* want it for themselves."

Marlowe nodded slowly. "I know that. I…I know that."

"Do you? Are you sure? Here you are showing more concern for someone than she shows for herself. You wouldn't do that if you really knew in your heart that what's happening with her is out of your hands."

Marlowe glanced at the couple walking past them in full dominant/submissive costumes. The woman was leading the man on a leash and the slap-happy grin on his face showed he couldn't be more content. "I guess not even a dominatrix has that kind of power over someone."

"That's right. Not even a domme."

"Man, today has been full of surprises." He glanced at her with appreciative eyes. Gena melted like chocolate squares in hot cookie batter.

He finished his drink and placed it on the table next to him. "Marlowe Chambers, meet Marlowe Chambers."

A flood of emotions washed over Gena all at once.

She could barely breathe and her eyes stung with tears. He'd had a breakthrough. She lived to help people do just that.

"Hey, are you all right?" he asked.

She nodded and then gasped and struggled hard not to break down in front of him. He'd just spoken the words she wanted every guest at The Epicure to say. He'd condensed her passion so brilliantly and succinctly. She wanted her clients to know and accept who they really were. Gratefulness and humility and amazement rushed to all parts of her body. The force of it overwhelmed her and she could hardly stand.

Marlowe tucked the notebook under his arm and wrapped his other arm around her as she faltered. "You're not all right."

In the battle between her tears and her overwhelming emotions, her tears won. She stopped fighting them and let them flow while she regained some of her emotional composure. After the pommel horse episode, Gena wondered if it was the beginning of the end. Her greatest fear was losing her ability to help others. But on the heels of that fiasco, here comes this success with Marlowe—a success she didn't realize she needed so badly.

"Should I call someone? Do you need Dr. G.?"

"No," she managed finally.

Gena stood straight and wiped away the wetness on her face. She stared at the tears on her fingertips, surprised by them. "I—I know Dr. G. If she'd heard what you just said, it would mean the w-world to her."

"Come on," he said. He led her to a seat not far from the buffet line. She took deep breaths and allowed all her strong emotions to culminate into one: happiness.

He motioned to Narcisa and she came over quickly, concern riding the contours of her face. She knelt beside Gena.

"What's wrong?"

"Nothing," Gena said. "And please, don't kneel."

"Yes, m-ma'am."

Marlowe took one of the glasses of spring water from Narcisa's tray. He handed it to Gena. "Maybe this will help."

She took a few sips. The cool water went down nicely, calming her even more. She glanced up at Marlowe. "Thank you."

Then Gena glanced at Narcisa, who looked concerned and reluctant to leave. "I'm fine," Gena said.

Narcisa nodded and stood back for a moment to make sure before heading back into the crowd.

Now, Marlowe knelt beside her. "So, you're an *emotional* VIP?"

Gena dabbed at her eyes with the tips of her fingers. "So true. So true."

This is exactly what Gena didn't want. All of her emotions open like a tattletale's mouth. Even her mask hadn't protected her. She didn't know why she assumed it would. This secret-shopper idea was not working at all. She took another sip of water and decided she was better off, and safer, in her penthouse.

"I think I've had too much excitement for one night. I should go back to my room."

Marlowe's disappointment showed in his eyes. "I wish you'd stay and have dinner with me."

"I shouldn't," she protested. "I really need to—did you say 'dinner'?"

"Yes. The buffet. It's on the schedule. And I could go for some pasta right about now. Back home, there's a huge Italian influence. So, when you eat out, spaghetti is an automatic side dish with your meal in some restaurants. Order a hamburger, it comes with a side of spaghetti. Order lasagna, it comes with a side of spaghetti. I could seriously hurt a bowl of shrimp lingu—"

The belly laugh came from way down deep and blasted out of Gena's mouth like Old Faithful. She couldn't believe it and couldn't contain her disbelief. Marlowe actually thought that the buffet was *food.*

Just as her laughter got really loud and obnoxious, the entrées finally made their entrance and came single file out of one of the conference rooms. They looked spectacular and scrumptious. From lingerie and masks, to lingerie only and masks only. A few of the guys got into position with their regular attire. Only a few had taken off enough for the women to get any kind of idea of what was really on the menu. The women, on the other hand, had gone all out. From body paint, to all manner of lingerie, to nothing but a smile, they stood proudly, waiting to be *ordered.* At the moment, their fantastic display didn't

Heaven help her, she was thinking crazy. Or so she thought. The intensity in his eyes told her that maybe not. Maybe she'd gotten to him the way he'd gotten to her. He had bold eyes. A lover's eyes. Eyes you can't wait to lie down next to. Eyes that made her wet just from one glance.

Ashamed of her thoughts, she quickly pushed them away and looked toward her feet. "I'm sorry."

"It's okay," he said. He smiled as if he'd just won the lottery. "I'm starting to get used to it."

"What do you mean?" she asked, his remark stinging her.

"That didn't come out right. Sexuality comes so easy here. People are open about what they want. So far, I've been a wanted man."

Gena sat back and checked him for arrogance.

He stood and frowned as if he didn't have a clue why every woman at the center wanted to hump him. "Just this morning, right after the Tease Me workshop—"

Marlowe glanced over at the buffet line and looked as though he was about to finish his thought. But instead, his mouth hung open and his eyes, those beautiful eyes Gena had just fantasized about, narrowed in disgust.

Shereeta grinned and batted her lashes as a huddle of men circled her. She stood proudly in the entrée line, breasts jutting inside a supertight dress that more closely resembled a long tube top. Her hips never stopped swaying.

"She is a piece of work," Marlowe said. The words came out venomous and full of disappointment.

"I can have her removed from the menu," Gena said, forsaking her mask for anything that would make Marlowe feel better.

"Nah. I'll just remove myself from the room."

"I'll come with you," Gena said, rising from the chair.

They stood next to each other. Close. Her arm against his. Heat radiated between them. Gena sighed from the warmth.

His eyes devoured her. The sensation was as intense as if he'd been inside her, making her slick, curling her toes. "You sure?"

Her entire body throbbed with anticipation.

"Very sure," she said. "Come with me."

Marlowe stared at her. A delicious shudder heated her body.

"I'm sure I will," he said.

Chapter Sixteen

"She's a slut, isn't she?" he asked.

"It's not my place to pass judgment."

"You don't have to. I saw the expression on your face when she queued up."

Marlowe paced on the rooftop. His mystery woman had led him up the wide flight of stairs he had wondered about when he'd first arrived. They'd taken a back elevator to the top floor. After that, it was another flight of stairs and they were on the roof of the resort.

The night wind cooled his skin, but only momentarily. Then anger flared inside him again and regret tossed thoughts in his mind like trash into a garbage truck. Sheereta was going to blow his cover. He was almost certain of it.

"She's not just any kind of slut. She's the no-good kind. The kind who'll sell her soul and yours to the devil if she thought it would get her what she wanted."

"She's gotta go. She can't stay," the woman said.

He stopped pacing and stared at the woman, whose whole face he'd never seen. "You said you know Dr. G.?"

"Yes."

"If Shereeta leaves then I have to leave, too, right?"

She kept silent for a moment then looked out toward the city. "It's a couples' event."

"That's what I thought."

He couldn't leave now. He was too close to getting what he needed. He'd narrow his human-interest focus from as many personal interviews as he could get to one. If he could just get one, he'd be ready to get the hell away from the Chocolate Chateau/Epicure and get his life back.

"I shouldn't have brought her," he said, speaking his thoughts. "But if I hadn't, I wouldn't be here."

Even in the night, he could see the woman's eyes on him. They were full of all the sadness he felt. "I don't mean to dump this on you."

"It's okay," she said.

"Are you sure you don't have a husband or a significant other you should be with?"

"No. I don't."

Marlowe walked over to her. He was tired of all the pretense. Ex-husband. Schoolboy fetish. ED. It was too much. He had to let something go.

She blinked and her mouth formed a delicate and sexy O.

"But you're flying solo," he said, clarifying his statement. "Are you are here by yourself because you and Gena are friends?"

"Yes. There's a guideline with parties like these. Single females are often permitted. Single males are often predators."

Marlowe believed that aside from a few native coyotes, his cousin was the only predator in the vicinity.

"I guess I'm stuck then," he said, plopping into one of the oversized deck chairs next to her.

"Please don't think of it as stuck," she said.

He didn't say anything. He couldn't say anything nice right then, so he decided to keep his mouth shut. Just one interview and he was out.

The mystery woman got up and walked to the edge of the roof garden. Light from the touchieres flickered off the side of her face, her arms and legs. It turned her dark chocolate complexion luminescent. It made her glow just like the mountains.

"When The Epicure first opened, this was a public space. Guests would come up here at all hours. Some would just talk, you know. They wanted to get away to someplace private. Others would come in groups, bring beer or wine, and have picnics on the roof. But most people who came up here came to make love. No matter what was going on downstairs. Workshops, body painting, water erotics, cowgirl games, bondage. None of that mattered. To people who came up here, the roof was magic. There was no humping or pounding like pile drivers. Just quiet. Just stillness. Just the slow heat of the sun still alive and radiating into the night. Even though you couldn't see it. You felt it."

She looked out over the city across to the mountains. The wind lifted her thin dreads, making them look like tiny fingers. She looked so at home. As if she belonged up here. Like she and the night sky were lovers.

For the first time since she'd brought him to the roof, he took a look around. The view was breathtaking. The backdrop was surreal—moon, sky, mountains and desert so perfect, it looked like an oil painting with acrylics that were still wet to the touch.

By far, the most beautiful thing in the night was her. Even though he couldn't see her face completely, he thought he could see her soul. She cared so deeply about Dr. G. and about him. About The Epicure. Someone with empathy that deep had a beauty that could not stay hidden behind a mask.

She turned around and he continued to stare and take her in. To want her. He'd seen her cry, but not the way he wanted her to. His good sense kept him in his seat. His desire kept him lusting. Kept him wanting her. Hell, she could keep the mask on again if she wanted. As long as she let him inside. As long as she came and cried and opened for him. The way he felt now. Wide open.

As if he'd called to her, she came to him without a sound. Her eyes full of lust and need. She knelt in front of him. Slowly. She placed her shaking hands on his thighs. Her heat swallowed him. It coursed off her body in waves. He couldn't move. He could barely take a breath. A dark storm of guilt swirled inside him. *What about the story?* it asked. That same guilt rushed with a torrent of blood to his dick and made him erect.

Marlowe could kiss his reputation completely goodbye if he messed this assignment up. "This probably isn't a good idea," he said.

"I won't go any further than this," she responded. Her eyes locked with his and bored into him like hot coals. "I promise. I won't go any further. I just—you look like you need to be kissed, Marlowe."

The heat of her breath was on him. His face. His mouth. They moved toward each other. She cocked her head and cupped his face with her hands.

Marlowe placed his hands on her shoulders. At first to stop her, but when his skin touched hers and the soft heat radiated off her body and into his, his resistance vanished.

"I won't go any further," she chanted.

Before she could repeat her mantra, Marlowe

touched his lips to hers. Lightly. Tentatively, as though he weren't sure how far he wanted to go. Breath to breath, he opened her mouth slowly, gently slid in his tongue. Desire drove him in deeper. He'd swear on any religious text in the world that she felt the explosions, too. He pressed deeper, their tongues dancing in slow, exquisite motion. He pulled her against him.

Her breasts pressed into his stomach. She groaned but never broke the kiss. Instead she gave more, opened more as if her mouth were blooming inside his. The nectar was sweet. He wanted more.

He wanted it all.

Their heads turned; their lips made S shapes against each other, and Marlowe moaned from the heat that made him hard enough to cut glass.

Her hands cupped his face more urgently. He pulled them away and pushed them down.

"How far?" he whispered and rested her hands on his dick. "How far will you go?"

"You're so hard," she moaned, kneading him gently though the fabric of his slacks.

He opened his legs wider to give her better access.

She unbuttoned his pants and tugged at the zipper. The deliberate and dangerous action brought Marlowe back to his senses. He pulled away from her lips and held her hands in his.

They stared into each other's eyes, and just as Marlowe had hoped, the lust tempered and better intentions prevailed on more level heads.

Fire stones ignited the wood in the clay pit next to them. The wood crackled and burst into tiny flaming torrents. Sparks leaped off the twigs and broke open into the air.

"This is wrong, isn't it?" she said, her eyes drunken with desire.

"You don't know how much I wish it wasn't," he admitted.

She glanced down at where her hands had been. The rise in the crotch of his pants steepled like a pyramid.

When she glanced up, her eyes were liquid with need. "I have an idea."

She stood and backed away. "Maybe we should go find Shereeta."

"I have a better idea. I think I should go find myself."

She walked back to where she'd stood just a few moments earlier and stared out toward Cathedral Rock. Her silhouette was mesmerizing. Her enigmatic nature drew him. Made him want to peel away every layer until he got to the physical and emotional center of her and set them both on fire. She was just the kind of woman in whose company he could go astray for a week or longer. That's how it always started. Then after a major missed deadline, he'd emerge with a richer story for his time but an irate editor ready to chop his head off.

She looked sad and forlorn. Her expression dug into him like razor-sharp needles. He went to her and held her from behind. He knew she was torn with guilt. After all, he was supposed to be a man reforming a relationship. What kind of woman comes on to an unavailable man? Maybe one who senses that there is something different about this "nonbachelor."

"I don't regret anything," he said.

She just sighed, kept her back to him and her hands on the rail.

He continued unswayed. "And you shouldn't regret anything either. I can't explain why now, but before the week ends, I will. "

For good measure, he kissed her again. Briefly on the temple. Then he headed off to his room while he still had the strength of character to do so.

Gena watched the traffic on the 89. Fast-moving whirs of light on a black slash of blacktop. For that moment, she wished she could travel like the light. Stretch out into the night and disappear into the horizon.

She didn't recognize herself anymore. Only a desperate woman goes after a man who's unavailable, and she'd never been desperate in her entire life. Kinky. Exploratory. Experimental. She admitted to enjoying being the dominant over a submissive and doling out a little *punishment* now and then. But this time she'd crossed a boundary.

A client.

A client involved with someone. Not only that, she was willing to ignore all the embarrassment and disappointment of her adult years to find out if the promise of a clitoral orgasm was in her reach.

Gena hugged herself in the cooling desert air. A pinch of late winter in the breeze.

Three more days, she thought. Then Marlowe and every bit of the temptation he'd brought into her life would be gone.

She just hoped she could forget how good his mouth tasted and how hard he had gotten. How deep he'd gotten inside her. She knew it would be three of the most difficult days of her career.

She wondered what he had to tell her. What in the world could possibly make this whole situation better? How long would he make her wait to find out? So far, Gena had talked herself out of running after him, but she didn't think she'd be successful for much longer.

Chapter Seventeen

"Where have you been?" Marlowe asked.

By the time he made it back to his room, Shereeta was there doing a frantic quick change. He caught her at the tail end of adding jewelry and slipping on a pair of the highest heels that he'd ever seen outside of adult pay-per-view.

"Told you I'm on the grind for a full-time sugar daddy. I want a *wealthy* one. I'm tired of putting up with these rich guys. They just don't do it for me anymore."

"Where are you going to find a wealthy man in here?"

As soon as he said that, he thought better of the remark. From the royal mahogany furniture, copper soaking tub and jaw-dropping view, their room had as close to five-star amenities as he had ever come. This place was not for the light of cash.

"Are you kidding me? Look around. These gentlemen are gentlemen. You hear me? And I'm trying to get paid."

Marlowe stepped in between his cousin and the door. "And I'm trying to get a story. So, at some point, we have to make appearances as a couple, or I'll start to look foolish."

"Uh-oh, too late!" she said and laughed at her own joke.

Marlowe didn't think it was funny. His cousin's wanton behavior was starting to get on his nerves. No telling what she was telling the men she was hanging around. For all he knew, his cover had already been blown.

"I need your help, Shereeta. I think we should be seen together—more than once. Now, what do I have to do to make that happen? Schedule an appointment?"

She had too much makeup on, too much perfume and too much attitude. "Maybe."

Blood boiled in his veins. The smug expression on her face pushed him into a slow fury. "You know, I should have followed my instincts and left your ass in Omaha."

"Really? And *your* ass would have been stuck in the Big O, scratching your head and trying to figure out life. You and your *writing.* If you want to write about life, g'head. Just get outta my way 'cause I'm about living it!"

"Shereeta," he began, hoping to appeal to her reasoning. "*LifeWire* is paying for your stay at this resort. All I ask is that you hang with your cousin from time to time and keep up the lie that got us in here. The rest of the time, you can do whatever the hell you want. Deal?"

"No deal," she said, checking her reflection in the mirror on the sliding-glass closet doors. "I have three more days to get one of these money trees to invest in my goodies. That's not a lot of time, considering they're all married. I need every moment I can beg, borrow and steal. Who knows when I'll get the chance to come back here again?"

"Shereeta—"

"Out of the way, *cuz!*"

"Quiet!"

Shereeta slammed her hands on her hips and stepped closer. "Or what? Cuz!"

Marlowe shook his head. He could see the family resemblance in her. Same reddish-brown hair, deep-set eyes and broad mouth. He hated that she favored so many decent members of his family, including himself. "How are we related?" he wondered.

Marlowe was starting to realize that it wasn't the cover he wanted to protect, so much as it was his cousin. He wanted to save her, even if it meant saving her from herself. Maybe if they just went to group together.

"Let's nail down one appearance before you leave, just in case it's checkout time before you show up again."

She waved him off. "You'll have to catch me when you catch me!"

"What?"

"Look, negro, contrary to this little charade we're runnin', I am *not* your woman!"

"Keep quiet." He stifled the urge to put his hand over her mouth.

"Why? We're here now. Like I said, I am not your woman! We are not a couple! And as loose as Grandpa was, we may not be blood cousins either. But anyway…you do not run *this,*" she said, circling an outline around her body wildly with her hand.

Right then, Shereeta looked like a peahen with too much plumage.

He knew better than to press her when she was in this state. Instead, he stepped aside and let her pass.

She opened the door and paused for a second.

"Look, Marlowe," she said, half in and half out of the room. "I'm not trying to rain on your parade. It's just that, I want a parade, too."

She sounded as if she was ten or eleven years old. Her eyes filled with tears that didn't fall. "If you ask me, you got all the brains in the family." She chuckled. "And all the heart, too. All I got was this." She spun around and showed off her body. "And this." She pointed between her legs. "So, I gotta take what I can get when I can get it."

Marlowe had always thought his cousin was just willfully wild and crazy, but now he wasn't as sure of that. Maybe she was just pitiable.

"You understand, don't you, cuz?" she said and cupped the side of his face. She rubbed his chin stubble with her thumb and then headed down the hallway.

Marlowe closed the door to his room, not sure whether he should pretend she wasn't even at the resort or he should try to convince her to talk to someone about her missing self-esteem.

"Cousins!"

The word bounced off the walls of her office and hit her full force. When she'd overheard them talking, she'd wanted to run up on them and cuss them out so badly they would swear they'd been hit with fists rather than words. Then she thought she'd just throw them out tomorrow at breakfast and expose them in front of everyone. After that, she considered suing them for misrepresentation. Her fury was making her crop hand itch.

She'd gone back to her office and sat perfectly still in her chair. All the while, her anger conjured ways to punish them for coming to The Epicure in such an underhanded fashion. After a few moments, she realized that her fury was primarily caused by Marlowe and how easily he'd been lying. She'd had party crashers in the past when she'd first gotten started. At least the party crashers came as themselves—however inappropriate. This offense went beyond that.

By the time she was able to think calmly again, half an hour had passed. She'd come up with an idea that would allow her to punish Marlowe and get him to fess up to his lie at the same time. She spent another fifteen minutes getting her office ready for something she hadn't done in quite some time. Eager to get started, she left and went searching. Finally, she found Marlowe in the spa chatting up more of her guests.

"Mr. Chambers, I have something that I think will make Mr. Happy ecstatic," she said. "Will you come with me, please?"

In her six-inch heels, Gena was almost as tall as Marlowe. He walked slightly behind her as she led him to her office. She walked a lot more calmly than she felt. Several times she fought the urge to kick him out on his imposter ass. But she had questions on her mind first. Questions and punishment.

Chapter Eighteen

"What's wrong?" he asked.

Gena pulled the keys to her office from the snap-back chain on her belt and opened the door. "After you," she said.

As he walked inside, Gena slipped in behind him, bumping him with her hips. He looked back.

She smiled, but only slightly. "Sorry."

The lights were off, but Marlowe saw everything perfectly. Candles sat on the numerous decorative bricks that extended from the walls in random locations. Shadows pulsed on the ceiling and floor with their flickers.

The smile on Marlowe's face dissolved into grave concern and uncertainty. He gave her another once-over, this one much more thorough, and understanding dawned in his eyes. She had plans to *do things to him.*

"Dr. G., look, I appreciate the special treatment and all."

He had no idea what he had gotten himself into. Gena checked out his reaction and knew she had him. He looked stunned, worried and aroused. A few more slow sways of her hips and he'd be hard. Shoot, it was too easy. She might not even be able to get to tie him up and have her way as she wanted to.

But she was determined to make him talk. Kicking him and his cousin out was not enough. She wanted to know what he did to get there. If there was a leak in her security—and obviously there was—Gena wanted to know who, what, where, when and how extensive.

She pulled her black crop slowly through her fingers. The cool, thin straps gathered then fell one by one out of her hand. Until then, her dominance-and-submission play had never been about sex. It had been a way for her to experience the thrill of power. But imagining Marlowe tied to her punishment wall, naked or not, made her so wet, she knew her feminine juices would start trickling below her dress at any moment.

"Dr. G.," he said, raising his hands and taking a step back. "I really don't think this will help the problem I have."

"Don't be so sure," she answered. Gena stepped close enough to feel the heat from his body. She made sure he could feel hers.

"Doctor, *doc-tor*...I thought you brought me here to explore my emotional issues, you know, ask me about my mother and write what I say on your little pad."

Gena stepped closer. He backed up some more. "Writing on a pad is not going to get you hard. And what I want more than anything right now is to get… you…hard."

She slid her hand straight down his body and grabbed his package. Damn. She almost needed three hands.

"Whoa, whoa!" he said, stumbling over his feet. "I'm off the market."

She got a good look at the bulge in his crotch forming just the way she wanted it too. That's when she felt the first drip onto her thigh rolling like a hot tear. The sensation made her tremble. Torturing Marlowe was getting her off in a way she hadn't anticipated. Since she knew what he was capable of, the feelings pouring through her trumped those on First Night and in the Chamber. Hungry for it now, she sought more.

"And before you leave here, Mr. Chambers, I'm going to make sure that you can honor your relationship by being able to satisfy your lady. As a matter of fact, I insist that you and Shereeta take center stage on Last Night." Her voice sounded deep. Needy. Smoky.

Marlowe stopped his retreat. The wall caught him before he could take another step back. Candles on the left and right of him threw dancing shadows across his skin. He looked sexy as hell.

"Say what?" he said.

"I've decided that you need a surrogate. Someone who's not Shereeta but can stand in for her. Give you feedback, guidance and encouragement. Make you ready for the real deal in the way an inflatable never could. So…just pretend like I'm Shereeta."

She pushed against him then. Her nipples already hard. They tightened as if they'd been pinched and rolled. She suddenly realized that her seduction was backfiring. Doing Marlowe wrong was actually doing her good. Gena moaned. She couldn't help it. His chest was solid and felt strong and hot and perfect against her oversensitive nipples.

His eyes darkened dangerously. Sexier than anything she'd ever seen. The sight of his eyes so erotic and raw shoved aside all the reasons why she'd brought him to her sanctum and replaced them with the shocking truth. She wanted him regardless of the lies. She wanted him in a way she hadn't allowed herself to want a man for way too long.

She'd expected him to put up some kind of fight. At least at first. Then she'd planned to strip him, tie him against the wall and use her favorite crop on his nut-brown skin until he fessed up. She never imagined that he might not push back, or worse, that she wouldn't want him to.

Gena reached up, traced the line of his hair that was perfectly edged against the side of his face. Her heart raced. Marlowe, in turn, ran the pad of his thumb against her cheek, turning her knees soft.

He gave her a sexy smile and bent down. His lips, stern and fleshy, pressed against hers so briefly, she almost thought she imagined it.

"I can't," he said.

Gena glanced down. The bulge was gone. She didn't know how he managed it. But the front of his pants were as flat as a frying pan's bottom. Gena's disappointment sickened her.

He traced her jaw with the side of his finger. "It's not you," he said, as though he knew what she was wondering. "It's me. It really is me."

Gena clamped her jaw shut for a moment. Not wanting to respond, or maybe just too afraid to.

She stepped back, realizing that the dominant person who loved being in control had vanished. She was replaced by this weaker person who just wanted to be told what to do for a change. *What has this man done to me?* She needed a moment and a new strategy.

"You sure it's not me?" she asked, hating the way her voice now sounded meek and babyish.

"I, uh, I have someone on my mind."

Gena's soul felt as if it was rolling over nails. Of course he had someone on his mind. He probably had a lot of someones on his mind. He could take his pick. Since there was nothing really wrong with that great big organ of his, he must have planned on using it, and not just with a masked woman who appears and disappears.

What was she thinking? He'd probably been busy since the moment he set foot in the resort.

She needed to work out. Flog someone. Run up a mountain trail. Do something to work out her frustration and get the old Gena back. Somewhere inside her was a woman who still wanted the truth out of this man. She just had to figure out another way to get it.

"As you wish," she said, fully taking on the submissive role, if just for a moment.

"Thank you, though," he said and offered a slight smile that looked like candy in the flickering light.

She watched as he left her room quietly. She went in the back to get a tissue to catch the juices cooling against her thigh.

Such a nice ass, she thought. Somehow, she'd find a way to teach that ass a lesson.

Chapter Nineteen

Marlowe felt as though he were a real student and had been called into the principal's office for being bad.

Day three and he'd had a great breakfast and great conversation. Instead of focusing on his article, he decided to just chill and enjoy himself. The fact that he didn't have to push so hard made for a great Sunday morning.

And then she came. Once again the good doctor asked him to accompany her to her office.

When he arrived, the room was completely different from the golden and red ambience of yesterday. Nothing about the soft hues and color tones felt inviting. But there was a reason.

He stared at the three items on her desk. Waves of revulsion washed over him. He wasn't sure what was going on. At least, he hoped he wasn't.

The first contraption was small and beadlike with tubes sticking out of its sides. The next object looked like a clear, palm-size missile with a hand pump attached to it. The third—too hideous to look at for any length of time—was a long needle, like the kind dentists use to shoot Novocain.

"Wh-what's all this?" he asked, sitting down before he fell down or ran cursing.

The woman, strapped, laced and zippered into a black corset dress, circled the desk slowly, every part of her body undulating, as if there was some roots music pulling her around. The movement looked so familiar. "Options, Mr. Chambers."

Marlowe wiped a brow, certain that sweat had formed a small pond there. "Options for what?"

"For your limp dick. I took the wrong approach yesterday, but I think I've got it now. You do want to correct your problem, don't you?"

He took a step back toward the door. "I'm sure it's only temporary."

"Well, let's make sure, shall we? Now, I've gathered some of the most effective equipment to use in your case."

Revulsion spun in his stomach like logs. "I can see that."

"This is a vacuum constrictor. It works by sucking blood into the penis."

"Uh-huh."

The doctor moved her hands over to the next contraption as if she was displaying items on *The Price is Right*. "*This* is a urethral insert. It deposits medication through the tip of the penis. You can have an erection that lasts thirty to sixty minutes. And this," she said, picking up the needle.

Marlowe's stomach curdled. "See, now you done lost your damn mind."

The doctor continued, unfazed. "This is a hypodermic needle. It goes into the inner part of the penis and—"

"Whoa!" Marlowe felt a sharp cut of sympathy pain for all the men who'd gone through that procedure.

He slammed his legs together and folded his lips in.

"—and then it scrapes out—"

"Stop!" He held his hand out. "Stop the world. Right now."

"But, Mr. Chambers—"

"But nothing. I'm good with the therapy sessions. Real good. They're actually helping me. As a matter of fact, I thought about Shereeta first thing this morning, and I didn't get the least bit nauseated. Now, that's progress, right?"

"Mr. Ch-am-bers." She drew out his last name as if it had three syllables instead of two. "I wouldn't be doing my job if I didn't present you with all viable options. My goal is to see you and Shereeta happily sexing each other up by Tuesday. And that doesn't give us much time."

Marlowe finally realized something. Behind that makeup, jewelry and sexy black outfits lived a crazy sadist. "Your, your goal?"

Dr. G. flicked her nail against the tip of the syringe. "Absolutely! Like I said, I want you and Shereeta to be our COA on Last Night."

"COA?"

"Center of attraction."

Marlowe pinched his wrist, and, damn it, nothing happened. He wasn't dreaming. "I don't get you."

"On Last Night, one couple, the one who's made the most progress during the week, is chosen to be the focal point—center of attraction. Sometimes, I'll choose an individual, but this time, I want a couple. It will be all eyes on you two. The rest of the guests support you, in any way you desire, from watching you to joining you. Eventually, the vibe gets strong enough where people break off and start to get into their own thing. But it starts with the main attraction."

The ED contraptions had turned the doctor's inviting office as cold as an operating room. Marlowe massaged his chin with his thumb and forefinger. He was three breaths away from admitting the truth. The good doctor looked on as though she expected him to do just that.

"With the performance problems I often have, there's no way I can get it up for an audience."

Dr. G. waved the syringe in a "now-now" motion. "If you simply try one of these, you won't have *any* problems."

Marlowe took another step back. "Ain't goin' there doc. Sorry. If you're that concerned, I'll take some Viagra or that Cialis I've been seeing on television."

Disappointment covered her features like a thick gray cloud. "I'm afraid those drugs can cause more problems than they correct."

He continued his retreat and offered her a weak smile. He had no idea such equipment existed. He'd definitely include the devices in his article. He pointed to the one in the middle, the one that looked least threatening.

"Let me see that one."

She handed it over. It felt like a cold dead thing in his hands, much like the organ it was designed to revive. He turned it over, watching the plastic chamber and hand pump rasp against each other. The damned thing looked like something you'd clap on and clap off.

"It hasn't been used, has it?"

Dr. G. gave him the Spock brow. "No. Will you consider it?"

He tossed up the device with one hand, caught it with the other and then placed it on the desk as far away from him as he could get it. "I'll get back to you."

Marlowe took a deep breath, amazed that the sight of the needle hadn't made him chuck up breakfast.

He pitied the poor souls who had to contend with these things every day.

Gena stepped around the desk, her superhigh heels making them nearly the same height. "I suggest you talk it over with your Shereeta. She might help you make the right decision."

Marlowe paused at the door, wondering what had changed. The normally warm, demure sex diva had suddenly turned colder than the north wind. Dr. G. seemed way out of character. Sharper. Almost condescending. She was handling him with tongs instead of embracing him as she had when he'd first arrived. A far cry from the vixen who tried to seduce him. He hoped that she was just having a moment or a bad day. If this was the real Dr. G., the rest of his stay would be hell.

"I'll see what I can do," he said.

He made a mental note to keep Dr. G. as far away from him as he could. *Ol' girl was on somethin' different.*

The morning sun came like a warm blanket into Marlowe's room. It wrapped him in heat, even at 9:00 a.m. Marlowe finished the last sentence in his notes for the morning, summoning visions from First Night and the Buffet to color his words. This whole situation was starting to test every sexual limit he had. The devices he'd seen on the tour, the ones that punish male arousal, were starting to make sense with each hour that passed. If there was a pill that was the exact opposite of Viagra, he needed it…bad. The surprising thing was, it wasn't all the skin and more skin, the curves of raw, open sexuality that was so thick he could write his name in the air, that was dealing him a fit.

It was the mystery woman who was driving him nuts. Everything about her attracted him—the music in her voice, her dreads, the way the red lights in the lower level had illuminated the golden undertones in her dark skin. It was the movement of her lips when she spoke. How her mind worked. The way her eyes softened when she saw him. Even through the mask, he could read her attraction.

Mostly, it was the way she seemed to want him. Bad. The bond between them was stronger than any golden cuffs in the gift shop could create.

If he didn't get a grip on all this lust, he might end up purchasing one of those blow-up dolls, or his hand would fall off from…overuse.

Marlowe wondered about the night's festivities. He didn't know how he would handle one more grunt, groan, moan, babble, cry of ecstasy or the Colonel tonguing his wife and then shouting, "Right shoulder…arms!"

He fumbled with the radio, trying to find a station that played soft jazz or easy listening. A few seconds of Luther singing "A House is Not a Home," and he knew music wouldn't cut it either. He needed hands-on and nothing but hands-on. He riffled though the amenities flipbook on the desk and found something that might help. He dialed the concierge, having no idea his fingers could move that fast.

"Narcisa? I need a woman."

Ten minutes later Marlowe heard a knock on the door. Nearly finished with his shower, he called out of the bathroom, "Come in!"

"You called for a massage?" a female voice said. He could barely make it out over the cold blast of water shooting out of the showerhead.

"Yes!"

"Would you like deep tissue, shiatsu or relaxation?"

Marlowe turned off the water and grabbed a towel. "Can I have it all?"

"Of course," came the response.

The accent stopped him between drying his arms and his chest. As if influenced by a spell he couldn't explain, he followed the sound out into the living area of his room.

The sight of Ms. Masquerade setting up the massage table momentarily froze him in place.

For once, he wanted Shereeta to stay away. After her disappearing acts, it would be just his luck that she took that very moment to reappear for a quick change. He decided he would deal with that if the time came. Just in case, he put the chain on the door.

She took in a good look of everything he had to offer and smiled approvingly. "Let me just go on record and say very nice. Ve-ry…nice."

That comment got him unstuck. "Thank you," he said and finished drying off his back.

The Epicure was a world unto itself. And in that world, modesty had no place, so he left his in the shower and walked closer.

The mystery woman kept her eyes on Marlowe's prize. "I hope you don't mind. When Narcisa said you called, I volunteered to come up."

Marlowe smiled broadly. The cool air prickled his skin and made him shudder. After the cold water awakened every nerve in his body, he was hypersensitive. He'd taken the edge off his need in the shower, but even the thought of her touching him was stoking the fire again.

"Well, now, I'm surprised a VIP like you would want to be bothered with little ol' me," he said playfully.

She gave his body a scorchingly thorough appraisal. "There is nothing old…or small about you, Marlowe."

He dried himself completely and then wrapped the towel around his waist. He noted the disappointment on her face. Apparently she liked the view. Well, that made two of them. This thing she had with white outfits worked for her. White tube top and white skirt against her dark skin was too sexy for words.

"You know this is dangerous," he said.

Their eyes locked. "Forget dangerous. Besides, I'll be good."

"I was talking about me."

She opened a medium-size pull case full of essential oils, warming stones and bottle warmers and set everything up on a service tray beside the table. She plugged some of the accessories into the wall then cleansed her hands with sanitizer.

"Climb on," she said, standing aside, a sly invitation riding her mouth and her hips.

Marlowe didn't know if she meant the table or her.

"Are you the masseuse for all the guests?"

"Just you," she answered.

He adjusted himself on the table, facedown in case Mr. Happy decided to wake up and get ideas. "Why me?"

"Because there's something secretive about you. And I'm nosy. I want to know what it is."

That statement knocked his sex jones down to zero.

"What's there to tell? Shereeta's a slut. When it comes to being with her, I just don't have it in me anymore."

She rubbed oil into her palms, "Really? So, if Shereeta was massaging you, and turned you over, she wouldn't see a big…hard…juicy…lip-smackin'…dick?"

"Well," he said, clearing his throat, "the big, juicy and lip-smackin' part can't be helped."

They both laughed and he closed his eyes, ready for her hands to be all over him.

She started at the base of his skull and pressed her fingers in small circles into his flesh. The cords and tendons she felt there were stretched tight. It took a moment for them to yield and soften.

"When is the last time you had a massage?"

"A year. No, closer to two."

"Two years?" Her mind couldn't imagine it. She never went more than a month without a massage. "I could never go that long," she admitted.

Gena moved lower, rubbing her fists against the sides of his neck, up and down in half circles. Then she opened her palms and spread the oil there against his skin. The deeper she pressed, the more the muscles gave and flattened.

"I can tell you work out," she said. "Your muscles obey quickly once they're given the command to relax."

"Uh-huh," he said.

His skin felt so good against her hands. Smooth and thick and toned. Heat radiated flesh to flesh between them, conducted by the oil and a current of attraction neither of them could deny.

She'd come to test him. To see if despite his claims, she could get him to tell the truth. If he could just admit it, she thought she could forgive him somehow. *Oh, how she wanted to forgive him.* If he would just come clean. And then…and then she didn't know. She hadn't planned that far ahead.

If she got his big juicy erect, what would keep her from tasting it, from taking it in her hands and squeezing it, from throwing off her panties and riding it? She wanted to flip him over right now and—

"Whoa," he said. "Too hard."

"Sorry," Gena said, embarrassed. She slid her hands down his back, fingers spread wide. All the way to the base of his spine. Then back up, right hand on top of left, in long strokes that arched out across his shoulders. She took her time, conscious about the pressure this time, and relaxed herself as she felt the tension lessen with each pass.

"Um," he moaned.

"I brought some warming stones with me," she said. "Have you ever tried them?"

"No," he said, voice groggy. "Um, can you not talk?"

"What?"

"Your hands feel damn good. I want to enjoy them to the fullest. In silence. Okay?"

Gena pounded her fists into the flesh just above his butt. His round, firm butt. Eager to see more, she slid the towel down to his thighs. He didn't move, but Gena felt what was left of her clitoris shiver with delight.

She continued to pound, and when Marlowe let out another moan, she moved down to the crease at his upper thigh. Pushing her finger in, making circles with her knuckles. That brought another longer moan.

Tingly and feeling the wetness between her legs, Gena kept going, kneading his thighs as if they were biscuit dough and reveling in the sensation of his warm muscles in her hands. Before long, she was holding her own moans inside, but she was determined to get more from Marlowe.

With open palms, she twisted up from his ankles to his knees. His muscles there like granite. The hair on his legs coarse against her open hands. He grew still and silent.

"Other side," she said, softly.

"Um," Marlowe said, turning in slow motion beneath the towel.

Disappointment dampened her lust. He was not hard. Big, juicy, lip-smackin', yes, but the payoff Gena was looking for was nowhere to be found.

Dismayed, but not defeated, Gena started part two of the massage, thinking he must have gotten off in the shower. She wondered what would happen when she massaged his chest, worked her fingers to his navel and then just below it.

She rested her hands gently on his face and remained still. She slowed her breathing to match his and held her hands in place. This was the technique that put just about everyone she massaged into deep relaxation. After a minute, she knew Marlowe had gone well beyond that.

When she heard his gentle snoring, she realized that she hadn't gotten him hard—she'd put him to sleep.

She shook her head and couldn't help the grin spreading across her face. Resting so peacefully against the white, cotton sheet. He was a beautiful warrior—with rocklike biceps, high-definition abs and thighs like marble columns.

She glanced at his prize package resting comfortably under his belly.

She sighed. As much as she wanted him to come forward, she would have to confront him after all.

Chapter Twenty

Marlowe watched transfixed as, yet again, Dr. G. worked her sex-coaching magic couple by couple in the therapy room. Not every couple had a breakthrough, but they all had some sort of breakout moment. She said over and over that foreplay begins long before the bedroom. And she helped the spouses understand how to be the best person for the other so they both could be the best partners in their marriages. For that alone, he could see the worth of a week at The Epicure. Erotic City and all it offered at night was truly icing on the cake. Or just pure gravy.

He dreaded the fact that she seemed to be working her way around to him again. He knew that he would eventually have to talk at length about the make-believe relationship and made-up problems, and then he'd have to fake his gratitude for the solutions she offered—or pulled out of him.

"How about it, Mr. Chambers? You've heard and supported others on their journey to wholeness. Give us the opportunity to do the same for you."

Dread sunk in the pit of his stomach like a heavy stone. He was so tired of the fabrication. He just wanted to get his story and go. If it weren't for Shereeta being MIA, maybe he would have.

"I've been so fortunate to be able to sit back and learn from all of you. I feel like there's hope for Shereeta and I."

"Really? Why?" Dr. G. asked.

"Ah well, just using you all as examples on how to move forward in a relationship," he hedged. Under regular circumstances, he might get away with that. He wasn't sure whether Dr. G. would let it slide.

Her brow furrowed. "So, everything's fine then?"

"Well, not everything. We still have a few things to work out."

"Like what?" she asked.

"Well, like—"

Dr. G. sat forward as though she were daring him to answer. "What's the biggest obstacle in your way?"

Besides this conversation? he wanted to ask. He glanced at the faces that were all eyes on him. They seemed genuinely concerned and interested. If he'd truly had a problem in that area, he had no doubt the clients as well as the good doctor could help him through it. He didn't have a problem, though. At least not with his performance in the bedroom.

However, he did have problems with his performance in his professional life. If he wanted a second opinion on things, maybe now was a good time.

"All right, here goes. There have been women."

"I knew it!"

"Told you!"

"A man that fine ain't faithful."

"Hey!" Philad said.

"Sorry, baby, but you ain't that fine."

Philad leaned away from his wife. "Ronalda, we will be back up in this place next week you keep talking to me like that!"

Ronalda speared him with a hard glance. "What? What you gonna do?"

"Please!" Dr. G. said, quieting the couple down. "Let's hear what Mr. Chambers has to say."

Marlowe cleared his throat and continued. "I can't resist a woman who's about something and going somewhere. The sexiest thing on Earth to me is a woman with a purpose and a plan." He imagined some of the women he'd hooked up with in the past and couldn't hold back the grin. "That's it for me, end of story, plant the flag, pull up the drawbridge, I'm done, man."

Mike put his hand up as if he was swearing on Bibles. "Dude, I hear you. There is a certain appeal about a woman who's on point."

One of the clients started singing, “Miss Independent.”

Marlowe smiled and shifted in his chair, which was surprisingly comfortable. “She doesn’t have to be balling. Just know what she wants out of life and is going for it in a big way.”

“So how does this effect Shereeta?” the doctor asked.

“Does Shereeta seem like that type of woman to you?” Marlowe asked.

“Yeah, man, but not in a good way,” Mike responded.

“When I meet a determined woman and we hook up, my whole world shuts down. It’s me and her for like weeks. I don’t think about bills, the internet, work, nothing. Just her.”

Jolisa sucked her teeth. “Sound like you whooped.”

“He’s not whooped,” her husband countered.

“Yes he is. If the lovin’ cancels his life like a check, he’s whooped.” Jolisa crossed her arms, smug in her convictions.

Marlowe blanked out everyone else in the room and stared at the beautiful sex coach. He really wanted her opinion. “What do you think, Dr. G.?”

“I think there might be some moth/flame issues going on here. It’s possible. Let me ask you a question. What are you dedicated and on the grind for?”

Marlowe nearly swallowed his tongue. In both the fabrication of his life and his real one, he couldn’t think of one thing he was dedicated to right then—except spending more time with his mystery woman. "I don't know," he said honestly.

"I believe you're drawn to a woman's strong sense of dedication, achievement, accomplishment because those are qualities you're missing. By submerging yourself into someone who does have them, you get dedication by association."

"Can you unpack that for the rest of us?" Jolisa asked.

"Why don't we let Mr. Chambers do that for us?" Dr. G. said.

Marlowe got reflective for a moment. "A big butt and a smile could turn my head like the next man. Like I said, what keeps my head in a woman's direction and makes me want more is vision, mission or some sense of purpose. And if she is somehow adding to the world rather than strictly her own pocket, then game over.

"The women I grew up with, my mother, my aunts, their friends, were all community activists. They got involved in things, and because they did, I saw neighborhoods change. I saw kids that life tossed away turn into good people. I admire that. I look for it."

"I get it," Jolisa said. "They remind you of your childhood."

Dr. G. leaned in. Stared into his eyes. As if she was boring inside and nothing could be hidden from her. "I think it's more than that. Mr. Chambers, what do you think?"

He tugged at the cross around his neck. Cleared his throat. "I've had the opportunity to travel the world. I discovered that I'm not one to stand by and watch a bad thing happen if I can do something to change it. Women who make things better are the ultimate for me."

Dr. G. smiled. "Make *things* better, or *you?*"

Marlowe sat back. He'd never considered that he needed to be "fixed" or that he latched on to certain women because he believed they could "fix" him. It was absurd. "Sorry, Doc. You were batting a thousand there for a while, but you struck out on this one."

"So, it's okay when she cracks other people open, but you're untouchable, huh?" Philad asked.

Indignation rose in Marlowe like a fast elevator. "Now, I didn't say that."

Ronalda rolled her eyes. "Yes, you did. You didn't use those words, but that's exactly what you're saying."

Dr. G. held up her hand. "Everything's all right. I don't force observations on anyone. I only challenge people to look within themselves and see the unfiltered truth."

"You all are not going to treat me like *Rescue 911.* If there's any rescuing to be done around here, I'm the mofo that does it," Marlowe said, yet he wondered who he was really trying to convince.

The glances in the room changed from curious and supportive to disappointed and snubbed.

"Look, nobody's threatening your manhood," Dr. G. said.

"Oh, I know *that!*" He slammed his notebook closed, all too ready to move on.

Marlowe knew exactly why his ego was on tilt. His father had wanted to be rescued by his mother. When she refused to keep doing it, he split. Marlowe had invested so much time trying not to be that kind of man. The idea that despite all his best efforts, he'd walked right into his father's footsteps chafed him like razors slicing into his gut.

"Look," he said. "Somebody else go."

Dr. G. closed her notebook, too. "This isn't an amusement park ride, Mr. Chambers."

He stood. Suddenly there was not enough air in the room. His gold chain felt like hands choking his throat. His skin was feverish. "Just the same, I want off."

He walked out of the room and headed for the lobby doors. He had to get out of the entire building, not just that room. Damn the scorpions. If he came back, *if,* he would need at least three hours with a good punching bag.

Well, that could have gone better, Gena thought. After group, she'd gone back to her office and double-checked the final arrangements for movie night. Between making sure that there were backup movies, enough chairs and working equipment and that the concession items were ready to go, her thoughts had been intersected by images of her group session. From the triumphs, like Mike and Jolisa, who might actually start having sex with the lights on, to the travesty, Marlowe, who'd stormed out of the room just when it seemed he was about to have an important breakthrough.

Years of being a coach taught her that not everyone was ready to delve deeply into their motivations. Some people would never be ready. But she didn't expect the reaction from Marlowe that she got. She would have never predicted that. Even superheroes had vulnerabilities, so mortal men—even as fine as Marlowe Chambers—had them, too.

As Gena checked the daily reservations database to review new arrivals and any checkouts, her concern surprised her. After everything she knew about his lies and the false pretenses that got him into The Epicure, he, like most people, suffered a pain from his past that shaped his current behavior. That directed his choices. As much as he pushed back from being fixed, Gena was drawn to the idea of fixing him. Instead of punishing him for his actions, maybe helping him was a better solution. It might keep him from repeating the same self-serving mistakes. As Gena Bivens, PhD, she eagerly looked forward to her role as his coach, if he would let her.

She took a look at the pile of rejected movie choices for the evening: *Shortbus, Eyes Wide Shut* and *Last Tango in Paris.* Suddenly, relief washed over her in big waves. Marlowe was available. She was much too happy about that. The crazy thought occurred to her to cancel the rest of the week, kick everyone out—except for the handsome Mr. Chambers—and spend the remaining days with him as the only client and her as coach, workshop presenter and Bantu Queen of the Lower Level.

When she'd first overheard his conversation with Shereeta, she was so angry, she'd been seconds away from throwing them both out. Why did that seem so long ago?

Reason took over her anger and she remembered the way guests behaved in the first days of the center. Marlowe and Shereeta had lied; that was true enough. There was a lot of that when she first opened The Epicure. People would lie to get invited in. But her clients soon became as serious about her code as she was. That stopped the gawkers, rubberneckers, and people who came just to look rather than learn.

With the tight control she'd once had on her security being threatened, Gena found herself at a crossroads. She could help Marlowe—the man obviously needed some coaching—or she could kick both him and his cousin out for being inappropriate guests.

Her mind flip-flopped like a fish washed ashore and gasping for air.

Gena unlocked the office safe. She rummaged through all of the labeled clear plastic bags. Most containing cell phones. She found Marlowe's bag. It held a cell phone, laptop and digital video camera. With a sigh, she pressed the call button on her phone. Narcisa's voice came on clearly through the speaker. "Yes, mistress?"

"Please find Marlowe Chambers and bring him to my office."

"Yes, mistress."

The line went dead and Gena felt as if she had, too. She'd been stirred silly by the thought there was some hope for her. That maybe she could be as free as she encouraged every one of her guests to be and share herself with a man.

Her experience so far this week had punished her for getting her hopes up. She knew better. But a handsome face, gorgeous smile, luscious body and dick for days had turned not only her head but her good sense with it.

"Shame on you," she admonished herself.

It had been so long since she'd been hopeful. So, long. The realization formed a lump in her throat. She turned toward the painting on her wall where the space between the man and woman had been erased by the artist. What drew the eye was the deep blur and how merged the two were. She wanted that so badly. She felt grateful that others had found it, but helping them find it brought her only so much happiness. Every now and then, she wanted some of that happiness for herself.

Gena sank with the feeling and held on to the

credenza to keep from losing her emotional balance. Instead of stopping them, she let the tears fall, allowed herself the grief that had been closing in on her all week. She knew crying would give it power and take it away at the same time.

She remained that way for what seemed like forever. In real time, it was less then twenty minutes. Then Narcisa poked her head inside the office.

"Mistress?"

"Yes," Gena said, wiping away the tears that hadn't dried.

"Mr. Chambers is gone. Emerald said she saw him leave the resort fifteen minutes ago."

Chapter Twenty-One

Despite her own best emotional judgment, Gena had looked for Marlowe each morning. She kept a reasonable professional distance—stopped by his table only to chat up the clients, be a good host and make sure breakfast exceeded their expectations. In truth, she came looking for Marlowe.

This morning above all she wanted to find him. According to Emerald, Marlowe hadn't checked out or called a cab. Gena spent the rest of the evening hoping he'd just gone for a walk.

He'd shown up in the dining area most mornings like clockwork. Punctual and traditional. No crepes or apple-cinnamon sautéed French toast. This man had scrambled eggs, hash browns, link sausage and

Navajo fry bread. He did put ketchup on his eggs, but Gena thought she could live with that.

She made herself stop at three checks in the mirror. Since Marlowe had arrived, she'd stepped in front of that thing five or six times each morning to make sure she looked good. But that was just ridiculous. Three times was more than enough.

After that, she would make her way to the dining area. By seven-thirty, he'd be making his way to the end of the line and angling toward a seat. She noticed he tended to sit with someone new every day. After the first day, his Shereeta never ate with him. Gena never saw her do anything with him, or vice versa. It was hard to believe they even knew each other. Forget about being related.

Gena stepped off the elevator and smoothed the front of her black catsuit. That nervous snacking she'd been doing since the security breach was doing a number on the fit of her clothing. Potato chips. The saltier the better. She figured she was carrying five pounds of water weight. When your wardrobe consists of skintight attire, there was no room for extra pounds.

"Somebody came to play today," Narcisa commented.

Gena ran her fingers through her wig. "Sure did."

She walked as she did every morning during an active week. Inside she wanted to run into the room to make sure he was there once again. To watch him with his notepad and pen. To see him smile with those gorgeous lips, those bright, white teeth, and to check out his open shirt and the creamy-brown abs she'd gotten used to seeing. The desert heat didn't have anything on the heat she felt coming from him.

She let her hips carry her swiftly into the room. She stood for a moment, giving a nod or two of acknowledgement to a few of her guests. A glance of approval to others. Smiling at her security people. She took in the scene. Voices bouncing off each other. Guests seated in clusters of four. Only a few couples were seated off to themselves. The largest group had pushed four tables together and was busy doing more talking than eating. To her disappointment, Marlowe was nowhere in sight.

"What is your desire, mistress?" Narcisa asked.

"Nothing, thank you."

"As you wish," she said, walking off toward a couple who'd decided to get the evening's festivities started early by pouring syrup on each other's fingertips and sucking it off.

Gena walked around, said good morning to guests, talked about the theme for the night. Thankfully, they all greeted her warmly and were pleased overall with the week so far.

"How are *you* enjoying the week, Dr. G.?"

Gena heard the question. It sounded as if there was a towel wrapped around it. Her mind was too busy wondering where Marlowe was. Had he slept in? Had he already eaten and left? Had he decided to leave? Maybe he'd found someone to play with.

Gena swallowed. None of those options did her heart or her peace of mind any good.

"I'm sorry. What was that?"

The Colonel eyed her suspiciously. "You don't look so good."

"I'll be okay. I just think I need some air."

"It's probably that suit. It's sexy, but how can you breathe?" Abigail asked.

"I don't know. Excuse me," she said, heading away from the dining room.

Anger flared inside her. She was furious for allowing an attraction to a man to cause her to act like a fool. It was unprofessional. What she needed was a walk around the grounds while the morning was still cool. And before she did that, she'd check out the pool, the sauna and the weight room just in case Marlowe decided to go there instead of breakfast.

Turner Garrison split the water like a sword being pulled through the waves. It was his daily ritual. Twenty laps and then lunch. Sixty-seven years old and the man was as fit as an athlete one-third his age. He was in the pool alone. His wife, Caroline, sat in the lounge chair on the side, watching him with eyes that said, as soon as you get out of that water, it's on!

Gena smiled, remembering that last year the energetic older couple was the COA on Last Night. They reminded everyone there that for some, the party doesn't stop in older age, it just gets hotter. Mr. Garrison's athleticism warmed her memory. She fanned herself and headed over to the sauna.

She passed through the courtyard to get from the east section of the resort to the west. The open area was rimmed with wrought iron gates and featured a cobbled sidewalk that split a garden of golden poppies and queen of the night cactus in half. Sweat formed a thin layer between her skin and the leather. The fabric was barely breathable in the Arizona heat. She went inside the square room. The sauna took inspiration from the natural surroundings outside the resort and mimicked the glowing red-rock mountains. One continuous redwood bench lined the perimeter of the room. Guests could sit or lie down to enjoy the eucalyptus-infused steam permeating from the center and the four corners. In the middle of the room, there were separate red cedar benches as well as contoured seats curved like hands to support the body.

Three couples took advantage of the morning humidity. Lying leisurely against each other, sweat pearling into beads and glistening off their brown skin in the rosy hue of the red, iridescent walls.

"Good morning," Gena said, voice heavy with disappointment. He was not here either.

"Good morning," came their collective response.

"Are you getting everything you need this week?" she asked.

"Yes."

"Absolutely."

One woman ran her hand against her husband's chest. "Ev-er-y-thing," she purred.

Pride lifted Gena's mood. "I'm glad. You let me know if that changes for you."

"We will," a man in the far corner said. He eyed her approvingly in her suit and winked.

Gena looked away politely and left the sauna. Next stop, the weight room. She felt like some foolish woman riding up on her man in the middle of the night at some other woman's house. Only it wasn't another woman. This was her house. A place where she offered an abundance of choices, only to discover that she needed only one.

She approached the all-glass room. It had a breathtaking overlook of the valley below, and in the morning the promise of a new day rose above the mountains in a slow bath of golden light. She caught a glimpse of Marlowe in the fitness room mirror. The knot of tension lodged in her stomach relaxed. She breathed more slowly. He was alone.

Blissfully, his shirt was off and he wore a pair of black biker shorts stretched tight around thick thighs. He lifted the iron easily while lying back against the bench. Looked like two hundred pounds on the bar. Nice. No wonder he lifted her in the demo without any strain. Images of him carrying her, sweeping her into his embrace, made her groan. She typically flicked away such womanish thoughts, believing they made her frail and weak. Not a strong black woman at all.

With Marlowe, she relished those thoughts. Her

body thrummed with the impulse of acting them out. Of being taken care of instead of being the caretaker.

How wonderful that would be.

She went inside, thinking about all the sweat she'd encountered this morning. From herself, the couples in the sauna and now Marlowe. It looked good on him. Tasty. Something Gena wanted to lick, swallow and be drenched by.

She approached him. His whole body filled her vision. She fought for control of the desire challenging her to straddle him and beg him to unzip her.

"Good morning, Mr. Chambers." Her own voice shocked her. It came out velvety smooth and as sultry as the sauna.

He continued his lift-and-lower, a steady rhythm catching her heat and turning it up. His breaths came out ragged and short. He'd been working awhile. His skin stretched tight over his arms and chest. The veins in his arms popped out, straining with the weight of the iron. Sexier than words or thoughts. Gena touched her throat and licked her lips. As though the mere sight of him drugged her, she felt sleepy and hella mellow.

"Good morning," he said through a powerful grunt. He placed the barbell on the holder and wiped his palms on his shorts.

Perspiration trickled from his brows into his hair. Gena managed to keep her tongue in her mouth and keep her lips to herself.

"I'm just making the rounds," she said, suddenly

feeling the need to explain herself. "I'm checking with guests to make sure they have everything they need."

Her statement was met with a grunt. He added ten pounds to each side then glanced in her direction. His eyes seared a path down her body as he checked her out. The extra time she took getting ready was worth the entire examination. For a moment, he didn't blink or breathe. Neither of them did.

"How do you manage to look that good this early in the morning?" he asked.

"I could ask you the same question."

He smiled and lay back on the bench.

Marlowe positioned his hands on the barbell and adjusted his grip.

"We missed you at breakfast today. And I can't help but notice how hard you're hitting the iron." She remembered how yesterday's group session ended. "Is something wrong?"

Marlowe removed the weights from the stand. Gena stood behind his head, taking the spotter's position. She placed a hand on each side of the rack. It gave her an excellent view of his darn-near flawless physique. The extra weight drew out his already taut muscles. Gena folded in her bottom lip.

"I'm just disappointed," he said. "I thought I could make some deeper connections here. Get to know people. But you've got these folks trained, Doctor. Their lives are on lock."

The iron went up and down again.

More sweat fell from his forehead like tributaries heading out to sea. Suddenly, Gena's catsuit didn't seem tight enough.

Marlowe lowered the bar slower than it went up. Exerting both power and control. She watched his chest contract at the top of the movement while his stomach tightened when his arms came down. Perspiration pooled between hard pectoral muscles, and each one of his six-pack muscles glistened like smooth, brown rocks after a driving rain.

"Considering the nature of what we do here, I'd say that's a good thing."

He pushed air out between clenched teeth. "Well, it makes getting to know people hard to do."

"Did you come to The Epicure to get to know people?" she asked, suddenly curious.

Her question was greeted with labored breathing and grunts. He was really into it now. Lowering the bar and pushing it up slowly. He made these same sounds when he'd been inside her. His body gave off the same drive now, with every motion cutting his biceps like tight rubber bands.

"I think you came here to get to know yourself." Gena took a deep breath and released it in the same way Marlowe had when she'd stepped into the fitness room. She spoke her doctor's truth no matter what. It was who she was. It was what made her want to become a doctor in the first place. Even with the mind-bending attraction she felt toward him right now, she still wanted and needed to help him if she could.

And that meant no lies.

Marlowe held the bar above him for a long moment. When his arms started to shake, Gena reached under the ends of the bar, just in case. It wasn't necessary. He set the bar back into the rack. It clanked into place.

His breathing came hard. His chest rose and fell. The sweat from his forehead had dripped onto the plastic mat beneath him. Muscles in his jaws flicked with tension.

He sat up and stared into the mirror.

"I should never have come here," he said.

The image of them together in the mirror was so perfect, it was painful.

"What makes you say that?" she asked.

"Because I came for the wrong reason."

Gena waited. Silence was often the best encouragement for self-revelation.

He looked at her, his brown eyes blazing with frustration. It wasn't the catsuit he saw then. It was her. As a woman. As a confidante. As someone who will not only listen but hear what he had to say.

"It's not about my so-called problem. It's that I thought this place was a freak palace times one hundred. The way people talk about it and then to finally be here, well, it's just not what I expected."

Gena took a towel from a basket behind her and slowly pulled it down his back, catching the wetness, watching how the cotton dried his skin to smooth brown perfection.

"Now, First Night was out there, but you do good work here. It's not about sexual deviation. It's about safe exploration. Hell, maybe I did come here to find myself. The dry air alone has done wonders for my lungs."

"Do you have asthma?"

"No. Black mold. I got it doing volunteer work in New Orleans. Three weeks ago I was in the hospital sucking air from an oxygen tank."

She stopped wiping off his back, concern rolling through her emotions like thunder. "I'm sorry."

Marlowe cast a glance at the barbell. "I couldn't even have squinted at this three weeks ago. Now, look at me. I'm all sweaty and thangs."

He laughed at his own humor. Gena joined in and then sat next to him on the bench. Her heart clapping like a big hand in her chest. She took a deep breath. "What about Shereeta?"

"We're not a couple," he said, calmly. "She's my cousin. We only pretended to be married to get in."

The bubble of anxiety building inside her for days popped. Cool exhilaration replaced it, and Gena fought the ridiculous urge to skip around the bench and sing, "Oh La La La."

The momentary celebration was replaced by sadness. Marlowe and his fake cousin had to leave. It was a couples' event. If she let them stay, she'd be breaking a rule.

If she ignored the rules, others might, too. Then the tight control she had over her sexual sanctuary would erode to who knows what?

Gena couldn't allow that to happen.

Marlowe must have read her mind. His expression looked as solemn as she felt. "I want to stay," he said.

"This week is for couples. If anyone finds out—"

"You don't have to tell anybody. You know and I know, and that's it."

"Shereeta knows."

"I'm hoping against hope that my cousin will carry that secret to the grave with her. Or at least to her next sugar daddy's bed. You know that's why she came."

"Well, it's obvious she didn't come for you."

Gena stood and took her place behind the rack again. It wasn't much of a barrier between them, but it was something to keep her from blubbering "Thank God you told me!"

"Gena," he said, using her first name for the first time since he arrived. She liked the sound of her name in his mouth. When he said it, the syllables made what should have been her clit vibrate. She squeezed her thighs together to see if she could force the feeling deeper.

"Something is happening to me in this place. Now, it could be the vortexes everyone talks about. It could be. It could be the energy of being around such confident and free people facing down their demons every day and setting themselves free every night."

His eyes grew soft and so sexy Gena was instantly wet. "It could be you."

Gena swallowed and felt light enough to fly.

"In group yesterday, you helped me move through something I didn't even know was holding me back. I can't do enough to thank you for that. I just—"

His hands worked to pull out the words. "I just want to finish what I started. I need to."

He stood next to her. His bare chest so near her own, if her nipples got any harder they'd be touching his. "You'll let me stay?"

"I'll think about it," she whispered, already anticipating the kiss that would come next. She inclined her neck. Not a lot. Just enough to start the heat. Marlowe bent down and kissed her forehead.

"Fair enough," he said.

He took the towel from her hand. "And thank you."

He smiled and strode off toward the door. "I'd better go get ready for group."

He took a manly sniff under his arm. "I need a shower, don't you think?"

Gena's jaw dropped. She couldn't believe he'd left her hanging. Not that she would have had sex with him right then and there without her mask. Well, maybe she would have. But a deep kiss and a feel-up would have been nice. And as far as needing a shower, she was the one. An ice-cold shower to lower her temperature from coochie inferno to something normal enough to facilitate group without touching herself.

Chapter Twenty-Two

Since 8:00 a.m. that morning, Marlowe had pranced through the day free of the lie that brought him to The Epicure. It was as though his ankles had been chained together since he'd arrived Thursday night, and now he could use both of his legs to wide-step freely throughout the resort. He'd learned that the undercover-reporter gig was not for him. He wanted—no, needed—to be straight up and straight on about everything he did from this point on. Otherwise, it wasn't worth doing.

The only pothole in his thinking was what to do about the article he'd been sent to write. He'd nearly finished what he'd come to do. It was an exposé as much as he could make it. He hadn't named names.

No one would give him any. But he had named industries and professions. Instead of debauchery, he'd painted a picture of sexual freedom reminiscent of the late sixties and early seventies. He'd put a twentieth-century spin on it so the exploits came across with more thoughtfulness and intention. It wasn't Freaknik on steroids as Tuck might have wanted, but it wasn't a *Cosmo* article either. There was plenty of lust to go around. Some of his descriptions were damn kinky, even if he did say so himself. Some that an over-stimulated teenager might even jerk off to.

But one thing was certain.

The article wouldn't get him the money he needed. It would probably cover the expenses of him staying five days at the center. But little more than that. If that's the price Marlowe had to pay for attending Dr. Gena's sessions and understanding himself better as a man, then so be it. It was worth every second and every penny. What he hoped now was that one decent article would turn into another.

Marlowe stared at the pile of notes that had turned into the article in the stack of sheets next to it. Just going by the notes he took, The Epicure could be construed as a sex palace. But putting his vision and his focus on humanistic details in the information produced a completely different piece. He was proud of what he'd done. He hadn't sold out too much. Whatever else happened after he turned in the article, he would deal with it then. For now, he just wanted to finish out the week and actually enjoy himself. And he knew just who he wanted to enjoy himself with.

He placed the article and his notes in his carry-on and headed out of his room to the lower level for movie night.

There were fewer couples than usual. Probably about twenty or so. He'd dressed comfortably in jeans and a polo. Most of the guests came in casual clothes, too. Shorts, flip-flops, artsy t-shirts and tennis shoes made the most-dressed list. Many still had masks, although they usually wore a different mask every night.

He inhaled deeply, filling his lungs with the smell of hot buttered popcorn. His mouth watered instantly. He followed his nose to the origins of the aroma.

Everyone looked so regular with clothes on. Not at all like the freewheeling sexual explorers who took over nighttime in The Epicure. With the exception of their masks, they could have been going to the mall or a mountain hike, or out to a casual dinner. Rather than to a 3-D, triple-X movie showcase.

"Chambers!"

"Hey, Ford," Marlowe said, sidling over.

Marlowe learned quickly. There was always group discussion before the main event. Most stood in clusters while others sat around the perimeter in big comfy chairs and love seats.

"Ready for this?"

Marlowe took a gander at his 3-D specs that had been placed on his pillow like mints. Compared with the paper punch-outs he'd used when he was a kid, the things he'd slid on top of his head were high-tech. Sturdy, hard-plastic frames with red/cyan plastic lenses in them. They were only a half step down from the drugstore readers his mother wore.

"Yeah," Marlowe answered the question, but he was distracted. He hadn't seen his mystery woman yet. He hoped she hadn't decided to skip movie night. He skimmed the crowd for her—checking out every mask. Unfortunately, none had the subtle hues or open plume of the one he searched for. His disappointment spiraled out of his body, along with his enthusiasm to see the movie.

"You know Asia Fire's in this movie," Ford said.

Marlowe frowned. "Who's that?"

"A rising star. Not big yet like Vanessa Blue or Marie Luv. But she's on the way."

Marlowe was obviously not up on his adult film stars. He didn't recognize any of the names.

"Anyway," Ford continued, "I heard a rumor that she's going to make a special appearance here on Last Night. She could be a secret COA."

"You don't say?"

"Yeah, man. And between you and me, if she gives me so much as a smile, I may leave the center with her instead of Birdell."

Marlowe shared a laugh with Ford, but he wasn't feeling happy. He felt anxious. As if something bad would happen if he didn't see Ms. Masquerade tonight. As if all the lust he'd been fighting off since their last intimacy would drive him nuts. There was only so much that Liquid Silk lube could do. After a while—a short while—a man needed a woman.

"Ford, I've got popcorn on the brain, man. I'm going to go get some with lots of butter. I'll check you later."

"Yeah, man. Later."

The buzz of conversation filled his ears. Marlowe checked his watch. Six minutes 'til showtime. He queued up behind a couple who just couldn't stop kissing each other. He knew The Epicure didn't allow dope, so the couple were doing a really good impersonation of having just popped E. They must have been shooting for the Guinness World Record for longest, sloppiest, noisiest kiss.

"I think they're trying to swallow each other's heads."

Marlowe let go a big breath of relief and turned to the source of those lovely, accented words.

"Hey," he said in a voice embarrassingly tender. He straightened his back, raised his chin and cleared his throat. His mystery woman came up beside him, looking good enough to eat. And he would, the first chance he got.

"Hey," she said, exaggerating his tenderness.

"Oh, you got jokes!"

"Yes. But that's not all I've got."

"I'm well aware of what you've got." Marlowe swept an appreciative glance over her body. Damn if she wasn't fine in a tie top and short wrap skirt.

He was so used to the mask now, he didn't mind it, barely noticed it and realized that it added to her sexuality and his attraction to it.

"No," she said, and then pulled the top of a tiny champagne bottle out of her skirt pocket.

"I thought there was no alcho—"

"Shh," she said, covering his mouth with her finger.

Instinctively, he licked the soft skin of her index finger and then pulled it into his mouth. He swirled his tongue around the slick smoothness of her nail then sucked rhythmic pulses against the tip of her finger. Her eyes darkened, but she didn't pull away.

His action caught the attention of a few couples on each side of them. He removed the woman's finger, and together they stepped up to the concession counter.

"More on that later," he said, content that her mind was in the same place as his.

"May I help you?" Narcisa asked.

"What would you like?" he asked her.

Even beneath the mask, her glance came across as sly and cool. "You know this is free, right?"

"Now, why you wanna steal my thunder like that? I'm trying to be gentlemanly over here."

"Gentlemanly?"

"Don't make me say it again. I'm not sure I can. There's a lot of syllables in that word."

All three of them laughed at the same time.

"Okay," she said. "I'll have small popcorn."

"You like butter?" he asked.

"I love butter."

"Narcisa, hook us up with a large popcorn, extra butter."

"As you wish. Anything to drink?"

"Nah. We're good," he said.

"Yes," Ms. Masquerade responded. "We're good."

"Yes," he echoed her. "So proper. Do you ever say 'Yeah' or 'Uh-huh'?"

"No. Where I come from, speaking proper English is important. The better you speak it, the more respected you are."

Marlowe was familiar with the belief. "Those who manage to lose their accents completely or at least disguise them well are revered in some places."

"That's correct."

"So, what part of Tanzania?"

"Tabora. My mother is American. She met my father when she was there with a group called Project Concern. She and my father worked on a clean-water mission together. When I was thirteen, my parents, my brother and I came to America. We've been here ever since. So, I'm saying all that to say, my mother tongue truly is my mother's tongue."

He chuckled and stared at her delicious mouth and fantasized about kissing it until it was swollen and calling him by his first name, accent and all.

Narcisa came back with a tub overflowing with hot popcorn. "Here you are, mistress."

Marlowe's head snapped to attention. "Mistress?"

The woman's gaze had changed from sultry to dismayed.

"I'm sorry," Narcisa said.

Marlowe was stunned. "You really are a VIP around here? You've been holding out on me. Are you a singer? Actress? Famous scientist?"

Marlowe had been hustling nonstop trying to find someone significant to interview, when here she was right under his nose.

She laughed, but the laugh didn't cover her discomfort. "Let's go watch the movie."

"Uh-huh," Marlowe said, suddenly feeling overly curious.

Marlowe thought that designation was reserved for the queen bee herself. Obviously Ms. Masquerade not only had friends in high places, she was a friend in a high place. Maybe that's how she got the hookup for the roof garden. He could see himself up there, with her again, in pitch darkness, taking her mask off and putting his love on her.

"What does that look mean?" she asked.

"It means I want to be alone with you after the movie."

She smiled. They walked into the theater together. He put his arm around her shoulders. She slipped closer into him, brushed against his body nicely as they angled up the aisle. Her hips felt as if they were softly kissing his.

"I want what you want," she said.

* * *

"Over here," she said, moving toward the top row. They took seats in the back in what looked like reserved seating.

"You sure we can sit here?"

"I'm positive."

From their two seats, they had an unobscured view of the screen as well as everyone in the theater.

He offered her some popcorn, Placed his arm around the back of her chair. "I heard Asia Fire might be here Tuesday."

"That's right."

"You know it for a fact?"

"Yes."

"She's the COA?" he asked, thinking that even an adult film star couldn't possibly have anything on the woman sitting next to him. Every move she made was sexy. From the way her chest rose and fell when she breathed to the way she walked as though her feet were kissing the ground rather than walking on it. Not to mention the positions. Hell, she even blinked sexily.

"If she wants to be. She may give a talk. Or dance in the lounge. She may sell DVDs and sign copies. If I know Asia, she'll come with a trunk full of products."

Her knowledge impressed him. Definitely more thorough than someone who simply was a regular guest. "You sound like you book the talent."

"Like I said, I've been here since the beginning."

"Yeah, but—"

"May I have your attention, please?" The Colonel came into the theater and stood down front while guests settled in their seats and got quiet.

"Welcome to Movie Night at The Epicure. Most of you know me. I'm Colonel Bootney Barnes, U.S. soldier, Second Battalion, Ninth Marines. My wife, Abigail, and I been comin' here for quite a few years. Dr. G. was kind enough to let me introduce the picture tonight. Before we get to that, how's the week so far?"

"Good!"

"Great!"

"I'm in the zone, man."

"Excellent. Well, I just wanted to say a few words before we get started. This film is by NeoNoir and stars Asia Fire. It's got that 3-D in it like *Avatar,* so don't be surprised if things seem to…come out at you. Heh-heh."

Cheers and applause greeted his statement.

"To shut down the rumors, Asia Fire *will* be here day after tomorrow."

Louder cheers this time. Mostly from the men.

"If you all behave yourselves," the Colonel continued, "we might be able to talk her into being our COA."

Rapid applause followed that sentiment. Mystery woman gave a thumbs-up.

"Without further delay, ladies and gentlemen,

please put your glasses on and enjoy tonight's cinema feature: *Mo' Better Bangin'*."

This time Marlowe and *his* COA joined in the applause.

The lights went down and the remaining guests took their seats. Marlowe noticed they left as much space between couples as possible. Privacy, he thought, and put on his glasses.

He placed the popcorn on his thigh. "This could get interesting."

"Oh, it will," she murmured, taking a handful of popcorn.

Surprisingly, the movie had both a plot and amazing graphics. The acting was bad, but he'd never seen an adult film where it wasn't. Besides the CGI and the occasional nipple that poked out of the screen big as a basketball and close enough to suck, the movie was boring. Not only was Marlowe not impressed by the women in the movie, who seemed to orgasm the moment they saw a dick let alone have one pounding inside them, he was almost offended. Thanks to his seventeen-year-old hormones and an older woman who could have written a manual on female climax, Marlowe preferred finesse and staying power to fisting and pounding to get a woman off.

He blew out a breath of exasperation.

"What's wrong?" she asked.

"Nothing," he answered.

She crinkled her nose. "Something."

He took a handful of popcorn. Tossed a few

kernels in his mouth. Glanced around to the men in the room. They seemed to be riveted by the pile-driving Paul and the surgically endowed Asia Fire, who had not stopped moaning since the flick started.

He turned to Ms. Masquerade. "Let me ask you something. And I want you to be honest. Have you ever had an orgasm like that? Now, I know we all like it rough once in a while. But this stuff here… tell me straight. Have you?"

Marlowe would have sworn that even in the dark theater, he saw the beautiful lush brown color drain from her face. Her body went rigid beside him. "No. I never have."

There was something guarded in her expression. It was the look he got on past assignments when his interviewees were just about to give up the goods. It was those times when his interviews took a turn for the better and the article he was working on took a turn for the award-winning.

The cool dude in him, that for all intents and purposes was on a kind of date, wanted to see the movie all the way through to the part where guests started acting out their own scenes and trying to outdo the actors. But the insatiably curious and concerned man wanted to get to the bottom of that drastic change in her mood.

"You wanna get out of here?" he asked.

There was silence at first and no movement. Only the "Ah! Ah! Ah-ah!" of the woman on the screen, who would probably be doing a repeat performance in person in less than two days.

"Yes."

"Come on," he said, helping her up. "You look like you could use some air."

Chapter Twenty-Three

The night air was chilly but not as cold as it could be. Gena was used to how the temperatures plummeted at night, but many of the guests who came to stay at The Epicure were not prepared for the sometimes near-freezing desert temps.

The moon proved to be king of the night sky as it shone without rival from any clouds. Gena stood, face turned toward the tall cacti and the high jutting cliffs in the distance. She needed the night wind to distract her from the other force of nature standing next to her.

"Another couple of degrees and we could see our words out here," Marlowe said.

"The price we pay for paradise," she responded.

And she meant it. If putting on a bolero at night and putting the occasional blanket on her bed was the worst part of living in Arizona, she'd take it. "No earthquakes. No tornadoes. No hurricanes. Just a trench when it gets cold."

"You're preaching to the choir. I'm from tornado alley. I'd give up four seasons and F4s for cool nights. No doubt."

He moved closer to her. Checked her out from the side. "So, you heard I'm single?"

"I heard."

"Does that make a difference to you?"

"Yes."

Marlowe decided to be bold. There wasn't much time left—only two days. If they were going to get as close as he wanted, he couldn't waste time.

He stood in front of her. Got close. "Wanna show 'em how it's really done? No fake instant orgasms. How about a nice, long, slow screw? The damn thing's been building up in me since the second I got here. Whadaya say? No strings. Just good lovin'."

She checked him out then. "You're awfully sure of yourself."

The outside balcony wrapped around the entire resort. The clay walkway and wrought iron railings often kept her company when she just needed time to think and get quiet. But now, what she would remember the balcony for is the place she let go of every nagging bit of hesitation inside her and surrendered.

The tips of his fingers pushed back a lock of hair the wind had carried in front of her face. She felt her pulse beat in her throat.

"Let me show you why," he said.

Gena held herself tightly and shuddered—not from the wind, but from the storm brewing in her heart. From the man she wanted to let inside her so badly it hurt to stand alone without him.

"Do you have something against adult movies?" she hedged, her head lowered. She kicked at loose pebbles on the ground with the toe of her gladiator sandals. Her hands were in the pocket of her turquoise sarong.

"No. I can't imagine my undergrad days without them. I've got fond memories. But I also know they can be pretty far-fetched."

"Isn't that the hallmark of most entertainment?" She walked away from him to the overlook.

"Maybe." He rubbed his palms together to warm them before he touched her. "But I need to ask you the same question. You looked like you'd lost your best friend in there."

"I wish."

"You wish you'd lost your best friend?"

"I wish what I've lost was as simple as a person. People often come and go. One sometimes replaces another."

Marlowe thought about the women he'd known. Brief encounters that changed like seasons. "Yes, they do."

"That is natural. That I can handle. But this—"

"But what?" he asked, surprised by how much he wanted to know. He'd unburdened himself of some of his pain recently. If he could help her do the same, he'd feel as though his visit to The Epicure had not gone in vain.

She stared out at the city. She seemed lost in thought and worry.

It had been windy all day. A couple of times, the wind had knocked on the windows like heavy fists. It lifted the ends of the mystery woman's dreads and parted the split of her sarong, revealing a thick, shapely thigh. Along with being a lips, breast and hips man, Marlowe was also a thigh man. And the thigh in his vision right now was beautifully thick, chocolate-brown with firm skin and a blazing torch tattoo.

What the heck? For a moment, he felt he could use a nice sturdy chair. Suddenly he remembered the very first time he saw just the hint of that tattoo. Either two women had identical legs with identical tattoos in the exact same place, or the good doctor Bivens was also Ms. Masquerade.

Events slid into place in his mind, the puzzle nearly solved. Narcisa calling her "mistress." All the information she knew about the place. How she insisted she'd been there from the beginning. The special seating in the movie. His massage. The tours. It all fell into place now.

He took half a step forward and swallowed hard.

She was the head of a center that exists to support sexual exploration, and yet she seemed so hesitant now to fully explore her own. The nobility of her dedication touched him on every level.

He stood behind her. Ran his hands down the sides of her arms. Goose bumps prickled her skin, and he rubbed them until they disappeared. She wrapped her arms around herself and locked her hands in his.

"I have to go," she said, belying her action.

He kissed her shoulder. The nape of her neck. The hollow of her jaw. She sighed and sank against him.

"Let me help you," he said.

She shook her head. "I can't be helped."

"Let me try."

She pulled away and marched toward the door. Marlowe's heart felt as though it were leaving with her. Suddenly it was hard for him to breathe, but he could think clearly enough.

"Gena!" he called.

She stopped. Stiffened as if he'd been a commanding officer calling "Halt!" to an enlisted. She wrapped her arms around herself again and turned slowly toward him.

In a second he was in front of her, holding her. Her dark brown eyes never left him. Never blinked. They just locked on to his gaze without looking away, holding as if they would forever.

In his mind, he tossed off the good doctor's wig, got rid of the contact lenses, wiped away her makeup.

He peeled off her catsuits, her minidresses, her latex costumes. He pulled off the straps of her superhigh heels and slipped them off her feet. The woman he had left was in his arms, staring up at him. Eyes searching for understanding. For acceptance.

"I may never leave here," he said and kissed her as gently as his raging passion would allow.

He wondered what she had been eating. It damn sure wasn't popcorn. Her mouth tasted like spiced milk chocolate—the kind spiked with cinnamon. The flavor didn't melt immediately, but stayed on his tongue awhile before it dissolved and flowed into every corner of his mouth. It was the kind of taste he'd keep searching for after the sweetness of it was gone—under her tongue, on the roof of her mouth, in the corner of her jaw, behind his lips. Just to have and savor again.

They pulled apart and Gena's eyes fluttered open—full of wonder and hope. "I don't…because I can't…"

She pulled away and found a spot on the walkway as far from Marlowe as she could get. He followed but kept a distance. Gave her the space she needed.

"In some parts of Africa, when a girl reaches puberty, there's a rite of passage…a ritual…" Her voice split in two. She held herself, took a deep breath and continued. "F," she began. "FG—"

"FGC," Marlowe finished. "I've heard of it."

Then a sadness greater than any he'd ever felt

gripped him. His legs grew heavy as if weights were tied to his ankles and were pulling him down into an abyss. Anger twisted around his heart and his shoulders sank. Rage and despair fought in the pit of his stomach and nearly doubled him over.

"Jesus," he said. Now every single thing made sense. Her desire to help others was so strong because she needed help herself.

Marlowe went to her and stood in front of her. He reached up and pulled her mask off. Line marks and impressions dented her face where the bottom of the mask rested on her cheeks. He cupped her face and kissed each one leisurely until he felt the marks smooth and recede.

Her breathing grew heavy. She moaned softly with his attention.

"So, you've never—?"

"Vaginally sometimes. With you…yes. But I just wish I could know what other women feel."

"Then come on," he said, ready to take her as far as her body would go.

Gena stepped back. "What if I can't?"

Her eyes searched his face, so full of need he found it impossible to believe she had this problem.

"What if you can?" he responded.

She rested her forehead against his chest and went light in his arms.

He stroked her hair and reveled in the warmth of her body against his.

"I hear you have the entire top floor of this place," he whispered.

She looked up, took a deep breath and led him back inside.

Chapter Twenty-Four

"Nice digs," he said.

She led him into her penthouse, so hot for him she could barely breathe, let alone speak. Her hand trembled inside his. She didn't bother to turn the lights on. Just walked past the gallery foyer, breakfast bar, the door to her skydeck and into her bedroom. Their breathing and footfalls mingling in the silence. She was so ready, ready to surrender to her desire. At the same time, fear charged through her and made her hesitant. What if—?

Marlowe squeezed her hand, stopping her, and pulled her into his body. He was solid muscle and hot flesh against her. The hunger she saw in his eyes doubled her pulse and quickened her breathing. He bent down and touched his lips to hers.

The sensation was magical. She tingled from head to toe with the promise of pleasure to come and hoped she would remember her own name when it was all over.

Gena crossed her wrists behind his head and held on. His breath sultry and humid against her lips. His mouth explored, devoured hers, saturating her body with bliss. In seconds, she was so light-headed she could barely stand. He held her face in his hands. His thumbs lightly stroked her cheeks.

He sure knows what to do with his lips. She wanted his mouth everywhere. With his strong lips parting hers, his tongue slid inside her mouth. Wet and raging like a storm. His passion drenched her to the marrow.

Her blood pulsed strongly in her lips as his hands reached around her back and undid the tie of her halter then unhooked the back, setting her breasts free. He let the top fall. It crumpled onto her feet. She shivered, his tongue still searching her mouth. Probing in and out, just the way she wanted to feel him inside her.

Her nipples tightened painfully and ached for his touch, but not for long. His strong hands cupped her breasts, massaging, pushing and gently pulling with his fingers. His thumbs stroked her nipples. She sighed and pushed her hips against him, grinding. Bringing heat to every place their skin met.

His hands massaged lower. Rubbing her sides and abdomen in luscious circles. Lower and mercifully lower. Gena ached everywhere. Need throbbed between her legs as if her heart had moved there, beating hard, pounding, demanding attention.

Marlowe unwrapped her skirt. It fell to the floor behind her. She stood against him naked except for a pair of white, lace panties. The air cooled her thighs. He picked her up, mouth still making love to hers, and placed her on the bed.

She pushed away all the pillows and stared at the man she'd craved so painfully. Her desire was back-built and had stoked so days felt like years. He removed his shirt, his trousers and boxers, revealing a body so sexy, he deserved his own statue. So toned, strong, and muscular, she ached for him to take care of her body the way he'd obviously taken care of his. She squirmed and twisted, so eager to get him inside her, to move with him and pray that maybe, just maybe…

"So impatient," he said, placing a hand just below her breasts and pulling his fingers slowly down. The movement chilled her out and made her tremble under his touch.

"Condoms?" he asked, kneading her flesh. The sheer pleasure of his stroke muted her. She managed to point to her goodie bowl on the nightstand. Considering she was the mistress of The Epicure, she'd always thought she should have one. Bodies arching in rapture were painted on the outside. The inside brimmed with condoms, oils, lubes and small toys of every variety. All items that she rarely used.

With one hand teasing lazy circles on her abdomen, Marlowe used his other to reach inside the bowl and pull out tiny tubes of massage oil. A whimper of anticipation escaped her lips.

Marlowe popped the top off the tube, poured the oil into his palm and rubbed his palms together. Gena watched and licked her lips. Where would he touch her? Her body quivered just thinking about the answer.

He straddled her. His balls pressed hotly into her crotch. His thick, heavy penis cast a shadow on her abdomen. Resting against his heels, he placed his hands just below her jawline and caressed the hollow of her neck. The heat radiated throughout her body. She gasped expectantly.

Pushing and pulling her skin back and forth, his hands slid masterfully against her chest. Kneading her breasts, her abdomen, her hips. Gena sank deeper into the mattress. Every ounce of tension flowed out of her body. His fingers left her tender and wanting. She stared at his brown eyes, which were holding her like hands. He was so chill, so relaxed, it drove her crazy.

He slid back. Massaged her upper thighs then slightly lower until she panted and called his name.

"Shh," he said, sliding to the edge of the bed.

His fingers slid across the silk of her panties and rubbed her feminine lips through the fabric. The moan that escaped her mouth came out raw and animalistic. She couldn't help it. She wanted him so badly, she could barely contain herself. "Please," she whimpered. "Marlowe..."

He slid her panties down and caught her ankles when she lifted her legs to come out of the silk, lace lingerie.

He slowly slid her legs apart. Alarm broke through her sensations and made her hesitant. She didn't want him to see how imperfect she was. She didn't want him to look at the place where remnants of her sex organ rose like uneven pockmarks in her labia. Her legs stiffened and froze in place.

"I want to see," he said.

"No," she responded. "It's too—"

"Do you think I would hurt you?" he asked.

Gena thought for a moment about all the times she was too reluctant to let a man see the stubble of flesh inside her. "No," she said, letting go of the shame, the resentment and the fear of not being able to come. The pleasure Marlowe had given her so far was already beyond what she could have imagined. If there was more, she would take it.

Marlowe spread her legs and kissed the sides of her knees. His kisses massaged her inner thighs. He drew circles with his tongue, spiraling up until his tongue slid easily across the slickness of her juices that had trickled onto her upper thigh.

He used his hands to push her legs farther apart. Gena let herself relax, sink farther into the bed and close her eyes. Ready to do whatever, to accept whatever.

He placed gentle kisses on her. Rolled her folds and lips into his mouth. Raked his teeth against areas so sensitive, she swallowed hard and clutched the mattress. Her wetness gushed and then poured like rain. Drenching his face, she spread her legs even wider. His tongue flicked back and forth inside her until her whole body jerked and her breath came in ragged gasps.

"I'm sorry," he said. His voice, a mixture of anger and sorrow, touched off the old pain inside her. "I'm so sorry this happened to you."

His words uncoiled a pain so deep she didn't think it would ever twist free. For so long, her pain had gone unuttered, suffocating her without hope. Now, years later, one man whispered the only apology she ever received. A surge of relief burst open in her soul. The misery beyond tears that she'd lived with since she was thirteen had been replaced by a bottomless sense of peace.

As Gena reached the point where she thought she would break from the pleasure, Marlowe slid a finger inside her. She cried out and arched wildly. He pulsed his finger back and forth then pulled it out. Gena cried out again. This time he slid two fingers in. His fingers against her slickness drove her wild. His lips made smacking sounds against her. The pleasure built in a way she'd had never felt before.

Afraid the sensation might end, she pleaded with

him. "Please don't stop. Mar-lowe..." She let everything go, casting all her inhibitions aside. "Don't stop."

Despite her begging, he shifted. His thumb took the place of his lips and tongue, pressing deeper against the place where her clit should be. His fingers worked rhythmically inside her. When his warm, wet lips pulled her nipple into his mouth, Gena thrust her hips against his hand and screamed.

Tears filled her eyes when she realized what was happening. Every nerve in her body vibrated. Heat rose inside her and pulsed on her skin in mind-numbing ripples. The room spun and the center of her body broke open in waves.

Gena writhed in complete ecstasy and let the sensations take her.

"Hold on," Marlowe whispered.

He took the other breast in his mouth and sucked lavishly.

Gena barely caught her breath and had begun to return to herself when she felt another wave rising up inside her.

"Oh, God. Oh, oh, God!" she chanted.

The second orgasm came much quicker than the first and was much stronger. Gena let go of the crumpled sheets in her hands and let the orgasm wash through her.

"Ah-ah!" she said, riding out the pleasure.

It was too good. It was too much all at once. Now she pleaded for Marlowe to stop. She didn't think she could take any more. But her body was so greedy. Her hips arched and rolled against his hand. She was so wet, the sheet clung to her butt as she moved.

"I can't, Marlowe, I can't—"

She was about to say "take it" when another orgasm stuck her so hard she felt as if she'd fallen off the bed.

Gena didn't know she could scream that loud or for that long. Every ounce of energy and resistance she had left her body with that scream. If Marlowe wanted to keep her coming all night long, he could. She opened her legs as wide as she could get them. Giving him all access. She didn't care what he did as long as he made her come again. In that moment, she didn't give a damn about her past bad choices or the imperfection between her legs.

She just wanted to come again.

His thumbnail gently raked the leftover, uneven place of her organ. Plucked it in exquisite tempo, as if it were a violin string. Each strum bringing her heat. Gena arched and fell back, arched and fell back in wondrous torment. She gasped and lay in his arms trancelike, turned out by the whisper of sensation that seemed all-powerful and unending.

When the pleasure took her yet again, she knew she had to stop him. Because she couldn't stop herself. This much ecstasy would make her crazy.

Summoning all the strength and reason she had left, she reached over to the side table and grabbed a condom from the bowl.

Marlowe slowed his finger movements inside her and let her breast slide out of his mouth. His gaze intensified with desire and he lay back on the bed.

His arousal lay thick and heavy against his upper thigh. She opened the packet, took his hot length into her hands and rolled on the condom. His dick stiffened in her palms. She took some of her own juices and rubbed against him, bringing him to full arousal.

Now, his moans filled the room. He turned toward her, kissing her shoulder, her cheek. She smelled her own desire on his lips. The scent amplified her eagerness to please him.

Marlowe climbed on top of her. They sank into the bed together. Gena placed her hands around his neck, the gesture so comfortable, as though she'd been doing it forever.

For a second, a slight smile broke though the lust on his face. He pushed her legs apart with his own. It didn't take much. She spread open, overly ready to have him inside her.

He pressed the head of his penis against her opening. She closed her eyes, imagining the fullness. "Be still," she said, boldly, then she guided herself down, taking him in inch by inch.

First she slid back and forth against the tip of his dick. He groaned and braced himself with the headboard. Using his neck and the bed for leverage, she pulled herself up and moved her hips up and down against his shaft. The sensation of his thick length taking up all the space inside her made her feel drunk and powerful. She ground her hips harder and took him in deeper.

With a kiss to her forehead, Marlowe plunged inside her. His full size filled her even more, and she shuddered at the immense thrill of it.

"No, be still," she insisted, wanting to tantalize him as much as he'd tantalized her.

"I can't," he groaned into her ear. The heat from his words warmed her neck. "I want you too bad."

At his words, she melted like caramel in the desert.

Marlowe took his time. His weight pressed down on her. Giving rise to her pleasure.

She started to believe nothing could pry her from his embrace. She'd never felt sexuality so deeply. She couldn't believe how much being intimate with Marlowe transformed her. All pretending and fantasizing aside, running her hands across his back, feeling the muscles flex strongly beneath her fingers.

The expression on his face was hot and smoldering above her. Heated her better than the sun ever had. She wanted so much to please him. She moved with his rhythm. Let him guide as in a dance and followed wherever his hips led. Faster. Deeper. Sweat glistened on his forehead and between her legs as they moved together.

Gena grabbed his butt and pulled him closer. She circled her hips in quick ellipses. Marlowe pulled out.

"You're gonna make me come," he said.

"That's the point," she whispered.

He slid inside her. His penis thick, and heavy and filling. "*You're* the point, Dr. Bivens. It's all about you."

His eyes bored into hers, setting everything inside her on fire. Gena sighed.

He adjusted himself on top of her, settling in and thrusting strong. Gena wrapped her legs around his waist for leverage and matched him.

The pressure built inside her again. The sensation was so acute it scattered her thoughts like lost words. She couldn't concentrate. She could only move and respond to Marlowe's masterful lovemaking.

Marlowe grunted and ground into her. His breaths throaty and short. With a groan, he pulled out again and held the head of his penis.

"I'm too close," he said. He leaned in. Kissed her neck, the top of her shoulders. "I want you to come with me," he said and pulled the tight bulb of her breast between his teeth. He flicked his tongue and sensations fired between Gena's legs. *Talk about making it rain.* There was so much rain coming down in that room, Gena would have sworn she heard thunder and saw lightning.

He slipped his hands beneath her. She felt his whole body relax. He breathed slowly. Got comfortable.

Marlowe kept a slow, steady rhythm, and her pleasure rose. It felt as if he was on top of her and in her soul at the same time. They breathed together. She bit her lip as the pressure grew acute.

Gena moaned and arched against him. She was going to come…again. Her juices flowed onto the sweat-soaked sheet beneath them. Excitement spiraled through her. Her legs trembled. She gasped and moaned loudly.

Marlowe kissed her lips, the sides of her neck. Kept his pace while she hurtled toward ecstasy.

"You gonna come for me? One more time?" he asked. His voice, thick with lust, excited her even more. He nuzzled her neck with his own. "Hmm?"

"Yes," she whispered.

"Tell me again," he demanded.

She didn't have the strength or the presence of mind to do anything except obey. "Yes," she said, realizing how true it was. "I'm coming, Marlowe. I'm coming again."

He moaned his approval into her ear. Made her wetter. Made her come.

"Yes! Marlowe, I'm coming." Her heart beat one hard throb after another. "I'm coming now."

"I want to feel it," he said, staring into her eyes again. "Let me feel it."

As if on command, her orgasm came in a dizzying surge of sexual force. Her muscles contracted and pulsed around him like a fist squeezing.

Marlowe released a deep groan and plunged inside her harder, faster. Seconds later he was slamming into her with an urgency that was almost brutal. She hung on while he called her name and shuddered through his own forceful release.

"I miss…being inside you…already," he whispered and collapsed on top of her.

Chapter Twenty-Five

Gena spent most of the night awake. At first, after Marlowe's lovemaking, she'd been out as if she'd taken six tranquilizers. Two hours later she was wide awake, lying beside the first man to take her all the way to a clitoral orgasm. She couldn't stop staring at him, as if he was the patron saint of climaxes. She kept touching him to make sure he was real. She touched herself to make sure the orgasm fairy hadn't flown in and given her a new clitoris. She wanted to make sure she hadn't simply dreamed about a missing clitoris and had one all along. For all that touching, she found strong arms and hands and the same old ripped nub as always.

She was like a little girl, pulling the sheet off him

to stare at her handsome liberator. Emotions cycled through her. She cried. She giggled. She squeezed her thighs together. She floated.

In his sleep, Marlowe would reach for her and pull the sheet up on them both. It felt so different adjusting to the weight on his side of the bed, the heat from his body, the space he took up. What fascinated her above all that was the smile that claimed his face. It glowed brighter and more vibrantly than all the red-rock mountains surrounding the center. She was bathed in it all night long.

But that didn't stop all the thoughts from racing in her mind. *What would happen now?* She'd been attracted to him before, but now, she felt merged with him. *Did he think less of her?* It had taken so long to happen. *Was he repulsed? Did he resent her for keeping her identity a secret? Did it really happen?*

And just as important: *Would it ever happen again?*

Floor-to-ceiling windows surrounded them on all sides. Gena pressed a button on her power shades to block out most of the sunlight. The multicolored tapestries and wall hangings that adorned her sleeping area celebrated sexuality with free-form expressions of sex and sexuality. But they couldn't compete with what Gena experienced with Marlowe. After last night, she might just give her treasured artwork away.

Marlowe rolled over and opened his eyes. The early sun crept in between the slats of the wooden blinds. The thin light made his eyes look like glowing warm honey.

"Jambo," he whispered.

She smiled and felt the honey drip down her body. "Hello to you, too. Did you sleep okay?"

He rubbed his temples and squinted. "Better than okay."

"I didn't sleep much at all," she admitted.

He slung his arm around her, pulled her into him. "I know."

"You know?"

"You touched me fifteen times. You pulled the sheet off me seven times, you—"

"Punk!" she said, slugging him in the arm.

"Careful. I just built that muscle up in the gym."

She was smiling like a giggly girl and couldn't help herself. "Why didn't you tell me you were awake last night?"

"I wasn't awake. You kept waking me up."

"Why didn't you wake up with me?" she pouted.

"Are you kidding? You wore me *out.* A brother needed his rest. I had to get some of my strength back."

That was exactly what Gena was afraid of. What man would want to be with a woman who couldn't get off unless he did cartwheels in her vagina? Her happiness drained away.

He jostled her playfully. "Hey, don't get all glum on me. That wasn't no ordinary lovin' last night. I put in *work.* Now, I love a good workout, but after a massage, some tongue, a hand job and some dick, you should be stompin' your feet, callin' all your girlfriends and bakin' me some cookies. I mean, how many times did you come?"

Gena shook her head in astonishment and turned to look at this amazing man in her bed. He was right, and she'd stopped counting at ten. "I've never met anyone like you."

He kissed her cheek. "Backatcha. An African, sex-coaching dominatrix. I gotta tell you, that's a new one for the kid."

"Are you teasing me?"

"Hell yeah!" He cupped her breast and twirled a nipple with his thumb. "But in a good way."

The beautiful and delicious Dr. Gena Bivens turned onto her back, giving him full access to everything he wanted. Her round breasts called to him. And those big hips of hers…he could live in them. Just pack up his condo and move right in.

The two of them were a lot alike. They didn't just decide what they wanted sexually. They grabbed it and held on tight. Her hungry eyes. Her body flushed with lust. She wanted him right now. He could tell. Despite morning breath, sheets that needed to be changed, their own funkiness, which he actually didn't mind, and her obligation to greet her clients for breakfast, she'd forget it all if he let her.

Oh, how he wanted to let her.

Just looking at the dark brown hourglass of her

body made him as hard as a pile driver. And the way she looked at his penis, as if it was magic or something, could keep him pleasing her for weeks.

But the truth was, he didn't have weeks. He had to figure out what to do with his life now that he'd decided not to turn in the article he'd written.

Gena's eyes lost some of their shine. She had to be wondering what last night meant. Hell, he was wondering that himself. He stroked her soft face with the back of his hand, determined to show her that what happened between them was not just *hit it and quit it.* At least, not for him.

For good measure, he fished out the tiny pack of miniature mints from her goodie bowl and popped one in his mouth.

"What are you doing?" she asked. He heard both eagerness and apprehension in her voice.

"Giving you what you want," he said, smiling and offering her a mint.

She accepted it, parting her mouth and licking the tip of his finger as he slid in the sliver of wintergreen.

He reached into the bowl again, trading the mints for a condom. Marlowe watched the rise and fall of Gena's breasts and chest. Her breaths came quick and she squirmed under his gaze. He kissed her collarbone.

"Last night was good for me, too," he said.

"Yes," she said, cupping the back of his head. Pulling her fingers through his hair. "Every second."

"Mmm-hmm," he said, moaned. He'd been so driven to make her come, just to get her off. The idea had consumed him.

Now, with sunlight slipping in through the blinds all around them, he was compelled by another need. He wanted to see it happen. Across her gorgeous face. He wanted to watch.

He slid his hands against the warm skin of her chest. He cupped her breasts, tweaking first one nipple then the other. While stretching his right leg across hers, he took a nipple into his mouth and danced his tongue back and forth over the bud until it tightened and Gena moaned.

She took the condom from him and rolled it down his penis. The sensation of her hands on him ratcheted his desire. Staying on his side, he slipped the head of his arousal inside her. Bumping the space where her clit should be, getting her wet.

Marlowe rolled a nipple between his fingers and continued to pulse back and forth inside her until her eyes fluttered closed and she whimpered with pleasure.

"Marlowe, you're so good at this. No one has ever made me feel so good. No one."

The combination of her words and her accent stoked the need inside him as if it were a growing fire. Pleasure caught him. He wanted so badly to close his eyes and sink inside her. But he knew she needed more. He pulled out slowly.

"No!" Gena shrieked, not wanting to be separate from him.

Her eyes snapped open. She clawed at him to come back to her, to join her again, to bring her heat once more. Her panic surprised her. The tenderness in Marlowe's eyes surprised her, as well.

"Don't worry," he said, inching her legs apart. "I got you."

He knew he couldn't get the friction she sought from his tongue, but at least he could start there.

He took his time, licking and teasing all the sensitive areas on Gena's body. He was careful with her breasts when he pushed them together, sucking both nipples at once. The act had her squirming beneath and him throbbing. By the time his tongue reached her opening, she was wet and trembling.

Marlowe raked his teeth across her feminine lips and sucked them as he would breasts until Gena grabbed the back of his head and chanted, "Marlowe, Marlowe, Marlowe."

He used his tongue to make figure eights inside her. Her legs opened and closed as if she couldn't control them. The scent of her drove him deeper. Her hips swiveled with each movement, and when he thought she was ready, he replaced his tongue with his thumb nail raking gently over the rough, nubby area of her missing clit.

A blazing-hot erotic current shot through Gena. Her body jerked up and she screamed his name. For a moment there was only Gena's heart hammering in her chest and Marlowe's kisses against her thigh. And then he did it again and again. Pulling his finger as if it were a long titillating string across the remains of her sex organ. She screamed and came with each stroke.

The sensation was intense, so acute it was as if she was crying between her legs. As though every emotion and feeling she had in her body pooled and broke open there again and again and again. She fell back against the bed, powerless. Marlowe had taken every ounce of her sexuality, and what he didn't possess, she gave over.

Marlowe kissed the tears flowing down her temples. Each time she came, heat coursed up and down his body in huge waves until he could no longer stand to be separate from her.

Before he lost all control, he opened her legs wider and slid inside. The heat radiating from her hot center made him lose his mind and forget his name. Gena's arms and legs hooked around him, pulling him closer.

Propelled by mind spinning need, Marlowe drove in and out his full length. He wanted all of him to feel all of her. Gena arched against him. He groaned with the pleasure of her hips pressing up to meet his thrusts.

"Gena," he said, slamming into her as the sensation overtook him—shooting them both over the edge and into oblivion.

* * *

They fell away from each other, panting and sated.

Gena covered her mouth. Almost embarrassed at the way she'd just behaved.

"What's wrong?" Marlowe asked, panting.

"You think anyone heard me?"

He gave her a cocky smirk and kissed her lips. "I think *everyone* heard you."

"Oh, my gosh," she said, concerned for the first time about others hearing *her* for a change.

"I think folks in Tabora heard you."

"Oh, you're funny," she said, giving him a gentle shove.

Before Gena could drift off again under the sedating aftereffects of Marlowe's lovemaking, there was something she had to know.

"Why aren't you married or hooked up with someone? And don't lie, please."

Marlowe breathed deeply and folded his lips together pensively. "I don't stay," he said finally. "I used to think that I just *happened* to find women who cared more about a cause than they did about a relationship. But thanks to you, I realize that it was me. I didn't want a commitment."

Gena wiped the sweat from her neck and shoulders. What he said made sense.

"I chose women who made it easy for me to leave them. Heck, they were so busy with their charities, community centers, cultural work, they wanted me to leave. I was a distraction. A nice one, but a distraction."

"How about now?"

His eyes took in every inch of her face. He looked like a blind man who'd been given thirty seconds to see and had to make sure he took everything in before his eyesight failed. Gena warmed from his appraisal. But part of it was halting, detached and made her shiver.

"I don't know," he said.

Gena's joy collapsed. She chided herself for being so vulnerable so fast. She could have taken that news yesterday, before last night and this morning. But now, in her book, Marlowe was a handsome man with a warm soul and a dick that delivered. It would be hard to let all that go.

"Don't get me wrong," he said, stroking her face, kissing her temple. "Being with you these past few days has kept me sane and horny as hell. I guess I'm just missing the real world."

Gena sighed, knowing that as of this moment, the world had never been more real to her.

"I'll be so glad to get my cell phone and my laptop back. I'll be glued to them for weeks. I haven't gone this long without the internet in over ten years. But more than that, I've got business to take care of when I get home."

Gena stiffened, remembering what he said about the women he chose. "Is that your way of saying I'm so dedicated to The Epicure that you have to leave?"

"Gena," he said. He'd dropped the formality last night, and she liked it. He stroked her cheek with the pad of his thumb. "What I have to do is important. I have to do it face-to-face. But I'm flattered that you wanna spend more time with a brother."

Gena listened, but her hearing and understanding stopped after the words "face-to-face." That had to mean a woman. All of her energy and excitement for the day drained away as she thought about Marlowe and the existence of yet *another* woman. She had to get it through her head once and for all, the man was unavailable. Seriously unavailable.

He looked around. "It's not like I don't know where you live."

Impulsively, she wrapped her arms around his waist. "Will you come back for another week? You can be my guest."

Uh-oh. Now she sounded as if she was begging.

She kept him in her arms but looked away. "I'm having a dramatic shift in my thinking."

"In what way?"

"I'm starting to understand why some women stay with their men no matter what."

He spooned her. Contentment spread warmly to all parts of her body.

"I hope that's a compliment," he said.

"In sessions, I try logic. I try exercises. I try plus/minus, future projection. For some women none of that matters. They choose to stay even when they shouldn't."

He pulled his finger through the sweat between her breasts. Followed the line all the way to her belly button. "Are you saying good loving cancels out good sense?"

She looked up, feeling the honesty bubbling to the surface. "Yes. I think it can."

"Lady, if you are trying to give me a big head—"

Her neediness had become unbearable. She knew if Marlowe offered her half a day, once per year, she would take it. Anywhere. Anytime. It was ridiculous.

"You have to go," she said.

Suddenly the penthouse was too small. It was swallowing her with Marlowe in the room. Too much had happened. He wasn't on a quest to get remarried. She revealed herself. Not only did she have sex, but she had it over and over, and it was good every time. And now, the thought of Marlowe leaving her was enough to make her want to close the center for a while and follow him to wherever and for however long. And she'd never taken a vacation since the day The Epicure opened.

She was thinking crazily.

"What?" he said, propping up on an elbow.

"Please go. I have to…I have to get ready for group." She lied. She just needed a moment by herself to remember who she was and what she wanted. Marlowe had managed a string of powerful orgasms to challenge her self-image, and she wasn't sure how to deal with that challenge.

His features grew solemn. "You want me to leave The Epicure?"

"I, I don't know. But you have to get out of my room. I need to be alone."

She stood, naked as the day she was born, and waited. Slowly, Marlowe put on his clothes and headed toward the door.

"That's cold," he said, his face hardening. "You know this is cold, right?"

"I know you need to get out of my room."

He scratched the back of his neck. "What's up? Why are you flippin'?"

"Please!" she insisted, with not much self-control left.

Marlowe regarded her bitterly. His face pinched tight and flashed with indignation. "As you wish, mistress."

He left without another word. The moment he was gone, Gena sat down on the bed and thought hard. She decided that the best thing for them both—or maybe just her—would be for him to leave the center. Otherwise, the wise and resourceful Dr. G. would forget any pride she ever had and beg him to stay.

Chapter Twenty-Six

Hours later, after obsessing over the night and morning she'd spent with Marlowe, Gena stepped inside the group-therapy room as if she had brand-new feet. She couldn't help herself. All eyes seemed to be on her and her quickstep. She imagined that everyone in the room knew what caused her new way of walking. She would just have to remind herself of the first thing she tells everyone the first time they come to The Epicure—the only rules for your sexuality are the ones that honor who you are. And who she was at that moment was a brand-new woman.

She was having an out-of-body experience. For the first time, she wanted to be the one talking. The one giving blow by erotic blow of the most amazing night of her life. She wanted them all to listen to her for a change and when she was through, she wanted to high-five everyone and break for the day.

Marlowe, along with the couples in coaching, was already there and waiting. She did as she'd done since the moment Marlowe had set foot in The Epicure. She dressed, overdressed, underdressed and redressed—trying to find the right thing that would make her feel good and showcase her assets. Her La Perla, Lascivious and Damaris styles were exactly as she would have worn them any other day. In the floor-length mirror in her penthouse, she looked the same. But under all the layers of fake hair, contacts and makeup, she felt like a brand-new woman. As she made her way to group this morning, she'd decided to focus on that, rather than the idea of never seeing Marlowe again.

Thinking about the good, and how after one delicious night and one scrumptious morning, Marlowe was able to guide her imperfect body into orgasm after orgasm, turned her into a woman of great hope—not just for herself, but for others, too. Gena had always been a positive soul, never wanting to give up or give in to adversity, but now she was even more determined. And she loved that feeling.

The couples welcomed her with good-mornings and hellos. Marlowe said nothing. He leaned against the wall, away from the circle. He glanced frequently out the window yet kept a wary eye on Gena.

"Aren't you going to join us, man?" Mike asked.

"Nah," Marlowe said. "I'm cool here."

Mike shrugged. "If you like it, we love it."

"How is the new day treating everyone?" Gena asked, trying to ignore Marlowe's sharp stare.

"Good."

"Great."

Still no comment from Marlowe.

"Rotten. Can we go first, doctor?" Philad Blue asked.

Gena looked around. "Anyone object?"

No one did and the man who looked like a sure candidate for a steroid junkie stood and began pacing. "Ronalda and I, this is our last time here. We keep coming because we, I, like trying things like ménage, swapping, you know, moresomes."

"Yes," Gena said.

"I was hoping that bringing Ronalda would help her understand how I feel about keeping an open community. But what it's done, doctor, is made it worse. She's so jealous—"

"I'm not jealous! I'm pissed!"

Gena held up her hand, looking from person to person. Both Philad and Ronalda turned away from each other, wearing thunderclouds rather than facial expressions. "Let's go one at a time. Now, Philad, you said Ronalda is jealous. What does she do to make you think that?"

"When we party, she half participates. Rather than get into it, she spends most of the time insulting our guest. She acts like nobody is good enough."

Gena held up her palm, signaling Philad to pause. "Ronalda, what do you say to that?"

"I say he's right."

"What's your relationship like when it's just the two of you?" Gena asked.

Philad's eyes grew wide. "What do you mean?"

"That's why I'm mad, Dr. G. It's never just us. He always wants to add someone or something. But don't let me suggest it. Just him. Then when we do, he spends more time with her or it than he does with me."

Gena glanced from husband to wife. "Is that true, Philad?"

He shrugged. "I don't know."

"Well, just be quiet for a moment and consider. Don't answer right away. Just think," Gena said.

The room grew quiet as they all considered, not just the feuding couple.

"Okay, well, yeah. I guess. I mean, that's what we're into."

"Not we, you!" Ronalda said.

Gena took a moment to consider, too. Their love life, if you could call it that, sounded like what hers would be like with Marlowe. Lopsided. She would be the clingy one—having to be jump-started and coaxed and needing so much attention to even get off, that Marlowe couldn't possibly be satisfied by, attracted to, or passionate for her. It was a good thing he was leaving.

"Philad, let me clarify something here. It's one

thing to add toys or guests if it's a mutual decision between the two of you. Please note that I said *add,* not *replace.* What I'm hearing is that this isn't enhancing your relationship with Ronalda, it's replacing it," Gena stated.

"But she agreed—"

"I only said yes because you wanted it so bad. But I don't need all those high-powered gadgets in my bed. And I certainly don't want some trick in my bed either." Ronalda turned to him then with concern welling in her eyes. "I just want you."

"Philad, I want you to think about why toys and guests are so important to you."

He shrugged. "It's just me. It's just who I am."

Gena crossed her legs, knowing they were on the verge of a breakthrough. "You're saying that, but I hear something different."

No one said anything. Marlowe kept his place in the corner of the room away from the circle.

"Let me put this on the table," Gena said. "I think the toys and the women are buffers—things you intentionally place between you and Ronalda. So, why do you need a blockade against your wife?"

"Yeah. What you scared of?" Ronalda asked.

"Ronalda, please. Let him answer. However, I will say your wife asked a valid question."

Philad took a deep breath and stared straight at Gena. "I, uh, I don't, I wonder if I please her. If I can please her."

"Don't tell *me,*" Gena said.

Ronalda rocked her neck. Gena wished that she didn't have such an attitude, but at least she was being quiet now.

"I get nervous when we make love. When we first got married, you just never seemed to enjoy it. I guess I started to doubt myself, and I covered it up by pretending I wanted to spice up our love life."

Relief washed over Gena in large waves. "Thank you for your honesty, Philad, and for being that open. That's a brave thing for you to say."

People in the room agreed.

"Ronalda, what are you feeling?"

"I feel like I want to tell the truth, too. When we got married, I really wasn't feeling you in bed. Hell, I'm still not. But, I guess I should have said something. Maybe then you wouldn't have brought all this unnecessaryness to our bed."

Guilt ate at Marlowe's gut like ravenous parasites. After last night and this morning, he couldn't ignore it. He felt bad about why he'd come to The Epicure. Gena wasn't the only one with a secret identity. The only way he could absolve the guilt and make the anguish go away was to tell Gena the whole truth.

He didn't know if it was the mountains, his near-death experience with black mold, the vortexes, Gena herself, or all of the above, but something had changed him. He'd had eager feet all his life, but being with Gena made him want to stay put. Find out what could happen between them.

Last night, he'd come out of himself completely, focused on her totally, and loved it. Seeing the beautiful combination of surprise, pleasure and joy on her face—he couldn't put into words or coherent thought just how powerful an experience that was. But he had to tell her that, too.

He had to tell her everything.

"We need to talk," he said to her, looking away from the mountains.

He'd interrupted the session. Inquiring eyebrows rose and jaws dropped. He didn't care.

"What? Now?" she asked.

"Yes."

She shook her head. "Sorry, you're going to have to wait until group is over."

"No."

"Wow," Birdell Jordan said.

Gena's eyes grew wide. The shock of his insistence hit her full force.

He straightened his back, regarded her coolly. "What's wrong, mistress? Not used to taking orders? Just used to giving them, huh?"

She shot him a look that could twist steel. He, however, was unscathed. "Don't make me call security."

He moved away from the wall then and angled in her direction, adrenaline propelling him forward. "On *me?* You're going to call security on me? After I made you come harder than you've ever come in your entire life? Nah, *mis*tress. I don't think you will."

Gena rolled her eyes. Tossed him a look of incredulity. "Unbelievable!"

"Not really, I just pushed your legs open and slid my tongue—"

"Okay! I'm sorry, everyone, for the interruption. Let's reschedule group for this afternoon. How about three? I'm sure Mr. Chambers will have found the mind he just lost or—" she gave him a look as sharp as ten daggers "—he'll be evicted from the premises."

"Wait! What about me and Philad?" Ronalda asked.

"Make it quick," Marlowe said. He wasn't really trying to roll over her, but he realized as a former domme, she'd might get off on someone telling her what to do for a change. Turns out, he was right.

Gena took a deep breath. "Here goes. Philad needs all those toys and the occasional guest star, because he has performance issues. He's using those things as a wall. Just tell him what you want and how you want it. Be gentle if he doesn't get it right the first time."

There were several sharp intakes of breath.

Ronalda nodded. "I sure will. Thanks, Dr. G."

Gena closed her notebook. "Ooh, me! Us!" Jolisa Titsworth said. "Do us!"

"Jolisa. you always want the lights off, but it's not your body you have an issue with, it's your husband's. Mike, you're too skinny. Jolisa wants a

Michael Jai White type. More like Philad. You look like Eddie Griffin. Eat some cheeseburgers."

The gasps were accompanied by a few muffled snickers.

Mike gave his wife a blank stare. "Is that true?"

She patted the back of his hand. "We'll talk about it later."

"I'll be back at three o'clock," Gena said, rising. "If any of you still want to have group, you're welcome to join me."

She joined Marlowe, who'd already made it halfway to the door, and then turned. "And Eleanor and Luke?"

"Yes," they said, fear and dread on their faces.

"You two are perfect for each other. What you have is real special. As soon as you realize that and trust each other, you'll be able to play all the bedroom games you want to without being embarrassed or feeling silly. You'll know that the person you're with would never—" her voice broke for a moment then she regained her composure "—hurt you or judge you."

Gena wiped her eyes and stepped out of the group room with Marlowe. He felt each tear as if it were falling on him—into his soul.

She marched ahead of him, wide, leather-clad hips swaying in short heavy bursts, head held high. He knew she was trying to get away from him. He caught up with her in two strides and took her arm.

"Wait," he said.

Her tears were gone, but the pain that caused them was still there. He couldn't help himself. He had to make that pain go away.

He leaned in and kissed her. Slowly, he pressed himself against her until they were against the wall, groping, panting and grinding. He grabbed her by her big hips and lifted her against him.

He nuzzled down against her ear. "All these hips, and ain't nobody been fillin' 'em on the regular. You know that's a shame."

She held on to his shoulders and bit down softly into his neck and began to suck. Marlowe groaned and eased them down to the carpet.

Members of the therapy group filed out of the room, watched for a moment and then gave Marlowe and Gena their privacy.

Marlowe placed gentle kisses on her forehead. "I'll go slow."

He tried to slide his hand underneath Gena's leather minidress. It was too tight. Flush against those hips of hers.

"Where do you get these dresses?"

"Narcisa orders them for me."

"Turn over," he said.

She turned onto her stomach without protest. She was quick to roll and together they tugged her out of her painted-on dress.

He pulled down the zipper, exposing the chocolate smoothness of her supple back.

"Who zips you up in the morning?" he asked.

"I have a pull wand."

His fingers traced the dark skin that became open and available as the fabric of the dress parted. "Of course you do."

"To be this leather right now," he said, suddenly envious of the fabric, "pressed against your body so tight all day. Mmm…I'd be one happy man."

He slid her arms out and then pulled her to him as he wiggled the leather down. Held her like a baby, supple and compliant.

Now that she was naked, Gena became strangely self-conscious. "Not here," she said, arms flailing.

Her left arm sent a nearby bowl of condoms flying. A confetti of Trojan Ramses and LifeStyles condoms showered the carpet around them.

"Not here," she insisted. Marlowe noted she hadn't stopped rubbing against him. Hadn't stopped panting.

"Why not?" he asked.

"Because—"

He frowned down on her. "Because everyone else can be free but you can't?"

She stopped moving then and stared into his eyes. He had to ask her an awful question. One he hoped he wouldn't regret asking.

"Who needs to drink from the cup now?" His voice came out gruff, heavy with frustration.

"W-what?"

"All this openness and freedom you preach. Be yourself. Go for it. Go for what you know. Isn't that what you tell your guests? So everybody can drink from your cup, but not the good doctor? Huh? What?"

Suddenly, she felt like an open wound. "I don't—"

He kissed her throat. Her neck. Her shoulders. "What about you? What about you?" he whispered.

Gena had never felt more exposed in her life. Instead of giving in to Marlowe's demanding advances or her own urges, she scrambled to her feet. She didn't get far before Marlowe caught her by the waist and spun her against the wall. His gaze bore down on her. Now she felt naked. All her feelings, emotions and desires open for him, for everyone, to see. His gaze made her feel more than naked. More like transparent. As though he could see through her to the fact that she didn't want Marlowe to leave. She didn't want to be the strong mistress. At least not right now. She wanted to be told what to do. Her sex was addicted to his sex, and the thought of going without it made her feel like a junkie facing the excruciating prospect of withdrawal.

Marlowe placed his hands against the wall on both sides of her shoulders. "Look me in the eye and tell me you don't want me, right here and right now. Tell me you don't want it so bad you can't think about anything else 'til you get it. Tell me you didn't want to touch yourself back there when you saw me. 'Cause I sure as hell felt that way about you."

Gena wanted so badly to look away. To lie. To get

him to stop reminding her of how lonely her life was before she met him.

She couldn't.

He got in her face then. His breath hot and moist against her skin. "Tell me you don't want to rip off my clothes right now and ride me 'til your thighs hurt."

Her resistance broke apart. She grabbed his face and kissed him greedily. Marlowe returned the favor, and their tongues fought for control inside an exquisite kiss.

She quickly pulled Marlowe's shirt over his head. She undid his belt, unzipped his pants, tugging and pulling until he was as naked as she. He pressed her against the wall. The hot weight of his body on her breasts combined with the cool hard plane of the stucco and made her shudder.

Marlowe massaged her breasts, still sensitive from earlier that morning. He kissed the space between them and then farther down, tonguing her belly button and then the space at the apex of her thighs. He moved lower, sucking her inner thigh, her knees. Finally, he picked up one of the strewn condom packets, opened it and guided the latex protection down the long length of his shaft.

Anticipation made her squeeze her thighs together and pinch her own nipples. Everything he said was right. She did want to touch herself, she did want to ride him as if there was no tomorrow, and she hadn't been able to think of anything else since she woke up that morning.

"That's good," he said, eyes glued to her hands. "Pinch 'em for me. Make them hard."

Guest after guest peaked around the corner, stared for a few moments and then went back to whatever it was they were doing. Word must have gotten around that the mistress was getting naked with the new guy. Even staff came around for a quick glance before getting back to work.

Marlowe licked his lips while she flicked her nipples between her fingers. After all the times she'd gotten off watching her guests, it made her hotter than ever to see someone so excited to watch her.

When he caressed her hips, she moaned at the feeling of four hands on her body. "I want you, now," he whispered and picked her up.

A knowing grin crawled across her face. She guided his hot length inside as he lowered her. They both moaned at the joining.

At first, Marlowe was afraid to move. The feeling of being with her again was so overwhelming, he knew he could come at any moment. He wanted to relax, calm down a second before the sexing.

Gena's hips had other plans.

The sweet twinge below her belly grew into a dazzling need to come. Passion flared between them as Gena worked her hips the way she'd always dreamed. She was no longer hesitant to seek out her own pleasure now that she knew she could have it. Gena grew as bold as she wanted to be—popping her hips like a pro and seeing Marlowe's eyes nearly roll back in his head as she did.

Suddenly she realized she didn't even have to come this time. Just being with Marlowe this intimately and this out in the open was beyond her wildest dreams of pleasure. And it was enough. It wasn't about pleasure-seeking anymore. It was about pleasure-giving.

Marlowe hissed and his whole body went rigid. "Slow down," he said.

"No. I want you to come."

He groaned and bounced her faster. "You first."

"No," Gena insisted, grinding strong against him. "You first."

"Ah!" Marlowe cried out, unable to hold back. Heat flooded his groin in a rush and slammed inside him again and again.

"Damn!" he said, catching himself and Gena as he slumped against the wall.

Chapter Twenty-Seven

Gena couldn't feel her feet. They were still in the afterglow, where she'd wanted to be all her adult life. But silly Marlowe had insisted they go to her office right away. If it was for another helping, she'd already canceled her plans for the rest of the day in her mind. No group session. No evening meet-and-greet. No Water Erotics night. No preparation for COA tomorrow. Just orgasms, as many of them as she could stand.

Then a terrible thought came to her mind. What if her sensation was temporary? What if having so many orgasms so quickly was too much stress on her fragile organ. She felt so good down there. It couldn't be short-term. It just couldn't.

"I want to have as many orgasms as I can for as long as I can. Are you up for it?" Gena asked as they stepped inside her office.

She'd been so inside her own thoughts, she hadn't noticed Marlowe putting on his clothes. He was already half-dressed. She grabbed a silk robe from her closet and pulled it on. The serious look on his face made her want to cover up.

"What's wrong?" she asked.

"I haven't been honest with you about something, and I want to be honest now. Before we do anything else."

Gena shivered as if she'd just walked into a deep freeze. She cinched the belt tight around her waist. "What is it?"

Marlowe looked around. He seemed uneasy. "I need you to move away from anything you can easily pick up and throw."

A vile combination of fear, anger and disappointment formed a hard knot in her stomach. "Aw, damn. Are you married? HIV positive? Gay? Got ten kids by ten different women? What?"

"No, no, no and, hell, no."

Relief flooded her senses. "Then it can't be—"

"What's up, Doc!"

Carmela Moore's shrill voice cut the tension in the room as a thin knife would. It was almost enough to make her forget what a good time her vagina had been having.

"Carmela. Back so soon?" Gena asked, thinking the actress wanted to cash in on her freebees as soon as possible.

Always, the young woman came in with an entourage. Gena would swear it was a new male review. Chippendales meets…thug life. All mute and a little vacant in the face. *What does she do, switch them out daily?*

"Marlowe? Wow. Who told?" Carmela shrieked.

All of the color and sensuality drained out of Marlowe's handsome face. He looked as if he'd just swallowed a mouse and the damn thing was alive and building a nest in his stomach.

"Hello, Carmela," he said.

Gena stepped back to where she could get a good view of the two of them. The lecherous expression on Carmela's face turned Gena's blood into cold, stabbing splinters. "You know each other?"

The actress stared at Marlowe's crotch. "Been there. Done that." She laughed lustily and waved a well-iced hand in his direction.

"We dated," Marlowe corrected.

"Got it," Gena said. She retracted her thought about Marlowe. The mouse was in *her* stomach nesting.

Carmela sauntered over to Marlowe, planted a way-too-familiar kiss on his cheek. "Well, since the Chocolate Chateau is on blast now, feel free to put me in the story."

Marlowe blew out a breath and gritted his teeth. "There's no story, Carmela."

Carmela whirled on Gena, ignoring Marlowe. "I can't believe you're letting Mr. *US News* here write a story. You could have asked me. I'm writing my autobiography, you know."

"There's no story, Carmela. Let it go."

Gena was still. She was sure of it. But she couldn't understand why everything around her was turning upside down. She could see it. Her office. Erotic City. All the suites and guests. Everything upended and tossed up, 8.9 on the Richter scale. All her hard work crumbling to bits. She could barely breathe, but she damn sure could speak.

"Marlowe, what is she talking about?"

Carmela frowned, deep confusion wrinkling her blemish-free face. "You know he's a reporter, right?"

Marlowe's chin dropped to his chest.

The floor shifted under Gena's feet. "What?"

He looked up quickly. "I swear on all that is holy I was just about to tell you. It was the next thing out of my mouth."

Gena struggled to keep her composure. "You've been here for days. Taking notes! Oh, my *God*."

Marlowe rushed forward. Gena backed up. He held his arms out as though he expected her to walk into them. "I came to get a story. But after I got here, I knew that wasn't right. I don't want the notes. I don't want the story. I just want *you*."

"Damn, that's deep," Carmela said. She crossed her arms over her high and oh-so-surgically implanted chest.

Marlowe sent Carmela a scathing glance. She sent one right back. "I'm serious. We've known each other for a minute, and when it comes down to a woman and a story—which it always does with you—you always choose the story."

Carmela looked Gena up and down as if she was seeing a new species. "You must have crack between your legs."

"Get out!" Gena and Marlowe said at the same time.

"Whatever," Carmela said, waving her hand. "I just came to be COA tomorrow. Can you hook that up for me, doc?"

Gena's hands shook and her legs trembled. "Yes. Whatever. Just go."

"All right, I'm out," the starlet said. She sauntered out with her entourage puppy-dogging behind her.

"Who sent you?" Gena asked in a calm tone she was nowhere close to feeling. They faced off like two gunslingers poised for a draw.

Marlowe looked her in the eyes. *"LifeWire."*

"Bull." Gena didn't believe for a minute that an upstanding magazine like *LifeWire* would want a story on the so-called Chocolate Chateau.

"They're turning a new leaf. Yellow journalism. The economy, you know."

Gena felt like spitting. "How much?"

"I told you. I'm not turning in a story. When I get back home, I'll owe them for everything they spent to get me here."

Gena crossed her arms. *Not again,* she thought, remembering Ward and other bad choices she'd made. She wanted to believe his change of heart so badly. Needed to believe it. "What changed your mind?"

He stepped closer. "*You* did. What you do for people here. How you change their lives. Hell, how you changed mine. I just couldn't betray something that sacred."

Gena stepped back. "What about all those notes you took?"

"They're in my suitcase," he said. His voice sounded flattened and weary. "We can go get them now. You can have them. Burn them if you want to."

Gena would take that as a sign that he meant what he said. And she would burn them. They *would* burn them together. "Let's go."

Marlowe had kept the notes to every story he'd ever written or thought about writing. They were all in a file cabinet in his home office. When he got back to Omaha, he had planned on adding the notes from his time at The Epicure to his collection. But if turning them over to Gena meant she'd believe he was telling the truth, it was a tiny thing to give up.

He hoisted his luggage on his bed and unzipped

it. Inside there were Sean John button-down shirts, microfiber shirts, socks, a grooming kit and a horsehair brush, some boxer briefs, souvenirs from First Night. The stack of notes that should have been on top of everything was gone.

"They're not here," he said, more to himself than to her.

Frustration grew like frayed knots in her stomach. "That's convenient."

Marlowe tossed everything out of the bag. "I put them right here on top two days ago. Maybe one of the maids took them."

"Not in a million years." Gena's words came out cold and slicing.

"Well, they didn't just *vanish.*"

As soon as he said the words, he knew exactly what happened. The cousin who'd *vanished* since they arrived had been up to no good once again. And there's no way to tell what she'd done with what she'd found.

He closed his bag. "Shereeta took them."

"Uh-huh."

"She's got a key to the room. I don't know if she was looking for money or what, but I know that's where they went."

Gena looked as if she was going to cry and explode at the same time. "You've been lying to me from the second you got here. You're still lying."

She turned away and stared into her hands. "I can't

believe this is happening. I worked so hard. It can't be this easy. I'm slipping."

She was talking at him, but not to him.

"I'm going to find Shereeta and find out what she did with my notes," Marlowe said.

Gena glanced up slowly. The pain in her eyes sliced him in two. "Don't bother. Just get the hell off my property."

Marlowe's plea for forgiveness was preempted by a knock on the door to his room.

"Mistress?"

"This can't be good," Gena said. If Narcisa tracked her down, something bad had happened. Her legs could no longer hold her. She leaned against the wall and slid down to the floor. Her butt smacked into the carpet.

"She's in here," Marlowe called, kneeling beside her.

Narcisa peeked in, her features gray with worry. "Mistress, we need you in your office."

"Is it bad?"

"Yes, mistress."

"Go ahead. What is it?"

Narcisa knelt beside Gena. "I shouldn't say it here."

"Say it, please say it. Whatever it is." She was too tired for anything else.

"BusinessInTheStreet.info has an article, and—"

Gena couldn't hear anymore. Her mind couldn't

take it. She just needed a moment to gather her thoughts and plan a beat-down for everyone who had anything to do with her entire life crumbling inside of an hour. If only she could stand, she'd kick some serious ass.

"What are you saying?" Gena asked.

Narcisa took a deep breath. "We're on the internet."

Chapter Twenty-Eight

He started by going door-to-door, knocking with purpose. By the seventh door in the center, Marlowe Chambers was banging and shouting for his cousin to come the freak out before everyone in The Epicure heard him describe her life on the pole.

"Shereeta!" he shouted, pounding harder. He'd lost his mind, he knew. He'd owe apologies all around, but it was the only way he knew to flush her out. When there was no answer at door number eleven, he moved on to door number twelve and raised his fist.

"What the hell are you doing?" Shereeta asked, strutting around the corner in a pink silk bathrobe and powder-puff heels.

"I was about to ask him the same thing," a nearby voice responded.

He spun to see Shereeta on his left and Gena on his right. The good doctor was flanked by three burly security guys. They appeared very professional in khakis and polos that looked ripped straight out of a Lands' End catalogue. Their builds said they worked out on the regular. Marlowe couldn't care less. Clearing his name was more important than anything they could bring.

"You need to leave now," Gena ordered. "Don't worry about packing. We'll ship your personals to *Nebraska.*"

He didn't care for the way she said Nebraska, but that was beside the point.

Shereeta struck a wide-legged pose worthy of *Hustler* magazine. "And you talk about me being a problem! What did you do to get kicked out?"

I will not choke the spit out of her. I will not choke the spit out of her. He walked toward her, fingers tingling. "You went through my luggage; you took my notes, and you sold the story to *BIS*. Tell her."

"Cuz, I don't know what you're talking about."

The words came out so sugary sweet, the air smelled like syrup. He stepped closer. Shereeta bit her lip and rested shaking hands against the sides of her robe.

"The truth now," he insisted. "For the first time in your life."

"Puddin'?" The Colonel came around the corner

in a white robe, white ankle socks, and brown leather slip-on sandals.

Shereeta turned toward him and grinned weakly. "I'll be right there, daddy."

"What's going on?" he asked, tightening the belt of the robe around his waist.

"Your puddin' here stole something that belonged to me," Marlowe said. "Stole it and sold it."

Suspicion drew the Colonel's placid features into a tight frown. "Is that true?"

Shereeta cupped her arm into the bend of his elbow. "No, daddy. Besides, his handwriting is whack. No one could read it good enough to turn it into a story."

"Good. I can't have my new star lying to me. If I find out you're a liar, I'd have to, well, let's just say I can't be daddy to a liar."

Shereeta's shoulders slumped.

Marlowe tamped down his frustration, but just barely. "Oh, she's lying. Believe that. If I have to carry the editor of *BIS* here on my back to prove it, I will."

The Colonel rubbed his hands impatiently. Marlowe had obviously interrupted something the man was eager to get back to.

"Puddin'?" the Colonel said. "Don't make me put you in a head lock."

Shereeta remained quiet, but her wide eyes betrayed her. "I wanted to buy you something," she said, voice as thin as paper.

"That hydraulic thing we saw," she whispered. "They're wiring the money to my savings right now."

The Colonel glanced down at Shereeta, disapproval pulling the corners of his mouth down like weights. "Guess you better find another place to sleep tonight."

Colonel Bootney Barnes, U.S. soldier, Second Battalion, Ninth Marines, turned and marched back toward his room.

"But, Daddy!" Shereeta said, rushing beside him. "I didn't lie. Just now, I told the truth!"

He reached up. Pinched her cheeks between his thumbs. "But you stole, puddin'. In my book, that's worse than lying."

He walked off, leaving everyone in the hallway in stunned silence. After a moment, Shereeta shook her head and dashed after him. "Big Daddy, don't leave me! Big Daddy, please!"

Cool relief washed over Marlowe. He'd done it. With the help of the Colonel, Shereeta had come clean.

Gena knew the truth now.

He turned to her with hope in his heart. His hope buckled at the knees when he saw the pained expression on her face. She looked more distant than ever.

He started toward her. "I told you. I didn't break your confidence."

"But you did," she said. Tears welled in her eyes but didn't fall.

She backed away from him. Each step like a blade to his resolve.

"Colonel Barnes is right. Stealing is worse than lying."

"What?" he asked, not understanding.

"You stole personal information from people. You wrote about The Epicure, about my guests, my presenters…about me without permission from anyone."

Marlowe's heart caved in. He'd done everything he could possibly do, and it hadn't mattered. He didn't know what more he could offer.

"I'm tired of telling you to leave." She glanced at the security guards. "Gentlemen…"

Chapter Twenty-Nine

"Man, if I had a place like this, I'd never leave. Even if I had to sell my ass to stay here, I'd be all up and down Leavenworth Street talkin' 'bout 'Come get you some.'"

Marlowe smiled. Rodney Chambers, aka "Sleepy," could always make him smile. He was the even hand in a family of extremes. One side of him was corporate-professional and the other side was wild and ran the streets. Sleepy—with his do-rag waves and b-ball attire—had street cred *and* a decent job. Marlowe thought of him as hangin' in the hood meets JoS. A. Bank.

"You want me to stay put, huh?" Marlowe asked, taping a box of books closed.

Sleepy placed the box on a dolly. “Yeah. I think you should stay.”

“Let me hold some money then,” Marlowe said.

Sleepy’s head popped up like a meerkat. “How much?”

Marlowe rubbed his chin and pulled over the next box of books. “Oh, I’d say ten K.”

“Man, you crazy!” Sleepy said, swatting the air with the palm of his hand.

The words echoed off the bare walls of Marlowe’s condo. Funny, he thought that by the time they emptied the sixteen hundred square feet of living space, it seemed much more expansive. From the ceiling-to-floor windows, hardwood floors and low-dropped ceiling fans, he realized the space had almost swallowed him. Not only did it seem larger, it was too big for what he really wanted to do with his life.

Marlowe thought about Sleepy’s words and wished he was crazy sometimes. He’d be able to deal with the changes in his life much better. Right now, he was perfectly sane. And very much aware that he’d needed a change in his life for a long time. He’d blamed the economy for a hot second. The truth was, the change he needed had nothing to do with the economy and everything to do with the man he wanted to be.

“I *got* ten K,” Sleepy assured him. “Don’t think I don’t. ’Cause, uh, you know me. I’m always holdin’. So, if you really need it, man.”

Sleepy pulled the packing-tape runner across the

top of book box number three to seal it. He kept his eyes on the shiny plastic as it unrolled from the spool. "You really need it?"

"Nah," Marlowe said. "It's like I told you. I just need to reorder my life."

"I hear you. I hear you." Sleepy hoisted one packed box on top of another and grabbed an empty one. "So, you thinkin' about getting a part-time job or what?"

Marlowe loaded his electric shaver, aftershave and all of his Sportin' Style grooming products. "I'm thinking about joining the Peace Corps."

The packing tape fell out of Sleepy's hand. "Get the freak outta here."

"I'm *trying* to get the freak outta here. That's exactly why I called them."

"What did they say?"

"After I filled out the application, they said they could use me. I could teach English as a second language…almost anywhere."

"Dang, man." Sleepy stood and scratched the back of his neck. "You gonna do it?"

"If they'll have me. They have to do a boatload of background checks. But if everything works out, I could get an assignment in a year and be gone for two."

"And give up your reporter thang? I can't see it."

Marlowe smashed a stack of designer ties into a too-small box. "Want to hear something funny? My favorite part of this freelance gig is traveling.

It's meeting people. More than that, it's helping the people I meet. Writing about it was just a way for me to express my passion. I can still do that. Heck, maybe I'll write a book or do a documentary."

Sleepy stared at him, unconvinced. "I don't know, man."

"I do," Marlowe said. "In my gut, I know this is right."

"Well, just be careful of them foreign honeys. I hear they'll turn a brother out."

Sleepy went back to work. So did Marlowe. He packed the rest of his cigar boxes and all of his old stories, thinking he'd already been turned out by an uncompromising diva named Gena Bivens.

He hoped Tuck emailed her a copy of the story he'd written along with a release to print it. On the plane flying back home, Marlowe had started working on a counterpoint article to refute the one printed on the *Business In The Street* website. He wrote it all from memory, experience and passion. It was just the type of article the old *LifeWire* would have published. It was full of the ways in which The Epicure helped people and supported their sexual growth. It turned the idea of the wild-and-sex-crazed Chocolate Chateau on its head.

By the time Marlowe touched down, he had half the story written. He'd stayed up all night with his laptop, a carafe of coffee and his determination. He'd finished the story by morning.

When Tuck got his email, he called right away.

"How in the hell did *BIS* get my story?"

"I have a stank cousin. She stole the article from me and sold it."

"Damn it, Chambers. I should have known not to work with you again."

"Did you get the new story?"

"Yeah. It's just the kind of thing we would have published seven or eight months ago."

Marlowe was hopeful. "What about now? You can hype it as a direct rebuttal to *BIS*'s article. Start a beef. That's good for the kind of readership you want."

Silence.

Marlowe pressed on. "Man, I got the source. Her contact information is at the end of the article. Call her. Send her a release. Ask her if she plans to sue *BIS*."

"Sue?"

"My cousin twisted everything I wrote."

Tuck cleared his throat. "So, it's really not a sex palace?"

"Far from it."

An unnerving silence stretched between them. Marlowe could only hope his years of producing high quality writing would convince his friend to give the article a chance.

"No more from you, Chambers. You hear me? This is our last go-round. If I were you, I'd get out of the journalism business."

Marlowe took a deep breath of relief. "I'm already on that."

"If this Dr. Bivens doesn't sign the release, you better call Thomas Funeral Home and tell them where to come get your body."

"Understood."

Marlowe figured the counterpoint article would pay for his expenses, but not much else. He was fine with that. But Gena hadn't taken any of his calls, so he had no idea if she'd sign the release.

"Mistress, there's an argument in Erotic City. Carmela and Asia both say they're supposed to be Center of Attraction tonight."

"Tell them to do a duet or get the hell out."

"But, mistress—"

Gena strummed her fingers impatiently against the top of her desk. "Narcisa, you really need to handle this."

"Yes, mistress."

Narcisa tiptoed out and closed the door gently behind her, leaving Gena alone in her office with her discomfort.

Marlowe Chambers.

Her mind sang his name all day. Her body had been reminiscing about his tongue, his touch and his tenderness for hours. Her whole body pulsed with the memories. The man had her thinking way too much. Making her second-guess herself and wonder if she'd done the right thing by making him leave. If it was the right thing to do, the right thing had never made her feel so terrible before.

All day, she'd wrapped her arms around herself, feeling as though there was a slight chill in the air. Ninety degrees outside, sixty-five inside, so that wasn't the case. She'd spent the better part of yesterday communicating exactly what had happened to her guests and giving them the option to leave if they chose. She told them she would refund any money at any guest's request.

Although three couples left the center, everyone else stayed, and so far no one had asked for a refund.

Probably the calm before the storm, her mind told her.

Gena held up the offending article. She'd gone online and printed it. The thing, from an uncredited source, claimed the Chocolate Chateau was a debauchery of freewheeling sex and wall-to-wall freaks. It identified a few guests by name, but mostly it painted a picture of a sexual fantasy island. *At the Chocolate Chateau, money buys the wealthy and powerful a suite, five-star meals and orgasms of every type and size.*

Gena fought the urge to rip up the article or use it as toilet paper. Maybe she should take it upstairs and burn it in the open pit.

She dropped the article on her desk and picked up the one next to it. She'd kept them side by side all morning. The second article came to her in an email from the editor of *LifeWire* magazine. Gena didn't know how he'd managed it, but Marlowe had written an entire article describing The Epicure perfectly. The picture he drew was masterful and exquisite, focusing on giving those who need it the freedom to be themselves in any way they saw fit.

At The Epicure, the red rocks of the Arizona desert aren't the only things glowing from the inside out. The clients who come by invitation-only leave with a new outlook on their own sexuality which shines like a light in the soul.

She had to admit, she liked it. If she was ever to hire or need publicity, that's the kind that she would want.

A release form glowed on her computer screen. The editor at *LifeWire* wanted permission to print the article. If she sent it back within the week, it would appear in the next issue and be fresh enough to neutralize the negative potency of the *Business In The Street* article.

"More publicity," she mumbled, getting up from her chair. She paced behind her desk, staring at the release form, her fingers itching to press Delete. In a gossip rag, there was still speculation, wonder and doubt about whether what was written was true. But putting an article in a legitimate magazine. That meant confirmation of everything she'd worked years to keep private.

As much as she wanted to, her mind told her it wasn't worth it to publish another article. But her heart, and the part of her that she saw reflected in the words of Marlowe's article, wanted to sign the release and set her business's business straight.

Her fingers trembled. With an anguished sigh, she placed her hand over the mouse.

Chapter Thirty

Marlowe picked up the last box from the living room and headed toward the door of his condo. Sleepy came in sweaty and hyped.

"I got it, man," he said.

"Thanks," Marlowe said, handing the box over.

The box contained his CDs and a mini boom box. Last on; first off. He figured when they got to the hotel room, they'd blast some music to unpack to.

He glanced around his home of the past several years knowing that this time next year, he could be in Nepal, or Argentina or South Africa. A slow smile curled across his face. Finally, after a nomadic past, he'd set down in a place for a while and be useful.

He walked to the window of his tenth-floor condo.

His place overlooked the southeastern part of the city. The river appeared close enough to skip a rock in.

Marlowe reached into his hip pocket and pulled out the last of his savings. Just under five thousand dollars. He was truly starting over. He felt mostly right about his decision. Mostly. There was still that part inside him where Gena Bivens lived that he could not shake no matter how he tried.

He shoved the bills back into his pocket. He'd have to find a safe place to put them. Too bad he hadn't put his heart in a safe place. If he had, he could get a good sleep at night and his guts wouldn't feel like they had rocks in them.

"Nice view," a voice said from behind him. The accent jolted him like an electric charge.

How the hell did she find me?

"It's not bad," he said, knowing better than to turn around. Seeing her might have him acting like a whipped teenager instead of a grown man in full control of—

"I've missed you." Her words echoed off the bare walls.

Marlowe blew out a breath. The tension he'd felt since he boarded the plane back to Omaha left him in a rush. He turned slowly, then. He needed to see her. Needed to know if she meant what she just said.

Without the mask, his mystery woman looked damned good. Her locks swung freely around her face. A tease of cleavage in a black lace halter. White wraparound skirt showed off the hips he loved. White and black heels that didn't turn her into a skyscraper. The perfect mix of sex and sensibility. He wanted her instantly.

She took a step toward him. With no furniture, there was nothing intersecting the direct line between them. He wanted to pick her up, spin her around, and thank her for coming to him. But he knew her intentions weren't altruistic.

"Didn't you miss me?" she asked.

He stroked his chin. She was up to something. "How did you find me?"

"Shereeta."

"Boy, she's giving up all kinds of information these days."

"Actually she is. She asked me to tell you that she's staying at the center for a while. She says she has some things to work through and thinks she can do it at The Epicure."

Marlowe would take his cousin's attempt to change with a grain of salt. "Good for her."

"She's not officially a client, but she'll be an extended guest, doing a sort of independent study."

Tension throbbed at his temples. "Why are you telling me this?"

"Because she asked me to," Gena said, that beautiful accent coming out of her mouth like music.

Marlowe stood his ground still wary of her intensions. "You could have sent me a text message."

"I wanted to see you."

Just then Sleepy bounded inside—an eruption of sweat and energy. "We all loaded up! Let's the hell outa—"

He swept an appreciative glance down Gena's body. "Aw, snap. Is this you, playa?"

Cousins, Marlowe thought. *Gotta love 'em.*

Gena put a hand on a round hip and stared at Marlowe. "Well? Aren't you going to answer the man?"

Marlowe walked over to Sleepy, grateful for his help. The two slapped palms and bumped shoulders. "Sleepy, why don't you come back through in an hour?"

Gena sucked her teeth. "An hour?"

"Make it two," Marlowe acquiesced.

This time he got a neck rock from the good doctor. Marlowe tossed his cousin the key to his storage. "Sleepy, I'll hit you up this afternoon."

"Daaaaamn. You got it like that?"

Marlowe just shook his head.

"I'm out," Sleepy said. "Bye, Miss Lady."

"Gena," she said.

Sleepy bounded out the door the same way he'd come in. "Bye, Miss Gena."

Marlowe closed the door and went back to the close scrutiny of his visitor. "You said you wanted to see me. Why?"

She shrugged her shoulders. Swept a glance around the empty condo. Her eyes looked up as though she were searching for the most appropriate words, but the words refused her.

He decided to save her from her trouble.

"I've got some buddies that will go all out to get some. Hundred-dollar dinners. Bouquets of roses. Auto repair. But to travel over a thousand miles? That's a good one. I mean, damn. I guess I should be flattered."

She hadn't come empty-handed. Marlowe saw the papers in her hand. "I want to talk about the article you wrote," Gena said finally.

"I have a cell phone, Gena."

"Okay, okay. I *want* you. I flew all this way because I've never connected with a man the way I have with you. I don't think anyone will—"

"Stop!" Marlowe said, holding up his hand. "As flattering as that sounds, it's far from the truth."

"Marlowe," she said, walking toward him.

"Stay over there," he ordered. "Look, I don't claim to know everything about a woman's sexuality, but I do know this. When you make love to a woman's mind, her body soon follows. I'll bet you haven't gotten there with anyone else, because your mind wouldn't let you. Your brain was so convinced that you couldn't get off, your body believed it."

Marlowe walked back to the window. "All I did was change your mind."

"That's not all you changed. You changed everything about me. You changed me from being controlling and reserved and hiding my real self behind latex and platform shoes. I learned it doesn't have to be all or nothing. I can be my sexual and nonsexual self at the same time. You taught me how to be myself *in public.* If I live a million years, I can never repay a debt that big."

She eased closer. He could hear her behind him. He kept his eye on the river. "Let's just say for the sake of argument that you were going to *try* to…pay me back." He turned to her then. Took a step forward. "What would you do?"

"I'd start by forgiving you for lying to me."

Two steps back. "Did I lie? I held back some things but—" Marlowe cut himself off. There had been enough half truths.

"You're right. I was dishonest. It was wrong. If you forgive me for that, well, I'm the one who would be grateful."

Gena unfolded the papers in her hand. "I'm going to sign this release form."

Marlowe wiped his brow and relief coursed through him. "Thank you."

"No. I came to thank *you.* You wrote a wonderful story. And it pulverizes that online article."

"It might at that." He took another step toward her. "What else?"

Gena took a step toward him eyes sparkling, so gorgeous without those dark contacts. "I want to make love to you. The way you have to me."

Marlowe allowed his arousal free reign without restraint. "Good answer."

The tension between them broke and so did

their reserve. They slammed into each other's arms kissing hard and tasting greedily.

Marlowe held her so tightly he had to remind himself that she needed to breathe. For a moment, he had to look away. He knew if he looked at her now, he'd be right back where he started, before black mold put him in the hospital for weeks.

Under the spell of another woman.

What's wrong with me, he wondered. Why couldn't he be like other men he knew who swam through decades of sex with a *hit it and quit it* attitude. But he knew the answer to that as soon as he asked it. He didn't get involved with just any type of woman and good women for him were not hard to find but they were definitely hard to leave.

"I'm leaving for New Orleans," he said. "I heard they could use a few good teachers, so I contacted a friend of mine down there. All I have to do is show up and go through the certification. I can teach there until I've been vetted for the Peace Corps."

"How long will that take?"

"A year."

She snuggled into him. He didn't move; only wondered what she was up to.

She slid her hands slowly up his arms and then back down. He sucked in a deep breath. Her touch undid him in every way. He wrapped his arms around her waist and pressed against her. Her firm butt fitting into his hands perfectly.

"You're going to leave me?" she asked.

He kept his hands still although all he wanted to do at that moment was kiss her until neither of them could talk.

She was breathing heavily and shaking. "Do you know what it took for me to come here?"

"Why don't you tell me?"

"I left my business in the hands of the staff. I've never done anything close to that before. If I think about it too hard, I'll probably pass out. But I had to get here."

Marlowe couldn't control his resolve any longer. He pulled her closer. "Why are you here? Tell the truth. You don't need me anymore. You can get off with anyone if you really want to."

She tried to look away. He wouldn't let her. He stayed in her face until their eyes locked.

"I came to ask you to come back to Sedona. I wanted to do it in person, so that you would know I mean it."

Her words rang coldly in his ears. "So, you can have a 24/7 stud?"

"I won't lie to you. I love the way you touch me. You brought something out of me that I never thought I'd experience. I can't conceive of another man touching me that way. I don't want another man to touch me that way."

Marlowe imagined that to some men that might be an ego boost, but not for him. This time, he was the one turning away. The words "Get out," tilting on the tip of his tongue.

"I also came to ask you about a project."

"What project? Servicing The Mistress?"

"No! Please, Marlowe, the cat's out of the bag about The Epicure. Why not let it all the way out?

"Why don't you spend your year before the Peace Corps with me? You could record what goes on at the center. Write a book about it or do a documentary. If the story is going to be out there, I want it through the hand of someone I trust."

"Sounds like you're trying to control things again," Marlowe said.

She dropped her head.

Marlowe was thoughtful for a moment. The idea was intriguing. "For me to even consider something like that, I'd have to run the show. The *whole* show, not take orders."

Gena looked him in the eye and then backed away.

Marlowe's hopes flattened. Even after everything, she still couldn't let go.

He watched her beautifully wide hips walk away from him and then stop at the door. "So, are you flying with me now or do you want to grab some things from storage first?"

In two quick strides, Marlowe was at her side by the door. He pulled her into his arms and kissed her deeply. She sank into him like velvet and felt like warm clay soft and ready to be handled.

He wrapped his arms around her, pulled her snugly against him.

"Marlowe...what are you doing?" she asked, breathlessly.

"I know you didn't think you were gonna leave here without getting *everything* you came for."

A smile lit up her beautiful face. "You still want those cookies?"

He gave her a swift appraisal. Liked every inch of what he saw. "Hell, yeah."

"So, what are we going to use for a bed?"

"Since when do we need a bed? Besides," he said twisting one of her dreds between his fingers and pulling her close with the other hand. "I was hoping we could try position forty-eight."

"You like that one, huh?"

He planted tender kisses on each side of her mouth, ran his tongue across her lips. "Oh, yeah."

He motioned to the duct tape next to the last empty box in the room. "I'll even let you tie me up."

Desire flashed in her eyes. She grabbed him by the collar. "Have you been bad, Mr. Chambers?"

"All my life."

Marlowe gently backed her against the wall. She threw her arms around his neck more than ready for the love they would make. "I think I can help you with that."

In the middle of his empty condo, minus all his possessions, Marlowe realized that everything he needed was right there in the room with him. He and

Gena had come together as two people looking for something deeper in life. He kissed her full on, with all his desire, knowing that they'd found it in each other. And they could get exactly what they needed anywhere…anytime.

* * * * *